Her FORGOTTEN HOURS

BOOKS BY LILY GRAHAM

The Summer Escape

A Cornish Christmas

Summer at Seafall Cottage

Christmas at Hope Cottage

The Island Villa

The Paris Secret

The Child of Auschwitz

The German Girl

The Last Restaurant in Paris

The Only Light in London

Her FORGOTTEN HOURS

Lily Graham

Bookouture

Published by Bookouture in 2025

An imprint of Storyfire Ltd.
Carmelite House
50 Victoria Embankment
London EC4Y 0DZ

www.bookouture.com

The authorised representative in the EEA is Hachette Ireland
8 Castlecourt Centre
Dublin 15 D15 XTP3
Ireland
(email: info@hbgi.ie)

Copyright © Lily Graham, 2025

Lily Graham has asserted her right to be identified as the author of this work.

All rights reserved. No part of this publication may be reproduced, stored in any retrieval system, or transmitted, in any form or by any means, electronic, mechanical, photocopying, recording or otherwise, without the prior written permission of the publishers.

ISBN: 978-1-83525-601-5
eBook ISBN: 978-1-83525-600-8

This book is a work of fiction. Names, characters, businesses, organisations, places and events, other than those clearly in the public domain, are either the product of the author's imagination or are used fictitiously. Any resemblance to actual persons, living or dead, events or locales is entirely coincidental.

1

LOIRE VALLEY, 1944

A match scraped against the night sky, setting the stars on fire.

Twelve-year-old Théo shifted away from his telescope, his planetary chart falling from his slim fingers, blood roaring in his ears.

Just past the small village of St Jude with its rolling hills and vineyards in the Loire Valley, a plane was going down.

It was about to crash in the field where the boy stood, momentarily frozen to the spot.

There are moments in every life that reveal who you are at your core. What you'll do when fear places its icy hands around your throat and begins to squeeze.

Théo began to race towards the falling plane, his eyes searching the heavens for a parachute – a sign that the pilot had ejected himself – but there was no parachute to be seen.

The pilot was trapped.

Théo looked behind him, to the village that rose from the hill like a wizened old man in a dark coat. It had been named after the patron saint for lost and desperate causes, St Jude Thaddeus. The irony was not lost on Théo at this moment. If ever there was a lost or desperate cause to find oneself in, this was it.

How long would it take the Germans to get here? How long did the pilot have? Twenty minutes?

Less if they ran, and if they'd seen the plane he knew they sure as hell wouldn't walk.

If the pilot was stuck, Théo needed to get to him before they did. He had heard the stories of what they did to downed pilots they captured. The tales made his blood run cold.

He clung to the chance that perhaps the Nazis hadn't seen the crash. There hadn't been a loud explosion and the fire wasn't particularly bright. It was a small plane, made huge by the magnified lens of his telescope. They might have missed it hurtling from the sky, if they weren't looking for it… particularly on a cold evening like this, well past midnight when they were likely tucked up for the night inside their stolen sheets and stolen beds and stolen homes.

At least, so Théo hoped.

All this and more raced through his head as he approached the crash site, and began to cough from the stench of burning oil, metal and smoke, his eyes turning red from the haze. He pulled his knitted jersey over his lips and nose, so that he could breathe. His heart lurched when he saw a shape in the grass. The pilot had climbed out of the smouldering wreck and was lying half out onto the ground.

Théo sank onto his haunches, fingers shaking as he touched the pilot and heard, to his enormous relief, a faint moan.

Alive.

As Théo's eyes adjusted to the smoke-filled haze, he saw that most of the pilot's face was covered by his leather helmet and flying goggles, apart from his lips which looked swollen and burned. Théo heard him groan, then mutter something too faint to catch. It was just one word. Théo leaned closer to hear and saw the pilot's eyes begin to shutter closed.

He was passing out.

Théo shook him urgently. He needed the man awake if they had any hope of getting out of here. The pilot's eyes flickered open.

The pilot said the word again, louder this time. It sounded like a name. Later Théo would realise that it was a plea. Or a benediction.

'Michael.'

The pilot began to speak, urgently, but Théo couldn't understand him. He was speaking another language. He recognised a few words. It was English, Théo realised.

'I'm going to try to pull you the rest of the way out, all right, Michel?' he said in French, hoping the pilot understood. Most of what he could say in English, he'd learned from an older friend, and none of it was polite; it would be no help right now.

The pilot didn't respond, so Théo began to pull at his arm. The man screamed and Théo realised in horror that his arm was bent at an odd angle – Théo had only been making the injury worse. He felt a hot flush of nausea hit him. The air went out of his lungs and he fought a wave of panic. After a moment, he wiped the sweat off his forehead, took in a deep, shaking breath, then made his way to the pilot's right side, and began to pull. There was some resistance from whatever was catching the pilot's right foot but nothing obvious that Théo could see. Then he realised that it was stuck because part of the boot had melted.

He closed his eyes for a beat.

'This might hurt,' whispered Théo, whose hands began to shake at what he needed to do. There was nothing else for it but to wrench him out. His heart thundered when the pilot came free with an awful squelching sound, followed by a bloodcurdling scream that sent shivers down Théo's spine and made his toes curl.

The pilot's right boot was charred along with part of his trouser leg. Théo swallowed. The poor man.

'Can you walk?' Théo asked him after he'd quietened. 'Or hop?'

The pilot grunted, it wasn't clear if that was a yes or not.

Théo shut his eyes for a second, gathering his strength. The pilot needed help, and to get away from the belching smoke which was as deadly as the fire itself. Théo had found this out only too recently, just as all the villagers had.

He thought about old Monsieur Dubois, a staple of St Jude, like the square that was carpeted in bluebells each spring or the sound of the church bells at noon, and who greeted everyone, even the German invaders, good morning when they passed. Days before, there had been a fire at the ironsmiths. Hours after everyone had thought he would live, he was taken by a silent enemy – the smoke that had built up in his lungs until he could no longer breathe at all.

It was this more than anything that drove Théo to force the pilot to move away from the deadly fumes. Théo couldn't watch someone die. Not again.

'Come, Michel,' said Théo, trying to drag him away from the cloying smoke, which burned the back of Théo's throat and caused his eyes to sting.

Using his name seemed to activate the pilot. He struggled to sit up.

'We need to get you somewhere safe.'

The pilot responded to Théo's urgency and tried to stand, crying out as he landed on his burned foot.

'I'm here, lean on me,' soothed Théo, in the gentle voice he used on the injured animals he found out on the fields.

Théo staggered under the pilot's weight. He was a slight man, but Théo wasn't particularly big for his age, thanks, in part, to the meagre war rations.

'It's not far, but we must go quickly, in case the Germans

saw your plane go down... My grandfather is a doctor,' he assured him.

He was a vet, actually, but even so, Théo knew that his grandfather would treat the injured pilot better than any Nazi doctor would.

Théo clenched his jaw; he wouldn't think about what would happen if the Germans caught *him* with the pilot...

Surely, it wasn't a crime to help an injured man?

He couldn't just leave him to die out here.

It took them twenty minutes to get to the farm. Every minute teetered on the edge of a blade, every second felt too long for Théo's racing heart. The pilot's small frame was something of a relief as Théo might not have managed to help him stand, otherwise, as his weight kept bearing down on the boy as he struggled. For every metre they hopped, the pilot breathed heavily, sweat dripping into his eyes, his blistered mouth pulled tight in torment but he kept pace alongside the boy, using whatever reserves of strength and determination he possessed as they made their way to an old stone farmhouse tucked away by a border of cypress trees. Their leaves swayed in the wind, whispering Théo's fears back to him.

Théo hammered against the back door, checking over his shoulder in trepidation. The wood was old and split and peeling blue paint the colour of a robin's egg. It wasn't locked but he needed his grandfather to help bring the pilot inside.

In a distant part of Théo's mind he knew that he would have to go back and get his telescope. If the Germans found it, they would know he had broken curfew, and when they saw the plane, it wouldn't take long for them to work out what had happened...

It was a small village, people knew about Théo and his passion for astronomy.

Suddenly, a light winked up at them from the bottom of the door, and Théo heard the anxious slap of his grandfather

Antoine's slippers on the stone floor. The door creaked open to reveal an old man with a shock of wiry grey hair sticking up wildly around his head in an improbable halo.

A pair of wide, pale-blue eyes widened in horror. 'My God, Théo!' he croaked, in a voice that was still half asleep. 'What have you done?' he whispered, taking in the sight before him, the blood draining from his whiskery face.

'His plane crashed in the field. I couldn't leave him there.'

The old man's face showed a panoply of emotions, from surprise to dismay – the boy was meant to have been in his bed, not breaking curfew and certainly not bringing home wounded pilots. His expression settled eventually on resignation and sympathy as he looked at the state of the pilot. It was clear he was badly injured.

The old man checked behind them, scanning the empty farm yard, and the shadows beyond, his eyes bright with fear.

'Inside, quick.'

2

By the time they dragged the pilot to the surgery room, he was unconscious.

Together they heaved him onto the steel table.

Antoine rubbed his lower back, knowing that he would pay for it in the morning.

I'm getting too old for this.

It was a handsome room, in spite of its purpose. The oak-panelled walls were filled with framed illustrations of animals and anatomical studies. A large mahogany bookcase housed textbooks alongside animal figurines and models.

Antoine had a brief thought about what the pilot might think if he knew he had been taken to a veterinary practice, but he admonished himself for being foolish.

He treated animals better than the village doctor treated most humans. A man whose hands shook from drink and muddled the name and cases of his patients. The thought of him caused Antoine's jaw to clench.

It was still too raw what had happened earlier that week with the fire in the village, and the death of the blacksmith Monsieur Dubois.

Antoine began checking the pilot over, maintaining a steady stream of rebukes for his grandson as he did.

'What were you doing out of your bed at this hour? I've told you that you can't just run out and do what you like – we have a curfew, or did you forget? The Germans won't treat you any kinder just because you're a child. The last thing we need is for them to start asking questions about your parents. Questions we don't have the right answers for, as you well know.' He scratched at his whiskery cheeks in contemplation. 'I think the villagers are right, I have been too soft on you. If they find him here, you know we can be shot for harbouring an enemy – did you think about that?'

'*Their* enemy,' hissed Théo, his small mouth twisting with an uncharacteristic flash of venom. 'Not ours.'

Antoine dipped his head in acknowledgement. That was true enough.

The boy frowned. 'I couldn't just leave him. There was so much smoke...'

They shared an unspoken look of agreement. The face of Monsieur Dubois seemed to float in the air between them.

Antoine had had nightmares every night since the fire. When he woke up he sometimes thought he could still hear Isabelle, Monsieur Dubois's daughter, wailing when they had found her father dead, hours after everyone thought he was fine.

The worst part was that when Antoine had asked the local doctor if he'd checked the blacksmith's and his daughter's lungs after the fire, he had looked at Antoine as if he was dirt beneath his shoes. 'I'm sure I don't need a pig doctor to tell me how to do my job,' he spat.

Except, it seemed, he did. He'd only bothered to check pretty Isabelle's.

Antoine's hands balled into fists that would like nothing more than to smash themselves into that smug doctor's face now.

The Germans had shown more care than the doctor had when they had returned from whatever it was that had called them away to Paris and found the smithy burned to the ground.

It would be Antoine's job to tell them that Isabelle, who had stayed with Antoine and Théo after the fire, had left this morning for the south of France to go to the only family she had left.

She'd looked as if she'd aged ten years since the day of the blaze.

Antoine had hoped that his life would go somewhere back to normal after Isabelle had gone, that he might even have a proper night's sleep after that horrible event, but thanks to his grandson's heroics tonight with this pilot, that didn't seem likely.

With a wince, he pulled off the boot on the pilot's uninjured leg, noting the burns on the other and the way that the leather was fused to his skin. That would need to be cut off. The pain would be considerable.

He swore softly to himself. Fifteen minutes earlier he had been in bed, drifting into an unsettled sleep and now... *this*.

Still, he couldn't fault the boy for being the sort of person who tried to help those who needed it. He knew he was wasting his breath admonishing the boy when he would likely have done the same thing himself. It was yet another reason to detest this war, it took too much. Sometimes he felt that he'd become a version of himself he despised, a pathetic thing that only cared for one thing above all else – survival.

He hated that his first instinct now went against his own nature. That was another cost of war that no one spoke about. The scars you gave yourself to get through it alive.

He couldn't deny that it would have been safer for them to have left the pilot in that field. Or to wish that the boy hadn't been there in the first place, that he hadn't broken curfew and sneaked out of the farm. Then they could have avoided this whole sorry mess.

It made him gruff with Théo. In another life, he would have praised the boy for his courage, for his humanity, now he cursed him for it.

Another scar.

'Fetch my bag, Théo,' he snapped. 'I'll need some warm water and fresh towels, and you will help – no squirming.'

Théo didn't have the strongest stomach and always had to look away when his grandfather operated on animals. Antoine wouldn't allow him that luxury today.

'Yes,' said Théo faintly, and rushed off quickly to do as instructed.

Antoine turned back to the pilot. One arm was hanging at an odd angle and his lips looked painfully blistered as well. Those would heal with time. He was lucky, all things considered. But the burns on his leg were another story. Those might affect his ability to walk, thought Antoine, as he stared at the melted boot with another wince.

He would have to get some whisky. Most of the useful medicines he possessed were long gone, thanks to the war. The thought of doing this without giving the man a dose of morphine or chloroform turned his blood cold.

There was no chance the pilot would stay asleep once he got that boot cut off, he knew. He would likely scream blue murder. His hands shook. It didn't matter how many animals he had helped free from poachers' traps, bits of rusted iron and jagged metal biting into their small, shivering bodies; when he freed them it caused further pain, and even when it was necessary to do, it caused his stomach to roil and cold sweat to break out along his spine.

He swallowed. He would need some whisky himself. He hated the stuff, really, wine being his preferred drink, but for shock there was nothing like it.

Antoine took a deep, steadying breath. Then he flexed his slightly arthritic fingers and continued his examination.

He unbuttoned the first three buttons on the pilot's grey shirt, surprised when he saw what looked like a thick bandage around his chest. He must have been injured before, Antoine thought with a frown.

He felt a stab of sympathy for the man. Up there, battling the skies, like fodder for the cannon. He picked up his stethoscope and listened to the pilot's heart and lungs. There was no wheezing, the lungs and heart sounded strong and healthy. The pilot likely had Théo to thank for that, for getting him away from the crash site so fast.

When Théo returned with warm water and fresh towels, Antoine turned to the pilot's leg and began to cut off the boot with a large pair of scissors.

As Antoine expected, as soon as the leather began to pull at the seared flesh, the pilot began to cry out.

'Hold his hand,' urged Antoine and Théo rushed to do so. The boy spoke to the pilot in a soft soothing voice. 'Michel, this might hurt but it's important.'

The pilot thrashed on the bed, his screams so high-pitched it caused the hairs to stand up on Antoine's neck and his toes to curl inside his old slippers. An odd thought made him frown, *Was the pilot—?*

No. He dismissed his overactive imagination with a shake of his head.

He just wasn't used to hearing that as he wasn't used to treating people. Wasn't used to their brand of feral sounds.

Yes, that's it.

'Théo, give the pilot some whisky.'

Théo rushed to give the pilot the bottle. The pilot grabbed it one-handed, from out of the boy's hands, then put it to his blistered lips with a grimace. He gulped it down, only to cough and splutter.

As Antoine saw to his wounds, the pilot passed out several times from the pain. After an hour and a half, the boot was fully off, the burned skin cleaned of debris, treated and bandaged, and at last, he sank into a deep sleep.

Antoine sent Théo to bed, too; the boy looked worn out, swaying on his feet from fatigue.

After the boy left, Antoine took the time to treat the rest of the man's injuries, including his broken arm. The pilot barely woke, even as Antoine reset the bone.

With the worst of his injuries seen to, Antoine turned to cleaning him up and making him somewhat more comfortable. He took off the goggles, then very gently began to ease off the leather flying cap, examining the pilot's head for any further injuries.

Antoine frowned. His fingers shook, and his heart began to race. The pilot's hair was matted and full of sweat and dirt, but suddenly a long, thick coil of chestnut-coloured hair fell across the pillow.

Antoine gasped, and then his eye fell quickly to the bandage across the pilot's chest and he swore.

There was a reason those high-pitched screams had turned his blood the way it had. The instinct he'd dismissed as it made no sense, had been right.

The pilot was a *woman*.

3

The old man's hands shook as he poured himself a shot of whisky. Antoine should have returned to his bed hours ago but his mind kept pestering him with questions that he didn't have the answers for.

He rubbed a gnarled hand across his whiskery, sleep-deprived face.

'A female pilot,' he breathed.

He didn't think he was the type to be shocked over such a thing, his own wife hadn't been the conventional type. He'd met her at veterinary college, for goodness' sake. But still... a *female pilot* was not what he had been expecting.

It also made the situation, if anything, more precarious. What would the Germans do if they found out there was a downed female pilot nearby? How would they treat her if they found her? His jaw flexed. A male would be taken as a prisoner of war, if he turned himself in, otherwise he would be shot. Something told Antoine that her options wouldn't be quite so straightforward...

Antoine didn't want to think of what they might do to her.

What revenge they could take against what they might see as some threat to their masculinity.

War brought out the very worst in some.

There was a short, sharp breath from behind as Théo came into the room, his eyes fixed on the sleeping pilot. 'A *woman*?'

Antoine startled to find his grandson there, his telescope case hanging over his shoulder. He must have slipped out to go and fetch it. He hadn't heard him re-enter the room. 'I was about to go to sleep when I remembered I'd left it in the field,' he said, indicating the instrument.

Antoine's eyes bulged. It could have led the Germans straight to them. Thank goodness he'd remembered.

Théo turned now to look at the sleeping pilot.

'She probably flies for the Resistance,' said the boy.

'What do you mean?' asked Antoine, in surprise, too tired to call him out for what he couldn't do himself – take himself off to bed.

'She spoke English earlier. I heard they are helping the Resistance. Maybe the British use female pilots to fly spies over?'

Antoine stared at his grandson in wonder.

Théo was a smart boy, wise beyond his years, and the war had sadly only amplified this.

It made perfect sense, of course – keeping male pilots for war itself, and using women for other tasks, but it would have never occurred to Antoine. But then the boy had been astounding him with his mind for as long as he could remember. He'd taught himself to read at the age of four and at age ten he could do complicated mathematics that Antoine had only grasped when he was in his late teens. Now at twelve, Théo was more precious to Antoine than ever; he was all he had in the world. He was most grateful that he had, so far, kept the boy safe and away from the Nazis.

When Théo's parents had died in a car accident when the

boy was a baby, he'd come to live with Antoine and his late wife, Jean. But after Jean passed when the boy was five Antoine had become mother and father to his grandchild, not something he expected in his late fifties. He had thought that he would live as an old man with his wife, never imagining that he would outlive her or that he would live to bury his only child, but life doesn't give you what you prepare for, it gives you what you least expect.

And Théo had been unexpected. In more ways than the obvious. He'd brought so much light into the old man's life. He'd saved him from drowning in his grief. It scared Antoine how much he loved the boy and how frightened he was of losing him.

He bit his lip as he looked at him. It was a wonder that anyone could look at a boy like that and not see just the kind heart, the mischievous brown eyes and the matching unruly mop of hair, but there were those, like the two Nazi officers who had invaded his village, like a creeping weed that choked out everything else, who if they'd known about the boy's heritage wouldn't see him the way Antoine did. Because Théo's mother had been Jewish.

No one in the village cared. The horrible pamphlets they had tried to pass around on how to recognise a Jew had been ripped up and destroyed. The stories of what the Nazis were doing, how they were rounding up the Jews and sending them away, were met with disgust. At least here in St Jude, sanity prevailed, but he knew that so many others in the valley, and further beyond, had been swayed by this idiocy.

Antoine knew no one here would ever give up the boy, but perhaps this new secret was one too many to bear.

A female pilot.

'Do you think the Germans know the Resistance use some female pilots?' asked Théo.

Antoine shook his head.

It was the sort of thing he felt sure they would have made a fuss about; he would have heard something, surely, if it was known...

The woman before him, with her blistered lips, looked young. There were no lines around her eyes and her skin looked youthful. She was possibly in her twenties or early thirties, if he could hazard a guess.

Roughly around Isabelle's age, he thought.

Then he frowned at the woman in contemplation, and an idea began to form in his mind.

'No, I don't think it's common knowledge at all,' he said, more sure of himself now. Then he looked at Théo and said, 'And that might just be what will save her life.'

Antoine hatched a plan that was just crazy enough that it might work.

The Germans had been at a rally in Paris on the night the fire had broken out at the smithy. Monsieur Dubois's daughter, Isabelle, had left for the south of France early in the morning, so that she could avoid dealing with the soldiers on their return.

She blamed the Nazi officers for the fire, as they were the reason her father had been working so hard and had nodded off. He'd hardly slept a full night in weeks while he rushed to complete the order they'd made for tools.

'Their precious tools are safe and waiting for them when they return – Father killed himself ensuring that he saved every last piece out of the workshop before it burned down. But if I have to look either of those two monsters in the face, they won't be.'

'But this is your home, Isabelle,' Antoine had implored the girl. 'You don't need to leave it just to avoid them. I'll take the tools to them, and explain what happened. You won't have to see them.'

Isabelle scoffed. 'You think they will just leave it at that? They will likely want answers. I managed to avoid them when they got back last night, but I won't be able to for ever. Not without Father there as a buffer, he always kept them away from me in the past, Antoine, because he was afraid of what I might say to them, how I might tell them how unwelcome they were.'

Antoine had nodded. Isabelle was known for being unfailingly direct. Something that could get her in trouble now.

She snorted. 'My father was worried before – now, well, honestly I don't know what I would say or do if they came to find me.'

'But—' he'd tried.

She put her hand on his shoulder. 'There's nothing left here for me,' she'd said, sadly.

He'd wanted to say that that wasn't true. They were here. Antoine and Théo and all the villagers that had known her since she was a little girl. But there was something in her eyes that stopped him. They had changed. Antoine had the thought that it was like looking in a pond and seeing no reflection.

If she stayed here and had to see the men she held responsible for her father's death every day, the light inside her might never return.

So he'd nodded, past the lump his throat.

Her jaw was set when she packed up only what she was able to carry with her. He'd watched her leave everything she had ever known, and set off to take the coach to Provence when dawn was just blinking on the horizon.

Isabelle's leaving, however, might be what saved this pilot's life.

Isabelle's hair was dark gold, not chestnut, but it was doubtful the Germans would have had much interaction with her to realise that it had suddenly darkened overnight...

As far as he knew, the Nazi officers stationed here likely

hadn't paid much interest to a female smithy with a dirty face when there were other temptations on offer, like the pretty baker's wife with her ruby red lips or the librarian with her waterfall of black hair.

Yes, thought Antoine now, thanks to Monsieur Dubois being afraid of Isabelle's outspokenness, and keeping her away from them, they likely hadn't noticed Isabelle much at all.

Thankfully.

The old man thought hard.

He couldn't turn the pilot out. She was mumbling in her sleep and obviously in a lot of pain. He knew that her situation would likely be quite different from the men – women weren't taken to prisoner of war camps…

There was no Geneva code regarding *females*, was there? Not that he knew, anyway. And he didn't care to find out if there wasn't.

He had been around long enough to know that it was likely that the Germans would take the idea of a female pilot attempting to disrupt their efforts as something of an insult, and they would treat her accordingly.

He didn't want to even imagine what they might do to her.

He shuffled blearily into his garden, his hands cradling a stone mug of coffee, the real stuff, that he had hidden beneath the floorboards.

It was a beautiful day in the Loire valley. Overhead, a pair of Egyptian geese were flying, and in the distance the river winked at him like light bouncing off a sapphire. There was the faint scent of the terroir, which he breathed in to calm his mind that raced with decisions, his senses flooding with lavender and thyme, and the *grolleau* grapes that would turn into perfect rosé wine. His small vineyard was a hobby project born of love. Some days he didn't know if it was a good thing or not that nature kept its own rhythms, quite oblivious at times to the madness of men and their wars. Today was especially beautiful, almost in spite of the night they'd endured.

Some days it felt like the world should stop, that the vivid green of their valley should dull, the lakes should dry up, the rolling fields of vineyards should wither on the vines in response to the evil that was present in this world.

But the sun beat on, the birds still sang their sweet song, the lakes were just as wonderful to behold and Antoine still had a child to raise. There was a job to do, and he was not done yet.

He took another sip of coffee, and then made up his mind over what to do about the pilot. There was an opportunity Isabelle's leaving presented but he couldn't manage the ruse alone. He would need help. But the pilot showed them that they weren't alone, didn't she? That over the sea, people were thinking of them, and trying to help, so perhaps they owed this to her. At least that was how he would phrase it.

His eyes fell on the small village of St Jude, at the top of the hill. He would need its help for this desperate cause.

And perhaps the help of the saint it had been named after.

4

The pilot opened her eyes and winced.

The daylight coming through the worn blue shutters was sharp and acid-lemon bright. It was burning her from the inside out. It took her almost a full minute to realise it wasn't the sunshine that was causing her pain.

Everything seemed to hurt, her face, her lips, her hand... but nothing was quite as bad as her left foot. She thrashed in the bed and warm tears stung her burned and blistered lips.

'Just breathe, calm yourself, Michel – it will only feel worse if you struggle,' said a voice she recognised as if from a dream, a dream that had been filled with fire and terror... though the details right then were hazy.

Apart from the fear. That was the one thing that was all too clear.

She could recall a field. A boy? Pain... excruciating pain. But beyond that there was something or someone she needed to recall; it was there at the tip of her mind, but the harder she tried to focus on that, the more it dissolved like a negative exposed to light.

'It's all right, you're all right, Michel,' said the voice, capturing her attention once more.

She blinked red-rimmed, hazel-coloured eyes and saw an old man hovering nearby. His white hair was sticking up wildly all around his head, most likely from the way he seemed to run his hands through it in a display of some anxiety.

He had the palest blue eyes she had ever seen, and they were filled with a mix of worry, and something she couldn't quite place. Later she would realise it was resignation.

'Burns,' he said in a heavy accent.

She could recognise that it was an accent but not which, at first. Just that she understood him and that he wasn't speaking his native tongue.

'You were lucky,' he said, switching languages. 'Most of them were superficial,' he continued. Then he paused. 'You understand?'

She nodded, realising they had been speaking a different language earlier, which had seemed more familiar. They were speaking French now, she realised, after a while.

She had to concentrate more as a result.

The old man continued. 'Like I said, the other burns were not as serious as the one on your leg. We won't know how much damage you have there – with your tendons and nerves – until you heal. There may still be some mild scarring elsewhere,' he said, indicating the side of her face.

She touched it. She didn't recall any of that, just the vague memory of pain.

'Who – who are you?' she asked.

'Antoine Giraud,' he said. 'You are safe, in my home in France. My grandson Théo found you after your plane went down.'

She blinked. 'My plane?'

'I think it is beyond repair,' he said, thinking she was asking after it.

She stared at him, perhaps she was missing something in translation. 'Was there anyone else with me?'

He shook his head. 'No, it was just you in your plane.'

She frowned, even though that hurt the skin on her face. 'Why do you keep saying "my plane"?'

The old man's eyes widened. It looked as if he was beginning to suspect something.

'Because you were the pilot.'

'I – I'm a pilot?' she breathed.

The old man looked at her askance. He seemed to realise before she did.

'D-do you not remember?'

She frowned, trying to recall. When she closed her eyes, there was a whirring sound. There was something... something just out of reach on the top shelf of her mind that she couldn't get to – something important, though she had no idea what it was.

'Is your name Michel?' asked the old man. 'Or Michelle, perhaps?'

She frowned. 'I don't – well, it must be, as that's why you called me that, isn't it?'

Antoine's eyes widened. 'We only called you that because Théo said you were saying the name over and over again when he found you. But you were saying it the English way. Michael.'

She blinked.

Michael.

For a moment, terror consumed her and she saw flashes of things before her eyes. A man with dark eyes looking at her with love. Men with guns. A forest where every footstep sounded like a bullet.

But just as fast as the flash of memory appeared, it was gone, along with any association she had with it. Except the vague sense of loss. Of missing something. Something important.

'I don't think that's my name,' she said, after a moment. It didn't seem right. Though she couldn't have said why. 'Mine is —' She blanked.

This is stupid, this is an easy one.

Or at least it should have been.

Her lips parted and she stared at the old man in a mix of confusion and a growing sense of panic.

Her heart began to pound. Blood rushed in her ears. Beyond the pain, the fear began to build. Her name shouldn't be a trick question... but she had no idea what it was.

'I – I don't know it.'

She searched her mind but nothing came to her. It was frightening. Her throat turned dry and she tried to sit up. A cold sweat broke out on her forehead.

'How do I not know my own name?' she whispered in alarm.

The old man's eyes were full of sympathy. 'It happens sometimes after an accident. Memory can go. It should come back.'

She clung to his words like a life raft.

'How long?' she asked, desperately.

He shrugged. 'In the last war, where I served as a medic in the trenches, sometimes it would take a few days or a bit longer... sometimes—' He broke off. 'Well, let's cross that bridge when we get to it.'

She swallowed. She knew what he was about to say. What he'd stopped himself from saying. Sometimes they never regained their memories. That wasn't something she needed to hear right now.

'It might take a few days or perhaps a little longer. You just need to rest.'

She nodded, trying not to give in to the waves of anxiety that were threatening to overwhelm her.

'Do you know why I am here?'

He knit his brows in contemplation. 'I believe that you may have been part of the Resistance.'

'The Resistance,' she breathed, as there at the edge of her mind, flickered something – a long stretch of tarmac, a hidden cottage, the full moon shining brightly and a group of people emerging from the shadow of night. But all too quickly it was gone.

She frowned. There was something there, some memory that his words conjured, though she had no idea what it was. It was a horrible feeling, the sense of not remembering, it made her feel anxious and a bit queasy. It was like leaving home and wondering if you'd left the stove on. The nagging feeling persisted uncomfortably. How did you forget your own self? She looked up at the old man. It occurred to her then that though he had treated her, he was taking a risk harbouring someone like her.

'Are you from the Resistance too – is that how you know about me?'

He shook his head.

This news did not fill her with confidence.

'Did anyone else see the plane go down?'

'Not as far as we know. No one has come knocking just yet.'

The words 'just yet' made her stomach churn.

'W-what are you going to do with me?'

'Do with you?'

She felt fear grip her throat. 'It can't be safe for me to be here. Are you going to turn me in?'

'No.'

Her relief was enormous. But still, it couldn't be safe for them.

'Why?'

He took a seat at the edge of her bed. He didn't say anything for a beat, then he ran a hand through his hair, making it puff out wildly around his head even more. He looked very tired, but his eyes were clear and determined. 'Because you landed at this door, and, well, I've never sent someone injured away before and I don't want to start now. We have a plan, don't worry. You are safe.'

'Thank you.'

Her eyes were growing heavy. The pain was taking its toll.

'Close your eyes, get some rest. I'll tell you about it later.'

She wanted to hear more, but almost against her will, her eyes began to close.

It could have been a few hours or the following day when she next awoke, she couldn't tell, apart from the fact that the light in the bedroom wasn't as bright as before. The pain was still there, though, particularly in her foot, but it wasn't quite as all-consuming as it had been.

She felt able now to take in things besides the pain.

The room was a simple one with whitewashed walls. There was a stone floor and a small green *Toile de Jouy*-covered armchair beneath the window. She could feel a cool wind coming through the open, pale-blue shutter, and as her eyes adjusted to the sun once more, she could now glimpse a partial view of distant rolling vineyards and a wink of a blue river or lake beyond. It was beautiful here, she realised.

Suddenly, a shadow fell over her. She looked up and saw a young face. It was a boy of around twelve with dark tanned skin, liquid brown eyes and a mop of brown hair.

'You're awake,' he said, in delight, revealing a dimple in one cheek. 'I'm Théo.'

'Théo,' she repeated. 'The one who saved me?'

He nodded, then grinned, and the dimple grew.

'Thank you,' she said, attempting to smile back, though it hurt her blistered lips.

He shrugged as if it was nothing, when it wasn't at all.

'My grandfather, Antoine,' he began, 'said you might be from the Resistance – but you don't remember?'

She nodded. 'He said that. I don't know if it's true myself.'

She searched her mind, but nothing came, just odd images that dissolved as soon as she tried to put them in focus. 'I can't seem to remember much of anything,' she admitted.

'But if you were a spy, isn't that what you would say?' said Théo, his gaze boring into hers.

She blinked in surprise. 'A spy?'

He nodded.

He looked very serious.

She shook her head, then winced, as that hurt too. 'I wish I was faking this, but I'm afraid it's worse. I have no idea why I'm here or who I am, or who I'd even be a spy for.'

'*That* I think we can probably guess, based on your accent, and the first words we said to one another when you first woke up,' said Antoine coming into the room with a tray, laden with bread and cheese and a bottle of pills.

She stared at him expectantly, raising a dark brow.

'The British.'

He began to speak to her in a different, though far more familiar language, she realised. She answered back. They had switched now to English.

Yes, that seems right, she thought. *I must be English.*

'Your accent is pitch perfect when you speak, unlike when you were speaking French. It gave you away.'

'Your accent is heavy too,' she pointed out, feeling strangely insulted.

He chuckled, then set the tray down on the chair, the skin around his eyes creased in his amusement, and for a moment she had a flash of another pair of eyes, much darker, that creased at the corners, too, but it quickly vanished.

'It wasn't a criticism,' said Antoine, 'or a competition.' He grinned. 'I only meant that if you were to try to pass as French, well, someone might be able to tell.'

'Oh,' she said, then snorted softly, her lips forming a tiny smile that hurt. 'So what you're telling me is that I'm not a very good spy?'

Théo shrugged, then pointed out, 'Maybe pilots don't have to be?'

She frowned. It was frustrating not knowing anything.

'You said I am in France?'

Antoine nodded. 'You're in the Loire Valley. In the little village of St Jude. Not printed on most maps, it is so small. Do you recall the war at all?' he asked. 'I'm wondering how much you know about what is happening?'

Her brows knitted. She got a flash of images, her mind seemed to whirl. Britain had declared war against Germany... there was an invasion... somewhere, she couldn't quite recall where. An archduke was killed? No, that wasn't it. That was... something else. Brown shirts. A stolen symbol. 'Nazis,' she breathed.

Antoine made a weird noise with his lips. 'It makes sense you wouldn't forget *them*.'

Whatever scorn there was in his voice, it wasn't directed at her.

She blinked. At least she could recall something. Even if it was awful. It was better to know than not.

'When France surrendered, the country was divided into an occupied zone and a free zone – but from last year, the Germans, to no one's surprise broke their word and occupied all of France. Now we live under their military command, and have to abide by their rules, including when we are allowed to leave our own homes at night.'

His words left her with no doubt how he felt about this state of affairs, and that it was a sentiment that was widely shared amongst the population.

Images filled her head. Somehow what he said didn't seem to be a shock to her; she recognised what he was saying, to some extent.

She frowned then, and looked at Antoine. 'You said earlier that you had a plan – a plan for what to do with me?'

Antoine nodded.

Théo suddenly began to speak. 'We are going to pretend that you are Isabelle.' Then he began to tell her a complicated story about a fire in the village that had happened the week before.

She stared at them in confusion.

The old man put a hand on the boy's shoulder. 'Don't tire her out,' he said. Then he tried to explain it as simply as possible. 'There was a fire nearby and the woman who survived it left for the south of France a few days ago. The Nazi officers in the village weren't here when it happened, they were away in Paris at some big rally. Isabelle left and didn't bid anyone goodbye, which gives us an opportunity, you see.'

She frowned, not following.

'For you to take her place.'

Her eyes flared. 'B-but the villagers would soon see I'm not her, surely, if it's as small as you say?'

Antoine shook his head. 'Quite the opposite. That's why it's been taken care of relatively simply.'

'What do you mean?'

'They've all agreed to pretend you're her.'

5

Antoine looked at the woman they had all agreed to call Isabelle.

She looked shocked and afraid.

'I know what you're thinking, we're a bunch of villagers, someone will say something, and you'll be betrayed... but they're not idiots. We have survived this war because we look out for one another. Besides, the thing about keeping secrets is that once you start with one, there are always more, and together we know so much about one another that it would be safer for all concerned to just keep quiet, all right, *Isabelle?*'

There was a faint smile at that, and a nod. 'Thank you,' she whispered. There was still some doubt in her eyes, but he could understand that. Hell, if he could have thought of a plan to keep her safe and not have to involve the villagers he would have – even though he trusted them.

There were other advantages to needing the help of others, though.

He handed Isabelle a plate with some bread and cheese, then opened the bottle. 'Painkillers,' he said. 'They're a bit old but they should do the job.'

The look on her face when she saw them – relief and hope – was worth it.

'I found them at the back of a cupboard,' he lied.

He'd traded Monsieur Delmaux, the curmudgeonly old falconer, for them with the last bit of salt pork he had. Now all they had left was beans and potatoes, but he couldn't let her suffer. There was only so much whisky she could drink.

She looked up at him now, and it was like she could see the lie.

'The Nazi officers in the village. How many are there?'

'There's two billeted here – but further afield, in Candes-Saint-Martin, there's probably about a dozen.'

Her eyes widened. 'Which means that when they find the plane they might come asking questions.'

He didn't deny it.

She looked scared now, and then something else stole across her face. Determination.

'I appreciate what you and your friends are trying to do but I am putting you all in danger, and it is unfair. None of you asked for this. I might not remember who I am, but if I was piloting that plane, well, that was my choice.' She struggled to sit up. 'I should go.'

Antoine stared at her in disbelief. 'Go where? You're injured and you don't have any idea who you even are!'

'Yes but—'

He pushed her back down, gently. 'Our plan is a good one. Besides, it is too late to try and put a stop to it now. Someone would have said that "Isabelle" has come to stay here – if you go now, and they catch you, or you confess, you will put us in even worse danger – if they realise who you really are and that we've all been lying about it.'

She blinked up at him, a look of horror flitting across her face. She stopped trying to get up, her face seemed resigned now.

'I can't thank you all enough for what you're doing for me, for a stranger.'

'Don't give it another thought,' he said. 'It's what anyone would do.'

She shook her head. 'I might not remember much, but I know that that's not true.'

Antoine had an illegal wireless radio. Isabelle could hear its tinny sound in the room down the hall, from the living room.

'We listen to the BBC, they broadcast in French, once they even had Charles de Gaulle on – he's one of the military leaders of the Resistance,' explained Antoine, bringing her a cup of mint and lemon balm tea for her nerves, both picked fresh from his kitchen garden. He was followed by Théo who had a book tucked under his arm. 'They haven't even really tried to look for it,' he said with a grin.

Isabelle knew some things about the war, like the name of the fascist regime that had taken over Germany – the Nazis, and so on – but as with most of her memories, there were gaps.

'Why would they try and take your radio?'

Antoine laughed as he took a seat at the edge of her bed. 'Oh, *cherie*. The Nazis try to control all information in and out of the country, especially the news. The easiest way to crack the polite mask they wear pretending to be our "friends" and collaborators is when someone is found with an illegal radio, or distributing books and materials they have banned.'

'How then do you have the radio?'

To her surprise, Théo laughed. 'They don't like to come here. Before they arrived, my grandfather decided to make our farm as unattractive to them as possible, so now they like to stay away.'

'Unattractive, how?'

'He opened the septic tank so that on the day they arrived

they were greeted with an awful stench,' explained the boy with a grin. 'He also switched off the water and built a flimsy-looking shed that he told them was our only privy. When, of course, we have two toilets inside.'

Isabelle gasped. 'You did all that – why?'

Antoine was the one who answered. There was a bite to his voice now. 'It's a beautiful old farmhouse that has been in the family for years, and it's the perfect base to house officers coming from further afield. I just didn't want to take the chance that it would be commandeered.'

'Has it come to that, though – the Nazis taking over homes?'

'Not officially, but yes.'

Isabelle liked his cunning, and she couldn't help but feel grateful for it.

That night, under cover of darkness, she heard her first broadcast in English. The programme began with the opening bars of Beethoven's Fifth Symphony. She felt as if she was on the verge of remembering something important, but before she could chase it, like a game of hide and seek with a child darting just out of reach, it was gone. However, the feeling of being haunted remained.

The music, she thought, before sleep claimed her once more, *it meant something*.

It was dawn when she awoke, and she caught its first glimmers through the open window. The sky turned from purple to peach as the cloak of night was shrugged off.

The beautiful morning was interrupted, though, by the distant rumble of an engine, followed by the slap of small feet on the stone floors in the hallway outside her room. She could sense the anxiety in the air, even before Théo rushed into her room, his face pale. His hair a messy riot of curls.

'The Germans are here,' he breathed.

Isabelle felt her stomach churn with sudden fear.

'Act natural,' hissed Antoine, from the corridor. He looked wan, and Isabelle saw his fingers shaking slightly.

'The radio,' she whispered to Théo urgently.

The boy shook his head, 'Don't worry,' he mouthed, 'hidden.'

Her relief, however, was short-lived, as the heavy sound of hobnail boots entered the house and made her bowels clench. It was followed by deep, masculine voices. 'We need to search the house.'

'Search?' said Antoine, feigning ignorance. 'What for?'

'A plane crashed in the field. Did you not see it?'

'No? Where? I haven't seen anything.'

It was, to be fair, the truth. He had not.

'I've been kept rather busy caring for Mademoiselle Isabelle, who suffered from the fire in the village. I thought when you came here, that you would be enquiring after them. Monsieur Dubois died while fulfilling your order, I believe.'

'Yes, we heard. Most unfortunate business.'

Another voice added, 'He didn't fulfil his order, though.'

There was a heavy silence.

'What do you mean?'

'I mean we are several tools short.'

'Well, I'm afraid there is nothing that can be done about that. His daughter is badly injured,' said Antoine in clipped tones. Even from down the hall, she could tell he was angry.

The first voice was quick to placate the old man. 'Of course not, forgive my colleague. It is all understandable. We were very sorry to hear about Monsieur Dubois and his daughter.'

The other officer snapped at his colleague. 'Stop dawdling, we have seven more houses to search and we're losing daylight.'

'I'm afraid we still need to search the area; I am sure you understand.'

'Yes, yes, of course,' said Antoine.

A few minutes later, they came into the room.

Isabelle looked up from her pillows as two men in uniform entered, followed by Antoine. One was tall and blonde with a boxer's build, the other had dark hair and very cold pale-blue eyes.

The blonde man stepped forward, then dipped his head at her. 'I am sorry for your loss, and for your injuries,' he said, in accented French, with unexpected kindness.

'Thank you,' she said, her throat constricting in fear.

The pale-eyed man came inside, then did a sweep of the room, opening up a cupboard, then bending down to look under her bed.

The blonde man shot him a look of annoyance, when he wasn't looking. When the pale-eyed one stood back up, though, his face was carefully masked.

Isabelle couldn't help thinking, beyond the fear she felt at having them in the room, that that was *interesting*. The tensions between the two.

The man with pale eyes and dark hair then turned and looked at her, at last. He didn't say anything for a while. Just simply stared. Isabelle's heart began to race. Did he know? Did he suspect?

Théo sat in the *Toile de Jouy* chair, his face impassive, apart from the muscle that flexed in his jaw.

The blonde man eyed the boy with a frown. 'Shouldn't you be in school?'

Théo paled.

Antoine hastened to answer. 'I home-school him. That way, he can focus on sciences. He wants to go into medicine like me.'

'Listen to the pig doctor – the boy is probably an idiot, like him,' scoffed the dark-haired man.

Isabelle blinked.

The blonde man shot his colleague a silencing look.

He came closer, edging towards her bed. Then he whispered to her, 'Are you comfortable here? We can take you to the hospital in town, if you prefer.'

'I – I am fine, I prefer to be here, th-thank you,' she whispered back.

The blonde man looked over his shoulder. Antoine was by the door and he seemed about to say something, then thought better of it. 'If you're sure... however, please do let me know if you change your mind.'

The other man looked impatient. 'When you're done playing Prince Charming over this piece of burned skirt, we should look through the barns. I've never trusted this old man, he always seemed a bit too sly to me, dirty too, I almost feel sorry for her staying here, the smell the last time we visited stayed in my clothes for days,' he told the blonde one, who frowned in consternation.

'Surprisingly, it seems clean enough now,' muttered the pale-eyed man. 'I wonder if it was a trick to get us to stay away? These tricky old dogs, we've got to keep an eye on them.'

Isabelle tried to maintain a bland look at their rudeness. She was bit surprised to see that Antoine hadn't reacted at all to being called sly. Or to the idea that Théo was an idiot...

'I hope you recover well, mademoiselle,' said the one who looked like a boxer.

Isabelle nodded at him.

When they left the farmhouse, she wasn't the only one to breathe a sigh of relief.

'They didn't suspect you. Thank God,' whispered Théo.

'Thank God,' said Antoine and Isabelle at the same time.

'For a second I thought he might, the way the blonde one stared at you and then that conversation the two of them had... it was like my heart was in my mouth,' said Théo.

Isabelle looked at him. 'What do you mean?' she asked.

'When they were speaking, I thought the dark-haired one might have been on to you. But then they left.'

'Me too,' whispered Antoine, who showed them his hand, which was shaking.

Isabelle frowned. They hadn't understood them. But *she had*.

It was only then that she realised why: they'd been speaking in German and she had *understood* them.

'They said they were going to inspect the barns.'

She left out the part about him being called sly. Or what they'd said about Théo.

Antoine swore. 'Well, there goes the pig.'

But Isabelle didn't hear. All she could think was, *I speak German?*

Later that day, after the Nazis had left, along with the pig, Isabelle was still trying to understand what she had learned about herself.

Was she German?

No, I can't be.

She thought in English. She knew that about herself, at least. She knew other things, too, like that this part of France was different to where she came from. There the summers were cooler. The landscape flatter. But she couldn't give a name to where she had lived. She knew things that she couldn't recall learning like language and mathematics, geography and history. Language. Or languages really. But anything personal – her name, her family, the town where she might have lived, the home she had grown up in, the face of her mother or father, was simply blank.

It was frustrating.

She was putting Antoine and Théo in danger and she couldn't even tell them who she was.

The sense of unease was ever present. The feeling that she was missing something haunted her waking moments.

Her broken arm was painful, but nothing hurt as much as her burned foot. The skin had stretched tight and it was painful just to move. Her injuries made everything difficult, particularly going to the bathroom, but at least she could do it herself.

Antoine had given her some clothes that belonged to his wife, Jean, who he said had died a few years after Théo was born. The clothes were old-fashioned. But, again, she didn't know how she knew that. There were a few house dresses, a thick cardigan, and a nightdress.

There was a photograph of Jean on her bedside table. Antoine brought it to show her.

'She would have liked you,' he said. 'She would have been glad that we helped.'

'She has a kind face,' said Isabelle, staring at the faded photograph of the woman reading, sitting in the *Toile de Jouy* chair.

'Yes,' said Antoine, in a slightly choked voice. 'That's what I remember about her most. She had the kindest heart of anyone, apart from maybe Théo.'

Isabelle nodded. 'She lives on in him, then.'

'Yes, and my daughter. She died in an accident, along with her husband when Théo was a baby.'

Isabelle's heart went out to the old man. So much tragedy in such a short time. It must have been hard. She hoped it wouldn't be too difficult for Antoine seeing her in his wife's clothes. Perhaps it brought her back a little.

'I'll leave you to get changed.' Antoine shuffled away, his blue eyes misty.

The mirror in the bathroom showed the face of a stranger.

The first time she'd seen herself had been a shock. She didn't know if the blisters and burns on her face made that worse – her lips were still painfully swollen, and her right cheek was purple with bruises beyond the burns. Her hair was long and dark, but it was also filthy and matted. She longed to wash it but she didn't think she would be able to manage that with her broken arm anytime soon.

But she didn't think it was the injuries that shocked her most.

It was her eyes. A person should recognise their own eyes.

She didn't.

But she forced herself to keep looking.

They were green and brown, like a forest with secrets to hide.

'You will remember,' she told herself.

She frowned, even to her own ears it sounded more like a wish than a promise.

She was shorter, too, than she would have thought.

When she climbed, gingerly, back into bed, it was with relief. Earlier that day, Théo had brought her a book to read, the one he'd just finished. It was *The Count of Monte Cristo*. She turned now to read it, needing a distraction from her own thoughts. But as she looked down at the first page, she swallowed. The letters seemed to scurry across the page like ants and she struggled to follow them. Instinctively, she laid a finger beneath one, like she was pinning it to the page, and as she did, a feeling of shame bubbled to the surface as a memory washed over her.

It was cold inside the room where they held Sunday school, yet she was sweating in her starched linen dress. The collar felt like it was choking her and she tugged at it uselessly, her throat turning dry.

Her hands shook as she turned back to the reader in front of her with dread. She placed her finger under the words and began to read.

There was a sharp smack of a ruler on the pulpit. 'No!'
She jumped.
The teacher's face was inches from hers, her flat grey eyes, over a hawk-like nose, were about to pounce.

'Are you a baby? Or are you a great girl of nine? I should expect your reading to be far better than this! Only babies use their fingers to follow sentences. Perhaps if you spent less time daydreaming and more time concentrating you wouldn't embarrass yourself so?'

Her cheeks flushed scarlet, and she threw the book down on the floor.

Next to her a pair of warm brown eyes flared. A husky boy's voice hissed, 'the only one embarrassing themselves is you.'

'How dare you, Michael!'

Isabelle gasped.

Michael?

The image of the boy had only been a flash. But it was enough.

Théo had said that when he found her she was asking after someone named Michael...

Her face was flushed, and her hand was clenched in a fist from the memory of that dour teacher but there was something else, something besides the rapid quickening of heartbeat and the dry feeling in her mouth. Something important.

She felt tears fall, and she frowned.

Whoever it was... her mind wanted to remember him.

6

The Germans were back. Isabelle's heart hammered inside her chest.

She could hear the panicked voices of Antoine and Théo in the corridor outside as they went to open the front door.

Had she been found out?

Her throat turned dry, and she struggled to sit up.

The man who entered her room was the same one as before. The blonde one who had a boxer's build. He held a small box in his arms. He was preceded by Antoine who had a grim expression on his face.

Isabelle swallowed.

'*Mademoiselle*,' he greeted her, with a small smile. 'I have brought some supplies – salve, bandages, painkillers, for your wounds,' he said. 'Also, in the kitchen, another box, with some vegetables, and some meat,' he said, giving Antoine a bit of a knowing look. 'It only seemed fair to share some of that.'

Isabelle blinked in surprise.

'Th-thank you,' she said, confusion mixing with relief.

'Dieter Frosch,' he said, introducing himself.

Before she could stop herself, she asked, 'Why are you

helping me?' only to wince internally – her French, according to Antoine, was close to fluent but her accent was distinctly English. She needed to be careful not to say too much and risk giving herself away. It wasn't only her life at stake.

Thankfully, he hadn't appeared to pick up on it yet.

She couldn't take the risk by speaking too much more. She hoped he would figure she was tired from her injuries.

He startled at the question, like he was genuinely surprised. 'Mademoiselle?' Then he frowned, a muscle flexed in his jaw. 'You think that we are—' He stopped himself and perhaps considered. Then he looked out of the window to the fields of vineyards in the distance and sighed. 'We are considered cold and unfeeling, this is understandable, I suppose,' he acknowledged. 'My colleague, he's a bit tactless, likes to play the brute. It only makes things worse, and is unnecessary. But that is not my way, or the right way to go about things, I do not want my time here to be a trial for anyone. I aim to make myself useful where I can.'

Isabelle couldn't help thinking of what she'd heard of Monsieur Dubois and how he'd worked himself so hard thanks to them. It had certainly been a trial for *him*.

She kept her face impassive. The real Isabelle may not have been able to.

There was a grunt of disapproval from his companion, the same dark, bad-tempered man as before. It was clear he did not share Frosch's goals.

His face betrayed his annoyance and impatience. Frosch dipped his head in farewell. 'If there is anything I can do, please don't hesitate to send a message.'

She nodded, then forced her lips into a smile.

Isabelle wasn't the only one shocked by his generosity. After they left, Théo came rushing back from the kitchen where he had pored over the basket of food.

'He brought enough to feed a family of ten,' he said in shock and confusion. 'I suppose not all of them can be bad,' he said. 'The other one gives me the creeps, though, the one with the dark hair with those ghostly pale eyes, you can see he's—'

Antoine made a *pfft* sound as he interrupted his grandson.

'He's *honest*. He doesn't come here pretending to be our *friend*, and he doesn't expect friendship in return. Frosch scares me far more. There are some men who delude themselves about their natures, and will remain convinced they are the good guy even as they beat you to death.'

Isabelle chilled at the thought.

'Maybe he isn't a bad person, though,' said Théo. 'Not everyone in Germany supports Hitler. I heard that if you said anything against him you could go to prison, and so it's possible some of the soldiers who were conscripted weren't really supporters, they're just doing what they have to.'

'That makes sense,' said Isabelle.

Antoine shook his head. 'Don't fool yourself – a wolf can look just like a dog until it bares its teeth. The Germans who were conscripted but not fully on board are the ones they send straight to the cannon. You don't get to Dieter Frosch's level, in that cushy post, without showing your support – trust me.'

Isabelle hadn't told Antoine or Théo about what she had remembered.

Perhaps it was because it wasn't particularly nice, or perhaps it was that she was trying desperately to recall more of it. But it wasn't until the next afternoon, when Théo was sitting at the foot of the bed, a board of draughts between them, while Antoine sat in the chair by the window, that she told them about the memory that had come to her, and how tinged with shame it had been when she'd tried to read aloud.

Antoine pressed his tongue beneath his lip, angrily. 'I always wonder about some of the people they allow to teach children. It's little wonder you recall *that* memory – many of the people who shape our childhood leave their mark, some only with scars, often due to nothing but sheer ignorance.'

They turned to look at him in surprise, and he explained. 'From what you described, it sounds a lot like "word blindness" – *dyslexia*,' said Antoine.

Isabelle frowned. 'Dyslexia.'

'My brother had it,' he explained. 'He might never have learned to read if my mother hadn't taken him to a specialist – he was misbehaving and acting oddly, and she had the sense to realise it was about something else. But how many other children are left in the dark, with teachers unable to help them just because they are different?'

Then he held up his left hand. 'The nuns used to tie my hand back so I stopped using this one,' he said.

She gasped. 'That's barbaric.'

Then, for just a moment, her lungs felt compressed, like she couldn't breathe, and she had a flash of a habit and there was the bitter taste of soap in her mouth. But before she could make sense of any of that, it was gone, leaving only the feeling of anxiety behind.

He shrugged. 'People fear what they don't understand.'

'People can be stupid,' said Théo, adjusting a black tile.

'Yes.'

Isabelle was lost in her thoughts. She had so many questions about herself. How did that shy, terrified girl, who clearly felt such a deep sense of shame at what she imagined was wrong with her become a pilot? *I wish I could connect the dots*, she thought. How did I go from that little girl who could barely read to someone who could speak three languages? Someone who flew planes, possibly for the Resistance.

. . .

Antoine switched the radio on with a small bit of trepidation. Ever since the Germans had come to visit, they had hesitated to play it.

Now that Dieter Frosch had taken an unwanted interest in her, they knew they were taking more of a risk to listen to it but none of them found that they didn't want to.

The radio was their only link to the unoccupied part of the world.

When Beethoven's Fifth Symphony came on, Isabelle frowned, and for a split second she remembered something. Something that had disturbed her the last time she'd heard it and not understood why.

'It's a code,' she said, surprising not just the others, but herself too.

They stared back at her.

'What do you mean, what code?' breathed Antoine.

She thought hard, pulling at the memory that was there, like a piece of thread.

'It has a meaning,' she said, 'this song. When they play it, it means...' She pulled at the thread some more. 'The British are sending secret agents over. There are code words, too, by the presenters that tell the Resistance how many to expect, and where.'

Théo gasped. 'What? Really?'

She blinked and clasped at her heart. 'H-how did I know that?'

Antoine looked pale as he gawped at her. 'It might be that the music triggered your memory. You might find that other things do the same, other sounds, scents or sights.'

She nodded, feeling a little shaken.

The memory frayed. Beyond the music and the fact that it was a code there was static, like she herself had lost signal.

She couldn't make sense of it at all. Why did she know that? Was it true? Was she in the Resistance? She didn't know.

But she knew that what she'd said was true somehow.

She woke up to the sound of barking, then Antoine's face as he peeped inside her room.

'There's someone who is dying to meet you.'

She had heard the dog in the corridor before, but they had kept it away until now.

'Gently, Saint,' said Antoine, and led what looked like a great bear towards her.

Isabelle struggled to sit up.

The dog was massive. A mix of black and brown and flecked with small patches of white with paws the size of dinner plates. Gentle brown eyes peered up at her and he whined slightly and looked at the bed then at her for an invitation.

'Absolutely not,' said Antoine.

'See, this was where he used to sleep,' explained Théo, a dimple appearing in his cheek.

Isabelle smiled at the dog. 'So you're missing your bed, eh?' she said, reaching forward to pat him with a bandaged hand. She was rewarded with the thumping sound of his massive tail.

Then he put his great big head on the bed beside her and sighed in pleasure.

Isabelle wasn't sure who fell in love first.

As she stroked the soft fur, she smiled. 'Saint. It suits you. I think you do noble work, sir, making ladies fall in love with you.'

The dog opened his large mouth and gave her what could only be described as a grin.

'I always wanted a dog,' she told Antoine, 'but my mother wasn't a fan, especially in the house. She was the strict one in our family. Emily and I used to try everything to convince her, but she wouldn't budge. But then one day we came home and found this wiry brown dog with three legs sitting on my mother's lap, she—'

She broke off, eyes widening, as she realised, she'd been remembering.

It had felt so natural.

But as before, as soon as she reached for it, the threads of her memory vanished.

'You were remembering,' said Antoine, excitedly.

She nodded, eyes shining. 'I could see it so clearly. The kitchen – it had this great big wooden table and flagstone floors and a vast stove in the centre. On the ceiling, there were a series of oak beams, where copper pots and pans hung.'

'It sounds like a farmhouse, maybe,' said Antoine.

She blinked. Was it a farm? Perhaps.

As she frowned, she remembered barns.

A barn. But she couldn't picture farm equipment. The image flickered out like a candle flame, and she was left snatching at smoke.

She sighed in frustration.

For a moment, she had seen her mother's face. Warm brown curls, hazel eyes. She was tall and thin, elegant, with a small mouth that might have looked stern but was saved from being overly developed in that direction by a sense of humour.

'You mentioned someone named Emily?' prompted Antoine.

She nodded. 'I think she was – is – my sister. But I can't recall now.' She sighed again, blowing out her cheeks. 'It was right there, Antoine, like I could smell my mother's perfume, see that little dog—' she gave a half-smile, 'but now there's nothing.'

'Don't try to force it – you'll just upset yourself. From what I've seen, they're coming out, your memories – you just have to give it time.'

Saint made a warbling sort of whining noise.

Isabelle grinned, then patted him. 'At least you know how I feel,' she said.

. . .

Isabelle had been with them for ten days now. The blisters on her face had begun to heal but it would be months before her other injuries fully mended. Antoine believed that gentle movement would help. Isabelle felt that there was nothing gentle about it. Every step was a new circle of hell. But she knew he was right, and the thought of getting outside was her motivation. Anything to get away from what had begun to feel like a comfortable prison cell, pretty, with a lovely view, but a cell nonetheless.

One sunny afternoon, when the scent of jasmine was heady and the jays were singing loud enough to drown out thoughts of doubt, Isabelle was led by Antoine, Théo and the encouraging barks of Saint, some five hundred steps outside to a table that had been set up near the house.

She paused midway, as if she had run a marathon. Sweat slicked her back, and where she placed her weight on her ankle, it was agony.

'This was a mistake,' said Antoine, noting her heavy breathing as she turned deathly white.

'No, I can make it,' she insisted.

'Nearly there,' said Théo, but it took at least another few minutes to get her into the chair. She sat down gratefully, although it was so hard it felt more like she was sitting on a bed of stones. It didn't matter, anywhere was better than being in her bed for another moment more.

She'd longed for the outdoors. For the promise her window offered, of green earth, fresh air and freedom. She closed her eyes as she felt the cool breeze touch her skin and run through her hair. When she opened them, she marvelled at the view. She hadn't been able to appreciate it on the painful walk to the table, and it was so much more than the frame her window afforded.

They were in the middle of a valley of rolling vineyards, under a sapphire sky. It was breathtaking.

The air was full of the smell of late spring. There was the jasmine giving the sweet notes but beyond that there was thyme, sun-baked earth, unripe grapes, dry grass, and the heady scent of roses from a pink rambling rose that bloomed so vigorously, it made one forget, for a moment, that they were at war.

Perhaps nature bloomed even harder to try and tempt us away from our madness, she thought for a moment. *If only it worked.*

'It is extraordinary, this place,' she said.

Antoine nodded, solemnly, as he uncorked a dusty bottle of wine. 'My family have always lived here,' he said. 'I knew it was special, even as a boy, but when I was older, and I saw more of the world, I came to see how lucky we were to call this place home.'

A dark cloud seemed to pass over his face. 'And why they would try to take it from us.'

Isabelle looked at him, thinking of how awful it must have been when the Germans marched through here, the shock of having their world upended, their land occupied by an invading army. She shivered. *Why* did she understand German?

For a moment, his hands shook as he poured her a glass of wine. 'You know what we need? Some bread and cheese with this picnic.'

She nodded, then forced a smile, taking her cue from him.

She watched him go back into the farmhouse, his shoulders stooping, like Atlas carrying the weight of the world, and she felt her heart go out to him. At her knee, Saint whined, then put his great big head on her lap.

Théo reached over and rubbed the dog's ears.

It was difficult in that serene moment to imagine the darkness that crested the beautiful rolling landscape. But she knew it was there all the same.

Still, as Théo got comfortable on the grass, with an old copy of *National Geographic*, her gaze was taken by a pair of swifts in flight, and she watched as they flew towards the distant spire of a church, and for a moment, it reminded her of another, grander building.

She frowned and had a flash of someone running.

It was her.

Boots slapping against the wet pavement as the rain sheeted down. Cold. Her hair soaked through. She didn't care. There was a roar in her ears, adrenaline coursed through her veins, making her oblivious to anything else. She raced inside the building. Someone inside knew where he was, she would make them tell her, if it was the last thing she did.

Isabelle sat up with a start.

Her heart raced inside her chest. The memory felt visceral and raw. She could feel the echo of pain against her ribs as she ran, the fear clinching her stomach. The desperation.

But the memory slipped fast, and the harder she snatched it, the faster it disappeared.

She was aware, in some distant corner of her brain that Antoine had returned and was busy cutting up slices of baguette and cheese. His words seemed to come from far away.

'Isabelle, Isabelle?' he called, trying to get her attention. 'Are you all right?' his voice penetrating, at last.

Her eyes snapped to his and Théo's who was looking up at her curiously over the top of his magazine. She was back here, in France, but part of her was still... running.

'Isabelle?' said Antoine again.

She shook her head.

'No. Yes. I don't know.'

He frowned, appearing concerned. He took a seat next to her and put the bread knife down.

'I had a memory, I was running and trying to find someone.'

'Who?'

She felt a wave of anxiety almost crush her.

'I don't know.'

7

Isabelle woke to find Saint's head nudging her. 'Hello, boy.'

There was an answering stampede of thumps from his massive tail as it hit the floor. Then he whined and went to stand by the door, only to look back at her.

She frowned.

He whined again and she got the message.

'I swear you and the old man are in league with each other,' she huffed as she got up and made her way painstakingly to the corridor, sweat beginning to pool at her lower back from the effort, as she grit her teeth against the pain while the dog wove around her thighs as she made her way down the hall to the front door, which she opened for him.

Instead of going outside to do his business he waited by her side until she followed him. Making sure that she got her exercise appeared to be his new job description.

The same pattern had been repeating every day this week. It was as if Saint had heard Antoine say that she needed more fresh air and movement in order to recover faster and had appointed himself as her trainer.

It was a cloudy spring day, and the village on the hill was

shrouded in fog. The temperature had dropped just enough that she shivered in her nightdress. The heady, almost summer-like weather from a few days ago now seemed like a memory. A bright spot in an otherwise cloudy week. Sunshine in spring, she remembered, was a fickle friend.

The air smelled of rain on dry earth.

She breathed it in and tried to ignore the throbbing pain in her ankle.

She turned when she heard the sound of footsteps. Antoine was making his way towards her from the garden. He was carrying a box, from which she could hear a faint chirp.

'Ah, good, you're following doctor's orders.'

'Dr Saint's, yes. Did you teach him to wake me up like that?'

The old man laughed. 'No, that's all him.'

She grinned, then scratched the dog behind the ears. He leaned against her and she had to plant her feet wide so she didn't fall over from his weight. He looked up at her and she didn't have the heart to move him.

'What's in the box?'

He came closer and she saw a blackbird, one of its wings bent at an odd angle. The bird looked like it was in pain – she could understand how it felt.

'Théo found it earlier. I'll need to treat it for a few weeks and set the wing. It won't like it. But Théo will take good care of it.'

She nodded. 'I can believe that.'

Antoine smiled. 'And you – are you feeling better?' he asked.

She knew he wasn't referring to her injuries this time but rather the memory that she had shared with him that had haunted her ever since. She had lain awake the night after she had that memory of her running and trying to find someone, tossing and turning as she tried and failed to get her brain to tell her anything more about who she had been trying to find.

It had been a few days since and it haunted her still as she tried desperately to remember. But so far there was nothing.

She'd had other flashes though, other fragments of memory.

A letter arriving and her excitement as she opened it. She would get to do something for the war effort at last! A blonde woman with an impish smile, who hooked her arm in hers and said, 'All work and no play makes Johnny a dull boy, and these boys are anything but dull, darling,' then she giggled, leading her into the dance hall.

'Yes,' she said to Antoine now.

It was hard to know the timeline of any of the snatches of memory that were coming back to her. Or what they were about either.

The memory flash with the letter was the one that frustrated her the most.

Her name was on that letter. She could see the envelope in her mind's eye. The stamp, the typing. But where her name was there was just a blur.

Later that day, she was in the kitchen, helping Antoine prepare lunch.

It was the first time she had visited this part of the farmhouse.

It had flagstone floors that dipped slightly in the middle by the hearth from centuries of people warming their bones before the fire. In the centre was a scrubbed wooden table, where she was sitting. Opposite this was a large oven, next to the open hearth. Hanging from the rafters there were copper pots and pans.

The windows were misted, offering only a partial view of the vineyards outside. It was like being inside a teapot, as the soup bubbled on the hob and the warm air circulated through the room.

Isabelle was chopping vegetables. She was fast and efficient. 'I've done this before,' she said, with a frown. 'Cooked, I mean.'

Antoine nodded, as he took the wooden chopping board from her and then scraped the potatoes into the waiting pot.

Théo was sitting next to her and had been assigned the same task. The little injured blackbird was nearby in its box, its wing bandaged now as it slept.

'I should think so!' exclaimed the boy. 'You peeled those potatoes like someone who meant business. I'm still struggling with my first,' he said, holding up a very sorry-looking spud that was now half the size it had been originally as he had cut away most of it with the peel.

She laughed. Suddenly, a memory sprang forth, unbidden.

'My mother once timed my sister and I – she said that whoever got the most done would get a prize. I remember my mother saying that if she had to take either of us to hospital for slicing off a finger, neither of us would get the prize. She set the kitchen timer and we got to work.'

Isabelle grinned. 'I think I must have peeled over thirty potatoes in about ten minutes, and when my mother gave me this silly wooden spatula that she'd drawn a funny face on with horns as our "prize" we all howled with laughter as that was the spoon she always threatened to smack us with. She said, "Well, Francesca there will be no smacked bottoms this week for you—"'

Then she gasped, her eyes widening. The potato slipped from her fingers and rolled across the stone floor. No one paid it any attention.

Théo stared at her open mouthed.

Antoine clapped a hand over his mouth.

Isabelle paused, laughter dying on her lips.

'You remembered your name,' exclaimed Théo.

She stared at them both. 'Francesca,' she breathed in wonder. The memory had come to her so easily. She could see her mother's teasing smile, hear her faintly accented Irish voice. See her sister Emily with her blue eyes and the tip of her tongue popping out from her mouth as she concentrated.

She frowned, then shook her head, 'No. That's not right, only she called me that. Everyone else called me *Frankie*.'

8

SUFFOLK, 1931

On the day she turned twelve, Frankie's father woke her up at dawn. He held a finger to his lips so that she didn't disturb her sleeping sister. There was a twinkle in his eye as he whispered, 'Come on, birthday girl, there's something you need to see.'

She rubbed the sleep from her eyes, then grinned, as she followed him outside. He led her away from the house, down the farm track towards a pair of barns where he restored old planes.

She shivered in her nightdress in the early dawn light. The air was crisp and fresh and the grass was that bright lime peel of spring, making her mouth pool with saliva as if she could taste it.

Her father's smile was infectious. He had deep dimples on either side of his mouth. 'Come on, Frankie-beans,' he said, bouncing on the balls of his feet as he led her inside the barn.

He steered her with some fanfare towards something vast covered by a sheet and declared, 'Happy birthday!'

He pulled back the sheet to reveal a lightly rusted biplane, with two wings placed one above the other.

'It's a Moth! A classic de Havilland Moth-DH.60. Light as a feather, perfect for you.'

Her eyes widened.

'For me?' she gasped, bouncing in excitement.

He nodded. 'They're named moths – because of the way their wings fold backwards, it makes it easy to store the plane in small places.'

Moth, she thought. Coming forward to touch a wing with reverence. For a moment she pictured herself flying under the moon like one.

She looked at him in wonder. 'I can't believe you did this.' She felt a rush of love, mixed with worry for her father. Her mother would be impossible to deal with, she knew.

As if he could read her mind, he said, 'Don't worry, I'll wear her down.'

Then he gave her a one-handed hug, squeezing her tight to him, and it felt like the safest place in the world.

He'd lost his other hand in the war. Frankie had grown up with the story, like a bedtime tale that was so beloved it had worn-out pages. But she never tired of it. After his hand and forearm were amputated and he was recovering in the hospital, one of the officers in his flying squad had remarked, flippantly, 'Well, there goes your flying days, old sport,' and her father had lain there in his hospital and felt the darkness closing in over him. Felt the words crush into him and weigh him down. Felt once more how different life would be for him. Around him, so many of his friends and peers were still trapped, mentally, in the horrors of the trenches, but so many more had lost their lives. Like his best friend, Tim, whose plane had been shot down in France. Her father knew it was silly to mourn the loss of his arm when Tim wasn't around – he just wished that he could have given it so that his friend was still there. So that there weren't two things to mourn.

The doctors told her father that he was lucky and at first,

he'd wanted to hit them for that. But over time, he saw how so many soldiers came back whole on the outside but couldn't escape the mental clutch of the trenches, or how others came back so broken the chance of them ever leaving the hospital at all was doubtful, and he understood. But it would be some time and a lot of mental work, he said, before he *felt* it.

'But something shifted for me the day that officer said that my flying days were over. Maybe it's because I'm a born contrarian, or maybe I just wanted to wipe that smug look off of his face. Either way, he did me a favour because it was the day I stopped feeling sorry for myself and started making plans on how I could prove that bastard wrong.'

Frankie always grinned at that.

By the time he was discharged and well enough, technically, to get back in the cockpit, he had run through everything in his mind so clearly, worked out all the ways he would be able to compensate for the loss of his hand, so that when he visited his old airbase and asked if he could take one of the planes for a spin, he was already in a plane and up in the air, flying, before anyone had a chance to object. When he landed, an hour later, and was read the riot act by a commanding officer, he'd found two things he'd long thought he'd lost to the war, his pride and his smile.

That was the day he *felt* lucky. The day he realised not only could you live with one hand, but you could also live well. He would do it for his best friend, Tim, who couldn't.

It did something to Frankie, having a father like that. Someone who looked on the brighter side of things, scanning the sky for opportunities, not bombs.

One of those opportunities, he discovered, was her.

Her father had a way of seeing things others didn't.

It was her father who saw how she was drowning. He noticed when something began stealing her spark. School had always been like death by a thousand cuts for her, but on one particular day that winter, when the snow was beginning to settle, she'd gone into her classroom, and made her way to her desk at the back.

There was a tutting sound from the front and her teacher snapped at her. 'I don't even know why you bother coming here, Miss Chalmers.'

She turned to look at the woman in surprise.

'Mam?'

The teacher was holding up a stack of student work that she had marked. She put it on the desk then picked up the first one with a look of disgust on her face. It was clearly Frankie's, by the way she shot her a look of pure disdain.

There were quiet murmurs around her as the other children stared at her. Frankie felt her cheeks warm. It was covered in red pen.

'I read your homework from yesterday, and to be honest I'm at my wits' end. You don't *seem* like an idiot, but I suppose looks can be deceiving. So either you're just lazy and careless or after five years of schooling you're basically illiterate. Which one is it?'

There were gasps all around.

Frankie stared at the floor.

'I'm waiting.'

She shut her eyes and tried not to cry. She couldn't say the truth. That she still couldn't really read.

'Careless,' she said softly.

There was a grunt.

Around her there were a few titters. Then one boy laughed. 'Nah, it's the other one, mam.'

And everyone joined in.

After that she became withdrawn. Her parents didn't know what was wrong and no amount of prodding would get her to tell them what it was, as she was too embarrassed. The failure felt bone deep, especially when she compared herself to her sister, Emily, who had always found school so easy.

Her mother tried tough love. 'For the love of God, child, either tell me what's got you so down in the dumps or snap out of it!' Which did about as much good as one would expect.

Her father tried a different approach. He sensed that she needed something else to think about. Something that might lift her spirits.

A few weeks later when the snow melted, he took her for her first flying lesson. She had felt a mixture of fear and excitement, and for the first time since that day in school, when her teacher called her an idiot, it was as if she'd shrugged off a heavy cloak that had been weighing her down.

By the time she was airborne and guiding the plane across the fields, her father's whoops of encouragement in her ear, she too had rediscovered her smile.

She'd also found something she was *good* at. It changed her overnight.

'A natural,' her father had said, beaming at her, after he'd guided her to land the plane in a fallow field that last year had housed sugar beet. There was pride in his eyes. 'It's remarkable! I had a feeling you'd take to it – you have such natural coordination, but I must say you've blown me away, my girl. You'd think you'd been flying solo for months already. You have instincts it takes some pilots hundreds of hours to develop.'

Frankie had felt the hairs stand up on her neck. It was the first time she'd ever been praised for being good at something. It was like entering a warm bath after a very cold winter.

And she never wanted to leave.

She turned to look at her father now and then gave him another hug. He knew how much flying meant to her.

'I'm glad you like the plane. It's not in too bad shape, should be flightworthy in a few months. Long enough for us to try and convince your mother to let you learn officially.'

She'd already had several unofficial lessons with him, far away from view of their farmhouse, and unbeknownst to her mother, who would, quite understandably, have murdered him if she knew.

Frankie and her father operated under a 'what your mother doesn't know, can't hurt her' principle. Her mother was anxious by nature. She worried as if it were her job. '*Careful of—*' the rain, the sun, keeping your dress clean, your temper – were regular reminders whenever Frankie set foot out the farmhouse door.

But today, perhaps in light of turning twelve and the wisdom that her new grand age afforded her, Frankie could see, a little, how reckless it might appear to put one's child in a rusty tin can and launch it into the sky...

Frankie winced. 'I can't see her changing her mind anytime soon, Dad. The last time I broached the idea, she went mad.'

'She'll come around, Frankie-beans.'

'It's your funeral,' she said. 'Might as well ask for a party.'

He laughed at that and tousled her hair.

Later that afternoon, as they sat down to lunch, Frankie was dreaming about the Moth, and how soon they could get her to fly, when her father said, 'Pass the potatoes, Frankie-beans.'

Her father called her 'beans' because he said she was full of them. She found it hard to sit still, ever.

'Will you, for the love of God, William,' her mother snapped, her Irish accent thickening in her anger, 'stop calling our daughter that? "Frankie" is bad enough. But "Frankie-beans" sounds like some gangster from a mob picture!' She slammed a dish of peas on the table and glared at him, her hazel eyes snapping fire.

Unfortunately, this made her sister and Michael laugh so

hard, that Michael snorted water from his nose, and they all began to imagine mobster names for themselves.

Michael was the son of her father's best friend Tim, whose plane had been shot down during the war. Her father had made a point of helping Tim's family however he could and often took Michael under his wing.

Scrappy, their wiry, short-haired Yorkshire terrier with three legs, had taken his position under Michael's chair, because wherever the boy was, was where he wanted to be. It didn't hurt that Michael was a soft touch and always shared secret tidbits with the dog when no one was looking.

Frankie's mother sniffed.

Frankie felt a twinge of guilt even as she laughed along with the others. Her mother had made all of her favourite food for her birthday lunch. Roast chicken and potatoes and her special rice with peppers. Even though she was usually strict on not having more than two starches at a meal, she'd made an exception as it was a special occasion. There were also two types of ice cream for dessert and a pineapple cake, another of her favourites.

Her mother had been working all day in the kitchen and the evidence of her love was there on the table, if not always with the sharp words that sometimes skewered Frankie in place for a moment, before she managed to wiggle out and away.

'This is delicious, Mum, thank you,' Frankie said, hoping to defuse things.

Her mother nodded,'You're welcome,'but the high spots of colour on her cheeks grew redder as her eyes narrowed as she considered everyone at the table who were continuing on with the game.

Her mother's outburst was too regular an occurrence for most of them to pay it any real attention. Her emotions burned close to the skin but they also burned away quickly too.

'You'd be Two-Bob-Em, because you're always after two bob for the cinema,' joked Michael to her sister, Emily, who hooted with laughter.

Frankie snorted.

Her sister's dark curls were burnished red by the late-afternoon sunlight pouring in from the window and her blue eyes shone.

For as long as she could remember her mother had been asking Frankie a question she often asked herself. 'Why can't you be more like Emily – look how neat her side of the room is?' or 'Why can't you be more like Emily – she never loses her temper like you do?' or 'Why are you so wild – your sister always does her homework straight after school, while the first thing you do is run outside.'

It should have made her resent her sister, but it didn't. Emily had a tendency to shut herself inside on beautiful days with her books, so Frankie cajoled her sister into reading outside in the garden with her.

Despite their differences, Frankie adored Emily, and wanted to be just like her. Emily loved the pictures, and her side of their shared room was covered in movie posters. She did her hair up like Jean Harlow, and so of course, so did Frankie... just with a bit less finesse.

If her mother wouldn't have 'given her a hiding' as she threatened to do if Frankie even thought about putting on make-up yet, she'd wear the same bright red lipstick her older sister wore on special occasions too.

Emily winked at her now and she grinned back, as she handed her father the potatoes.

'Mum would be—'

'Careful, be very careful, now—' warned her mother, shooting her sister a look. But now there was the faintest twitch of amusement from her lips.

'Careful Carmine?' suggested their father, a twinkle in his eyes.

They all howled. Frankie always thought her mother's favourite word was careful. She said it so often.

Even her mother laughed.

'Michael could be Mikey Shoeshine,' Frankie suggested. 'You know, because whenever he comes over to visit he always says he was late because he had to shine his shoes.'

They all giggled at that, including Michael, who was fourteen with dark brown hair and eyes and the sort of smile that the postmistress in the village had said was going to cause a lot of heartbreak someday.

Michael was often around at theirs whenever he was home from boarding school, because his mother was one of those people who put her name down for everything in the village and was hardly ever home because she was so busy running everything else. When Frankie was younger, she'd just accepted this without question, it hadn't occurred to her that this might have been a source of pain for Michael, and that he was bound to feel neglected by his mother.

But a few years ago, Frankie had heard her parents whispering about it, when they thought she and Emily couldn't hear.

'Sometimes I feel like I want to go and wring Irene's neck,' her mother had said. 'Some people don't deserve to be mothers.'

'Car, you know she had it rough after Tim died, she could barely function... he was the love of her life.'

'That doesn't mean she gets to abandon her son in all but name. Her boy needs him.'

'He has us.'

'Aye, that he does, thank the Lord. We might not have been blessed with a boy of our own. But he's as good as.'

'That he is.'

It made Frankie see him differently after that. Saw how

lonely he seemed sometimes. Or the way he stared at her parents, as if in awe, at times, and her heart couldn't help widening just that bit more for him.

Emily thought of him as a brother, but Frankie didn't. Mostly because she'd long harboured the secret hope that when she was older, he would marry her. Thankfully, he had no idea about her secret desire, and if he did, he was kind enough to feign ignorance.

Michael looked mock-affronted. 'I happen to care about my appearance, unlike some people,' he said.

'I care!'

He shot her a look. 'If you had your way you'd wear overalls all day and help your father build planes.'

'You might have a point about the *day*, but at night I would make up for it by dressing up like Lana Turner and wearing the most outrageous red lipstick I could find.'

They all laughed at that.

Frankie might have worn overalls a lot while she helped her father work on his planes but she also adored dresses and pored over her mother's copies of *Woman's Own*.

He laughed. 'Touché.'

Later, her parents went to wash the dishes, giving the children a rare break from the daily chore. As they sat in the living room, listening to the radio, they soon heard the sound of raised voices coming from the kitchen blocking it out.

Emily shot her a look of sympathy as it became clear what they were arguing about.

'You're actually planning to teach Francesca how to fly some old rusty plane you found? You can't be serious.'

Next to her, Michael turned white. He looked at her askance. 'He bought you a plane?'

She nodded, then bit her lip. This was not how she wanted him to find out.

His eyes turned dark. Beside him, Scrappy put his head on the boy's knee, and looked at him in concern.

He patted the dog absently.

She felt her stomach twist slightly. Michael had lost his father in a plane and had always been a bit apprehensive around them. She knew he worried about her father's safety in the old planes he fixed up, and she could just imagine what he was thinking now... it was likely similar to her mother. Frankie opened her mouth to try and explain, to say that they would be careful, but she was interrupted by the sound of her father's voice from the kitchen.

'I promise you I won't let her take it up until we've got rid of every last speck of rust, then when it's ready, we'll start with some short lessons close by. She's old enough now, and you know how much she loves planes,' said her father.

'And whose fault is that William Chalmers! You encourage her foolish ways.'

'Carmine, sweetheart,' said my father softly. 'She needs this. It'll be good for her.'

'*GOOD* for her? Can you even hear yourself?'

Michael looked as if he'd been struck speechless. It was clear that he was on her mother's side.

Then her father said something that made her squirm uncomfortably.

'She's struggling, Carmine.'

Frankie felt her cheeks flush pink. Emily looked at her, then looked away. Unfortunately, she knew exactly what she meant. It was no secret that she wasn't doing well at school, but even Emily didn't know how bad it really was. The last person she wanted to know though was Michael.

Michael frowned, looking puzzled.

Frankie was horrified at the thought of him knowing her secret shame.

If she could have, she would have bundled him out of the farm and back to his cottage in the village before he could hear another word, but there was no stopping this.

She looked at Michael, askance.

But he didn't look back at her.

'What she needs, William, is to focus on her reading and writing, to spend less time trailing after you and focus on her schooling. Her teacher says that she struggles with most of her letters and can barely read more than a few sentences. At *twelve!* By her age, Emily was reading novels in French, as well as her mother tongue.'

Frankie sucked in the air sharply. She was used to being compared to Emily but her mother had never stated her shortcomings in comparison to her sister so baldly before.

She closed her eyes in mortification.

'She's exaggerating, Frankie. I could read a few picture books. Maybe we should go out into the garden,' suggested Emily, kindly.

The last thing Frankie wanted was pity. She wanted to run upstairs to her room and slam the door but she didn't as she also wanted to hear what her father said next.

'Carmine, she tries, it's just hard for her. It doesn't help you comparing them like that either. They're different, but different doesn't mean wrong.'

'I know that! And I don't compare them, Bill! I'm just pointing out the facts. Francesca needs to focus, or she will get even further behind and you distracting her with this will only make things harder.'

'It's not a distraction, Carmine. It might be the motivation she needs; we can make it so that the price of her flying is making sure she does all her homework.'

At this Michael gasped, his face turned red and the next

thing Frankie knew, Michael was storming into the kitchen where he began to launch into her father, right alongside her mother.

'So, watching someone else you love die in a plane is a price you're willing to pay, Bill, just so she improves at school? Was my father's death not enough for you?' he hissed. 'You want to lose Frankie too?'

9

It took ages for Michael to calm down.

He left that afternoon, and they didn't see him for days. But they felt his absence in everything. In their silent meals afterwards, in the way Scrappy would lie on the mat by the door and whine, and by the haunted look that had stolen into her father's eyes.

Frankie had expected her father to go running after him, to try and explain. To put his arm around him and talk to him in that soft, patient way he had that always put the world to rights. But he didn't do that. He stayed glued to the spot in the kitchen, his hand dripping wet dishwater onto the floor, looking as if he'd been cut in two.

After that he did what all wounded creatures do, he disappeared to lick his wounds.

As the days passed, Frankie watched her father's figure in the distance on the farm as he wandered aimlessly through barns he hadn't been inside of for years, and took a sudden interest in the farm he'd long left the manager and his team to run while he got on with his business of restoring planes. A situation that suited everyone apart from her mother who had often lamented that it wasn't right for her father to ignore his family business the way he did. Perhaps she was regretting that now.

In this corner of Suffolk, her mother always said that they grew sugar beet and potatoes and ways to test her patience.

'He's just annoying Henley now,' said her mother one afternoon as she attacked the potatoes with a knife, her cheeks pink from the heat of the steaming pot where she dropped each one as if they had caused her some personal offence. 'Your father has asked him five times now why the east field is fallow, it's clear he doesn't listen. The last time Henley got fed up and told him that it's so that the fey folk can host their midnight picnics and your father just nodded, and said, "Good, good." I swear that man is going to send me to an early grave.'

To be fair she said that about all of them. But her words about how distracted he was pierced Frankie's heart.

He didn't go near the barn where the Moth was.

Frankie felt bad for Michael, and hated how hurt he was. But she also couldn't help resenting the boy for the pain he was causing her father now.

It hadn't been fair what he'd said. Her father had nothing to do with his best friend's death. But grief and guilt defy reason and logic and she also knew that in his heart of hearts her father had always thought that somehow, he might have prevented Tim's plane from being gunned down, even though he hadn't been flying with him on the day he died.

'Right, I've had quite enough of this,' said her mother, on the third day since the rift with Michael, from the top of the stairs when she watched him put on his wellingtons with an expression that looked to Frankie, from her post on the top step, like he was a man about to face the hangman's noose.

She went marching down in her slippers, heading towards him like an exclamation point.

'It is time for you to get your act together, Bill Chalmers. I know I've been at you for years to take more of an interest in our farm but it's clear your heart isn't in it! The only thing worse than you ignoring the farm all these years is your poxy interest in it now!'

Then her voice softened. 'It's my fault, for pushing you. You know I don't like admitting when you're right, but you were right about that. Henley knows what he's about so it's time now to get back to normal. I'll never pretend to know why you enjoy restoring planes instead of being out in the fresh air—'

'Well, it's the feeling of accomplishment – of bringing something back to life.'

She looked up at him, and a tender look passed over her face. 'And you're good at that. So why are you abandoning it now?'

He frowned. 'I'm not.'

She raised a brow.

'Michael is a just a boy and he's probably feeling awful for what he said. You need to make this right.'

A shadow passed over his face. 'What I need to do is get back to work.'

Her mother snapped. 'Despite all evidence to the contrary lately, Bill Chalmers, you are the grown-up, which means you are the one who has to act like it. Don't tell me you're afraid of a fourteen-year-old boy, whose only fault has been to worship you since he was a lad – and the first time he sees you as human and vulnerable, you're going to hold that against him for the rest of his life?'

'Of course not.'

'You know why he was upset. Frankie has always been his favourite. We're the only family that boy has – his absent mother notwithstanding – and the thought of losing her like he lost his father must have sent him overboard.'

Frankie's heart twisted at that. Sometimes her mother knew exactly what to say.

She saw her father surreptitiously wipe his eyes, then nod.

Later that afternoon, he left and when he returned, Michael was with him.

'He's going to teach me to fly too,' said Michael, seeing Frankie loitering near the barn that housed the Moth. She had been feeling unaccountably nervous about approaching him after his absence.

She looked up at him in shock now. 'What?'

He nodded, then smiled. 'It might be fun, us learning together.'

'Fun?'

He nodded, but the look in his eyes didn't match his words. She'd known him too long; she could tell when he wasn't quite telling the truth.

Why did he want to learn?

She felt a stab of guilt that it had something to do with her.

'Michael, you don't have to. I – well, I know how you feel about it.'

'It's all right, Frankie.'

She hadn't seen him for days, and she looked upon his face now, as if seeing it anew. He looked thinner, there were shadows beneath his dark eyes, and his dark hair wasn't quite as perfectly combed as it usually was. Her heart went out to him, imagining him all alone at his cottage. This hadn't been easy on him either.

He was somehow even more handsome than she remembered, too. She tried to push that thought away.

She frowned. 'But why do you want to learn, when you told Father that he was going to get me killed?'

He blew out his cheeks. 'I shouldn't have said that. I didn't even mean it. Well, not really. Rationally, I know he would be careful, but it just sounded so... reckless. The thought of losing you like my father, I... well, I don't know if I could bear it.'

She looked down, touched. She would feel exactly the same if she lost him. They all would.

'Look, I know you probably think it's riskier for me learn to fly because I'm a girl—'

'I don't think that! Blimey, you're tougher than many of the boys I know – I know you could handle it.'

She was confused at that. She didn't feel especially tough. 'How am I tough?'

He smiled, then leaned against the barn, shading his warm brown eyes from the late summer sun.

'I love your mum, you know I do, but well, I think a lot of people would crumple at criticism like hers, and yet you always seem as if it just rolls off your back.'

'That's because I'm too used to it.'

He raised a brow. They both knew that was only half true.

'Also, any sign of weakness and she goes after blood.'

He grinned. Pointed a finger at her, then winked. Then his face turned serious. 'Then there's how you handle the situation at school – I know it can't be easy, but you keep trying—'

Her cheeks turned red. She didn't want to talk about that. She hated that he knew how much she struggled, and she couldn't help feeling ashamed. It was something everyone else managed, so why couldn't she?

'If you really think I'm tough, why did you think it was crazy for me to learn to fly?'

Michael sighed. 'I just couldn't understand why he'd want to risk your life that way, after what happened to my father.'

She frowned. 'But your father didn't die in a crash. He was an excellent pilot, that's what Dad always says.'

Michael ran a hand over his eyes. 'Yes, but if he wasn't in a plane then he wouldn't have got shot down. It sounds stupid, I suppose, now, saying it aloud. He might just as easily have been shot in the trenches.'

Frankie nodded.

The one place on the farm he never ventured was the barn where her father restored planes. He never showed any interest in them at all. It was as if they just didn't exist. Whenever her father spoke of flying, a troubled look would cross over the boy's face, like he was terrified he might lose the closest thing to a father he'd ever had.

It was the reason, even from a young age, Frankie had never pressed him to join them in the barn. Even though as far as she had always been concerned any room that contained Michael was always improved by his presence.

'Why did you ask him to teach you to fly?'

He bit his lip. 'So I could get over my fear of it, or at least that's what I told him.'

'Isn't that the whole reason?'

He shook his head. 'I know you – you're going to learn either way, and I just figured if I was here, learning too, maybe I could make sure you didn't get yourself killed.'

That was what she was afraid of – that he was making himself do something that terrified him because he thought he might somehow protect her. That he would risk his life just to look after hers. It made her feel guilty for even wanting to learn.

But not guilty enough to want to stop. Which was a different kind of guilt anyway.

10

It took them just over a month to restore the Moth.

They worked on it every spare moment they had.

Frankie would race home from school, drop her bag in the hall, shout hello and 'bye to her mother and be out in the barn before her mother had a chance to shout, 'Change into your overalls!'

Michael did the same.

As they worked, they listened to her father's radio, humming along to songs by Louis Armstrong, their paint brushes and sandpaper sliding along to ragtime and swing music from the previous decade.

The news was full of stories about the economy, and the depression sweeping across the globe, but there in that barn, it was hard to imagine such things.

Working on the Moth was the high point of her day.

Her mother, however, would not let her father forget that he had promised her that Frankie's schoolwork would come first.

Ten years earlier, the Education Act had extended the school leaving age to fourteen and now most children were expected to be at school all day. The syllabus now included a range of subjects, but Frankie's worst was still reading and writing. Considering how little she seemed to get out of her schooling a part of her wished that her mother shared the opinion of some neighbouring farming families who grumbled that their children were needed to work on their farms, not learn things they might never need.

'In a hard world like ours, what a child needs are options, Frankie, and an education will provide that. You might not see that now. But I've known many people change their fates because of it. My great-grandmother and grandmother were maids, and my mother would surely have followed the same path, if she hadn't decided to train as a secretary. It gave her options that her mother would never have dreamed of. That's all I want for you too.'

Frankie nodded. It wasn't like she didn't want to learn, she just didn't seem able. She tried her best to honour her mother's wishes. She would do anything to be able to work on the Moth and begin flying lessons properly.

When she wasn't working on the plane, she stayed up late trying to get her homework done. But though she tried her best to make sense of the letters, and to progress, it was just as baffling and confusing as it always was. No amount of time seemed to make it easier, and one night when everyone else was asleep, her mother found her in the dining room crying over her worksheet.

'I just can't get it,' she sobbed. 'Maybe I *am* just stupid.'

Her mother blinked back her own tears, then gathered her up in a fierce hug.

'You are many things, Francesca Rose Anne, but stupid is not one of them. You were the first one of my children to talk and the first one to walk, and by God, did you love the word "why?" growing up. But unlike children who just ask that word over and over again you really listened to the answers. So I won't be having any of that sort of talk, you hear me? It's why I push you so hard, because I know you have it in you. But we have to do things differently. We can't keep trying the same thing over and over, as we are getting nowhere fast. There's something else going on here, and that's what we need to figure out.'

A few days later she came home with a solution.

It was a retired teacher by the name of Mrs Bell, who smelled of violets and old books. She resembled a dove but had the eyes of a hawk, who missed nothing. It was she who finally put a name to Frankie's struggles.

'You have what is known as *dyslexia*. And it is far more common than people imagine. Now, I'm not an expert but I have taught several students successfully over the years and I have some methods we can try that have made a difference – some I learned from researching how to help, and others I devised with the help of my students. One even became our Vicar—'

'The vicar struggled with reading?' cried Frankie in shock, thinking of how long his sermons were and how easily he seemed to read them.

'Indeed! Even today, you can see him pause over certain sections. Frankie, it won't be easy but it will get better, I promise you.'

For the first time, Frankie felt hopeful that she really might be able to learn how to read and write properly.

Mrs Bell was kind, but firm, and had a vastly different approach to her regular teacher who seemed to think that Frankie was just careless and uninterested and that if she insulted Frankie enough, or threatened her enough with her willow switch, she would somehow 'buckle up' which only had the opposite effect, as Frankie only learned how to shrivel instead.

Mrs Bell was not like that.

She had strategies and tricks up her sleeve. There were

different coloured papers and pens and ways to break sentences down. She used white space around words, so that they stood out more clearly.

Her sharp eyes grew kind whenever Frankie found herself using any of her old tricks – the ways she had fudged things and pretended to know words she didn't.

'Don't do that, Frankie. Don't pretend, we'll get there soon enough.'

By the end of that summer, it was like the clouds had parted, and she was able to see the road ahead. It would never come easy, but it was no longer an obstacle, it was just a challenge, one she could work with. In time, she would even surprise herself by learning to enjoy spending time with a book, instead of seeing it as some enemy that had to be feared.

It was a hazy summer's day, the grass was dry, and the birds were trilling in the trees, when Michael flew with her father for the first time.

He had to be helped out of the cockpit, and stumbled across the field on unsteady legs.

Frankie worried that he might be sick.

'I'm proud of you,' she said. 'Deep breaths,' she added, handing him a tin mug of water.

His fear was coming off him in waves, and it felt like she could taste it. Acid sharp.

Frankie knew something about fighting one's fear and doing it anyway, she knew how much harder it must have been for him to get behind the wheel than it was for her.

The fact that he did it made her respect him all the more.

Her father clapped a hand on his back. 'When you opened your eyes, you seemed to be enjoying it for a while? It'll get easier, son.'

Michael's hand shook as he brought the cup to his lips,

He raised a brow. It was clear he wasn't going to stop.

She sighed. 'There was a book I wanted to try reading, *Jane Eyre*, but my teacher... well, she didn't think I'd ever manage it.' She took a deep breath, feeling her cheeks redden with shame. She was too embarrassed to tell him the part where she'd suggested she stick to picture books instead.

'She shouldn't have said that,' whispered Michael.

'It's fine, I've had worse days, honestly.'

He nodded, a frown between his eyes.

She picked up a sheet of sandpaper and joined in, and soon she was singing along with them to the songs on the radio. Her hips swayed in time with Michael's as they sanded and the day melted away, so that the earlier sting faded to a dull ache.

A few days later, she heard Scrappy barking joyously at the front door. It was barely past dawn, and she got up to investigate. She opened it to find Michael standing there, a sheepish look on his face.

There was a package in his hands, which he had been in the middle of leaving on the front step.

His brown eyes widened and he gave her a lopsided grin. 'Hi.'

She grinned back. 'Hi? I thought you were heading back to boarding school today?'

'I am – I was just going to leave this here for you before I go.'

She blinked. 'For me?'

He straightened up, and passed the package to her. It was wrapped in brown paper. 'Open it,' he said, the tops of his ears reddening slightly.

She unwrapped the paper to discover it was a book.

'It's only second-hand. I got it from the bookshop in Woodbridge.'

She looked up at him in surprise. That was more than an hour away.

She turned to look at the cover. It was an older edition than the one on her teacher's shelf. It was a hardback, dark with gold lettering.

Jane Eyre.

Her mouth opened in surprise. She looked up at him in shock and he shrugged, as if it was nothing, when it wasn't, not at all.

'I thought you should have it.'

She opened the inside cover and saw his inscription, and felt a lump form in her throat.

'Thank you,' she said.

She reached out to squeeze his hand, feeling a bit overcome. He held on to hers.

11

PRESENT DAY, LOIRE VALLEY, 1944

It was only natural that soon enough one of the villagers would come past to meet the woman they were all pretending was Isabelle.

But as Antoine muttered beneath his breath, 'Why did it have to be *him?*'

It was the doctor, Monsieur Leclair, who came to call one afternoon when the spring weather had taken another turn. Rain lashed at the windows, and they were settling in for the afternoon in the living room when the doorbell rang.

Frankie was sitting on a green sofa, Saint at her heels, while Théo worked on a puzzle at the coffee table. The little blackbird Théo had rescued had been named Pip. After days of coaxing, and training with worms, Théo had gained the bird's trust and now Pip perched on the boy's shoulder, one beady eye on the board with interest, another on Saint in case the great beast made any sudden movements.

Antoine had been enjoying a nap in the faded velvet armchair, a book slipping from his hands.

But now, the new arrival had shattered the earlier peace and brought with him a blast of cool air that settled into the bones of the house, causing Frankie to shiver. It was clear from the look on Antoine's face as he showed the visitor inside that he wasn't pleased to see him.

The doctor was a short, dapper man with eyes that were rather close together, like a hawk. Even from some distance away, she could detect a faint, sour smell of alcohol, like it was seeping from his pores. He had a mouth like a razor cut and she soon discovered that his words were just as sharp.

He looked at Frankie, took in her blistered lips, the burn on the side of her face, and shook his head, making a 'boff' sound. Then he gazed at Antoine in disbelief. 'Have you lost your mind? This girl looks nothing like Isabelle! People will notice.'

Antoine's lips folded in on themselves, turning white in his irritation. 'We spoke about this already, Leclair. The Nazis never saw the real Isabelle, and if they did, Isabelle was always in the ironmonger's, working, a layer of grime on her face.'

Monsieur Leclair raised a brow, not convinced. He turned to address her in English. 'You should turn yourself *in*.'

'I offered to, but if I did then everyone else would get punished.'

Antoine snapped. 'Do you want more deaths on your conscience, Marcel? Was one not enough?'

Monsieur Leclair reddened. 'You cannot blame me for that! Monsieur Dubois's death was not my fault.'

Frankie knew that Monsieur Dubois was the real Isabelle's father, who had died from smoke inhalation. But she hadn't been aware of the tensions between them or that Antoine blamed the doctor for the man's death.

'If you had checked his lungs—'

'I did.'

'When it was too late to do anything!' spat Théo, who stood up, his face turning red. Pip flapped his wings at the sudden change, and the boy cupped the bird in his hands to stop it from hurting its injured wing, shooting the doctor a filthy look in the process.

Saint began to bark.

Antoine and the doctor were circling each other, like a pair of puffed-up old roosters.

Until Monsieur Leclair appeared to sag. 'I should have checked his lungs earlier,' he admitted. His face looked haunted – it was clear that deep down he blamed himself too.

Antoine stared at the man then let out a sigh. The fight seemed to go out of him all at once too. 'I'll pour us a drink.'

He decanted them each a whisky, apart from Théo, who had taken a seat next to Frankie now, his arm around the dog, Pip back on his shoulder. The boy didn't look at the doctor. Maybe he didn't trust himself to.

Monsieur Leclair took a reluctant seat opposite Frankie.

'Shouldn't you be in bed?' he asked, his eyes raking over her injuries once more, and settling onto her bandaged foot.

'Antoine thinks I will heal faster if I don't stay there all the time. He said I should get up every so often so that the blood flows and my muscles don't wither.'

The doctor sniffed, to show what he thought of that. But he didn't contradict him, not now that the peace had been so tentatively brokered.

He sighed. 'What you're asking of us is a lot,' he said, looking from her to Antoine, who came back in with a drink in each hand. 'To expect the whole village to keep her secret, to lie for her, is too much risk.'

'No, it's not,' snapped Théo, his brown eyes cold. 'All we have to do is keep quiet.'

Monsieur Leclair stared at the boy. 'It's not that simple, Théo. You're risking all our lives for this. If the Germans find out we have been lying to them we could all be in danger.' He turned to Antoine. 'You should just tell the truth. Yes, maybe you'll go to prison, but well, it *is* a crime to harbour an enemy.'

'She is *not* the enemy. They are!' cried Théo, making Pip squawk at the noise.

Monsieur Leclair shrugged. 'They will not see it that way.'

Antoine set his whisky glass down and a dark cloud passed over his face.

'It is simple, Marcel. You *will* keep your mouth shut.'

'Or what? You'll tell everyone that I was responsible for killing Monsieur Dubois – you've done that already. Despite the fact that even if I had checked his lungs earlier, he more than likely would have died anyway.'

A muscle flexed in Antoine's jaw. 'Perhaps, but at least we could have known for sure that you had done everything in your power to save him.'

Monsieur Leclair only frowned at that.

Antoine continued. 'I am surprised that you feel that keeping this secret would be difficult, when I know for a fact that you are very good at keeping them. Some for decades.'

Monsieur Leclair blinked, but his expression grew guarded. 'What are you talking about?'

He was starting to look a little worried.

Antoine raised a brow. 'She came here, that farm girl, knocked on my door when her time came. She told me everything while I helped her deliver a son. Including who the father was.'

Monsieur Leclair blanched. 'I don't – I don't know what you're talking about.'

Antoine scoffed. 'Yes, you do. Everyone remembers the child that was abandoned at the church. The young servant girl that got herself in trouble and then disappeared overnight from the village. What no one seemed sure about was who got that girl in trouble. I'm sure your wife and children must have wondered, too, though I doubt they would have suspected it was *you*.'

Monsieur Leclair's mouth opened and he blinked rapidly.

'It's a small village, Marcel, everyone has secrets they wouldn't like to share.'

'You wouldn't.'

Antoine's eyes flashed in warning. 'I would.'

Monsieur Leclair stood up. 'Fine. I will keep your secret.'

'Good.'

After Monsieur Leclair left, Théo turned to Antoine. 'How come you never told me that he was the father? I remember that girl, the day she came here to have the baby.'

Antoine sighed, then rubbed his eyes. He looked tired after dealing with Monsieur Leclair.

'It wasn't my secret to tell.'

Théo's mouth gaped open. 'But all this time, he has a child out there they know nothing about? That doesn't seem right!'

Antoine nodded. 'It's not.'

'So why didn't you say something?'

Antoine sighed. 'It's complicated, Théo.'

The boy scoffed. Pip chirruped in response.

'Marie – that was the young woman's name – she didn't want to hurt Monsieur Leclair's family. She thought it best if she gave the baby up, and leave, and so I never said anything because she begged me not to. I promised her that I would only reveal the identity of the father of her baby if it was necessary, if someone's life depended on it.' His eyes flicked over to meet Frankie's gaze. 'And now someone's does.'

That night, when Frankie went to bed, she slept fitfully. Her dreams were haunted by the events of the day. She dreamed that the two Nazi officers from the village had come for her. She heard booted heels, like a drum that never ended, marching her to her death. The blonde officer, who looked like an overgrown schoolboy, that had come to visit her, bringing food and supplies, Dieter Frosch, loomed at the end of her bed, his friendly smile twisting into a snarl that made her heart thunder inside her chest. 'You have taken us for fools! But now we know the truth! You are a double agent. You thought you could collaborate with us and report us to the British. But you work for us!'

She shook her head in denial.

It wasn't true, she couldn't work for them!

'We have the paperwork.'

A mountain of papers landed on the bed.

She turned to look at it. It was school homework. Each one with a fail mark on it circled in red.

Her cheeks reddened in shame.

'How else do you know German?' demanded Frosch.

'I don't know.'

'You do! Because you're one of us.'

Suddenly, hands were grabbing at her, hurting her, and she was now in a cell, shivering cold, in only a nightdress. Monsieur Leclair was there, pointing at her from the other side of the bars. 'I told you to turn yourself in! Now look!' he spat.

She turned to look and saw Théo and Antoine in chains.

'You worked for the Germans this whole time?' cried Théo.

She screamed, 'No!' and woke up bathed in sweat.

The dream had felt so real.

As her heartbeat thundered in her ears, dream Frosch's question loomed inside her mind.

Why *did* she speak German?

She had to know the truth.

12

SUFFOLK, 1933

The plane was going into a tailspin.

Michael's heart went with it. 'She's going to crash,' he whispered, feeling the blood drain from him. He turned to the man at his side, his eyes wild and accusing.

Bill let out a soft chuckle that was completely at odds with Michael's panic. 'Frankie's just showing off.' He pointed at a local farmer, a few metres away. 'He made the mistake of saying that a girl couldn't fly as well as a boy and now she's teaching him a lesson he won't forget in a hurry.' He grinned widely, chewing on a sprig of wheat.

It had been two years since Bill, Frankie's father, had taught them both to fly. Michael had become a decent pilot, safe, cautious, and skilled. But Frankie was always pushing things to the limit. Always ready to try out a new trick, with no apparent thought to the consequences.

What was worse, Michael thought, was that her father encouraged it.

Michael had been away at boarding school for the past six months, and he was shocked at how reckless they'd become in his absence. The plane that would dust crops was some new venture of Bill's. In the letters he'd received, Bill had said it had seemed sensible to put Frankie's skills to use this way, but now he wasn't convinced at all. It seemed unbelievably risky.

Bill cocked his head in the farmer's direction, whose face mirrored Michael's; it too had turned white as milk.

Michael swore beneath his breath.

As his fear mounted, Michael wished he could wipe the smirk off Bill's face, when suddenly the small plane pulled up, only to climb high up into the sky where it proceeded to do a series of tricks.

Bill cheered loudly, as did a few of the other onlookers. 'Told you,' he said, winking at him, as if Michael was only imagining the danger Frankie had put herself in.

Bill, as usual, was cheerfully oblivious. He gave Michael a wink and then made his way over to where the farmer was standing, looking slightly green himself. 'I think maybe we can talk him into taking her on now, for a rather favourable fee,' he said with a chuckle.

It was a beautiful Suffolk day. The sky was a periwinkle blue and the fields were bathed in lemon light, but right then Michael felt like he could have cheerfully committed a crime.

Michael watched Bill head inside the hangar with the farmer while discussing Frankie's fee to dust his crops. He didn't move. He couldn't. He didn't trust himself.

When Frankie finally came in to land, and jumped out of the cockpit, she took off her leather helmet and her long chestnut hair fell like a waterfall around her. She pushed her goggles onto her forehead.

A part of his brain registered how beautiful she had become. For some reason it irritated him.

Her hazel eyes were shining as she made her way to him, 'Michael!' she called. 'We didn't expect you for another week at least.'

'I decided to come home early, I'm beginning to see that maybe it was a blessing I did. You almost lost control!'

Two high spots of colour appeared on her cheeks. 'I did not!'

He stared at her incredulously. 'You waited until the absolute *last* second before pulling up – the throttle could have jammed! You're being an idiot, Frankie, and what's worse your father is encouraging you.'

Frankie was still steaming when she got home an hour later.

She wasn't an idiot. The word was a low blow to her, as that's what many children at school had called her when she struggled with reading.

She just believed in herself up there. It was one of the few places she did. She wasn't going to let Michael try to take that from her. Michael, who would likely only do exactly the obligatory number of hours needed to get his pilot's licence and not a second more. Who didn't love flying like she did and so would never understand how the plane was like an extension of herself.

She knew flying was difficult for him, he would never have her pure love for it, and that was understandable, after what had happened to his father.

She sighed. She would have a talk with him later. Try to get him to understand that she didn't want to upset him, but he had to show more faith in her.

She found them in the living room where she could have cut the tension with a blade.

'Francesca Rose Anne Chalmers, what is this I have been hearing – that you almost crashed your plane to prove yourself to some farmer?' shouted her mother, as soon as she locked eyes with her. 'And that you were behind it all?' she spat, looking at her husband with snapping eyes. Bill winced as he came up behind Frankie.

Frankie pursed her lips in anger, glaring at Michael. 'You ran straight here to tell on me?'

Michael pinched the skin above his nose. 'Tell on you? *Jesus*. Grow up, Frankie, you can't expect me to stand aside and not say something when you're being completely reckless!'

'I'm not—' she denied, just as her father said, 'She's a bit hot-headed, I admit, but she knows what she's doing.'

Her mother's eyes flared. 'So you don't deny it, then? Frankie was performing tricks again?'

Bill blinked.

Her lips went razor thin 'And, of course, you're careful to do it far away from the house so I don't see... right? Neither of you were ever going to stick to your word, were you? You just thought that as long as I didn't know you could get away with it.'

She looked hurt and upset and Frankie couldn't help the creeping sense of shame that spread over her. Her mother was right. They had gone out of their way to keep it from her.

There was the sound of someone sucking in a breath of air. It was her sister Emily.

Frankie caught her sister's eye and swallowed. She had promised her, too, that she wouldn't do tricks ever again. Emily had always been her biggest supporter. But when she started doing tricks, Emily had got worried.

'What if something goes wrong, Frankie, I couldn't bear it if I lost you.'

When her mother had heard about it, she had threatened to send her away to boarding school like Michael if she ever did it again.

She'd promised them both that she would stop. She couldn't meet their eyes now. She didn't mean to worry them, but when she was up in the air, the urge was irresistible, she knew they wouldn't understand. She didn't blame them, not really. She didn't know how to explain it.

'It was just a small one,' she lied, lamely.

'Michael said the plane was going into a nosedive! He said you nearly crashed.'

'No, no, I promise I had it all under control.'

'Are you so arrogant you think that you couldn't possibly make a mistake?' snapped Michael.

Frankie's nostrils flared, her fists balled at her side. 'It's not arrogant when you know what you are doing!'

'Frankie—' warned her father but it was too late. She was seeing red. 'He just doesn't get it. I've done it a hundred times before!'

There were gasps all around.

'What do you mean?' said her mother's cold voice.

Frankie realised her mistake too late.

'I just—'

'So you've been lying to me this whole time? Performing tricks, risking your life, the pair of you, making a mockery out of me?' said her mother.

'I – no, it wasn't like that.'

Her father shook his head. 'Frankie is talented. I wouldn't let her put herself in danger.'

'Do you even hear yourself?' snapped Emily. 'She's fourteen years old! Performing stunts because you think she is some genius – and maybe she is – but now you want to get her to dust your neighbours' crops and possibly kill herself in the process?' she snapped at her father, who turned pale.

Emily then turned to look at her, her eyes filled with worry. 'Maybe you are amazing up there, Frankie, but what happens when you push it too far? Everyone can make a blunder. I've never thought of you as a fool – never, but you must be one if you think you can't ever make a mistake. I think maybe Michael is right. Maybe you have become a bit arrogant and reckless.'

Then she turned and glared at her father, 'And you are encouraging her in it, Dad. If something happens to her it will be your fault.'

'I—' said her father. Then he shut his mouth, and nodded, his face falling. 'You're right. I'm sorry.'

Frankie stared at him in shock.

'I think you're right, she should go away to school,' said Michael, his mouth down-turned, not meeting Frankie's eyes, who gasped.

Her mother sighed, her lips pressed together like she was trying to hold back her tears.

'Yes, I think we're at that point too.'

Frankie's eyes widened in horror as they all began to nod around her.

'Dad?' breathed Frankie. He was her last hope, surely he would intervene, like he always did.

He closed his eyes and she felt the ground shift beneath her feet. 'Frankie, they have a point. It's my fault, Lord knows. We can drive you up to St Cuthbert's in the morning.'

Frankie gasped, her vision blurring through her tears. 'No!'

'It's done, Frankie,' said her mother.

'It's for the best,' said Michael, reaching out to touch her on her shoulder.

She wrenched herself away and glared at him.

'I will never forgive you for this,' she spat, then turned and ran from the room.

13

Sister Mourdell said she was doing God's work. She was going to cleanse Frankie's soul and rid her of the demon inside her.

The one that made Frankie think she had a right to answer her back.

'I'm doing this for your own good, child,' she said, as she dragged Frankie kicking and screaming into the bath and turned the tap on, holding her head under the deluge.

The water hit her eyes and mouth, and she struggled to breathe. She tried to fight back but the nun was strong. Sister Mourdell shoved a small sliver of soap into her mouth. Frankie gagged but managed to gasp a breath.

The soap suds trickled into her eyes, making them sting.

'Eat it,' the nun commanded.

Frankie shook her head violently.

The nun picked up something else from the rim of the tub. 'If you don't, you will eat this one too.'

Through her burning gaze, Frankie could just make out that it was another bar of soap, this one full.

Frankie felt her stomach roil.

Since the moment her parents left her at St Cuthbert's the

day before, she had been made to understand that her life here was to be very different.

The ward sister who looked after the dormitory she was assigned to had made that clear.

Sister Mourdell was a tall woman with a face like a blotchy red apple. Her eyes were like two black seeds pushed into the flesh and her hands were raw and red and strong.

The dormitory housed twelve girls; the beds were laid out in a long row. She was assigned a bed at the end, closest to the corridor, which was heady with the scent of bleach.

There was a small wooden chest at the end of her bed, where she could keep her belongings, and a row of wooden cubbyholes at the back of the room which served as a wardrobe for all the girls.

The uniform was the colour of January. Grey and white. The fabric, heavy and itching.

As Sister Mourdell explained the rules and schedule that she was expected to follow, Frankie's head swam, and she felt like she was experiencing everything from under water.

The sister was speaking to her, but she had tuned her out. Then she felt a gnarled finger poke itself hard into the centre of her chest, and she snapped to attention.

'Mother Superior told me about you. How you have been brought to us for disobeying your parents—'

'That's not true—' Frankie began.

The nun's eyes widened. 'Don't lie to me, girl, and don't answer back! I know everything.'

Frankie had swallowed.

'What was I saying before? Repeat it back to me.'

Frankie frowned. 'You said I was sent here for—'

'Not that girl,' she snapped. 'Pay attention! We rise at six, prayers, then breakfast, lessons begin at eight, we pause for luncheon at twelve and the lessons continue until three...'

'This is a mistake,' said Frankie wildly.

This wasn't a school, it was a prison.

'I'm not meant to be here.'

Sister Mourdell raised a brow. 'You are exactly where you're supposed to be.'

Frankie felt a crashing wave of despair take over her, as she was told to get into her uniform, and head straight to her first lesson. She was shown into her classroom and introduced. She turned her face away when the other girls looked at her curiously. She didn't want to engage with anyone, she didn't trust herself not to cry.

The day felt like an eternity.

A few girls looked like they were thinking of coming over to introduce themselves but changed their minds. It made her feel self-conscious and trapped. She had never felt more alone. Or more desperate to leave.

As soon as she could, she climbed into bed and pulled the covers over her head. She heard them whispering about her but eventually she fell into an exhausted sleep.

In the morning, while the other girls made their way to church, she stayed behind, making up her mind. There was just no way she could stay here. Her mother would calm down; she would see that this was a mistake. She would walk home, even if it took her a week.

She shoved the clothes she had been forced to fold neatly the day before into a bag and was preparing to run away when Sister Mourdell's shadow loomed behind her.

Frankie jumped in fright, spotting the older woman, whose beady eyes glittered like an insect.

'Where do you think you're going?'

Frankie swallowed. 'I can't stay here.'

Sister Mourdell's eyes flared. 'You can't stay?' she scoffed. 'Did you think this was some hotel? You don't just get to check out. This is your home now.'

Frankie shook her head wildly. 'This is not my home. I hate it here.'

Sister Mourdell blanched. Her voice grew cold and dangerous. 'You hate God's house, child?'

It happened so fast. One moment she was standing next to her, the next she was dragging her down the hall to the bathroom, kicking and screaming.

That was the moment Sister Mourdell told her that she was going to cleanse her soul.

Then beyond the sound of rushing water, and her cries for help, she heard the hastening of footsteps on the linoleum, which squeaked as someone else entered the bathroom.

'Please Sister, she's new—' piped a girl's voice.

Sister Mourdell turned her head, but she kept a firm hold on Frankie, who was being given a kind of baptism.

The nun's eyes bulged. 'I'm well aware of that fact. Do you want to join her in this tub, Beatrix?'

'No, sister, I just meant she doesn't know the rules. I could help her learn them.'

The water was going into Frankie's eyes, but she could make out a figure near the doorway. A small girl with very pale hair.

She recognised her from the dormitory. She had smiled at her the night before, but Frankie had gone straight to her bed and shoved the covers over her head, wishing to go home.

The nun sniffed now. 'You wish to help her?'

'Yes, please, sister.'

Suddenly, Frankie was released, and she fell to her knees, gagging on the floor, spitting the shard of soap into her hand, where she clutched it. Something told her that if it landed on the floor Sister Mourdell might still make her eat it.

'Very well, Beatrix. But if she disobeys me again, next time you will join her here.'

'Yes, sister,' said the girl.

The nun stood up, sniffed, then said, 'You can start by cleaning up this mess.'

Then she turned on her heel and left.

Frankie stared at the girl. 'Thank you. Why did you help me?'

The girl's eyes widened, 'Call me old-fashioned, but I don't really fancy watching someone get tortured with a bar of soap.' She winked. 'I mean, if you have to eat one, at least make it something posh from Harrods.'

Frankie's lips twitched. 'Thanks,' she said, again.

The girl shrugged. 'You're Francesca?'

'Frankie.'

The girl gave her a wry grin. 'I'm Beatrix, but everyone calls me Trixie. I say, what did you do to get Murder's back up so fast?'

Frankie guessed that Murder was the sister's nickname. It was apt too.

Trixie grinned. 'Must be a blooming record. Usually most girls only get her "baptism" in the first term. I never heard of someone getting it their second day.'

Frankie snorted. 'I have a talent for getting myself into scrapes. I told her I hate it here.'

'Ah. Yes, I can see why that sent her round the bend. She thinks this little corner of hell is hers. And she's probably right.'

Later that morning, at breakfast, Trixie said, 'Come and meet the gang,' and herded Frankie towards a big, shy girl with short hair and a kind face named Marie and a fey-looking girl with pale skin and dark hair named Eugenie.

'I – w-wanted to come over and say hello yesterday, but—' broke off Marie.

The other girl interjected with a wry grin. 'It looked like you might devour anyone who approached.'

'Eugenie,' said Trixie, shooting the girl a look.

Frankie winced. 'No, she's right. I might have,' she said. She hadn't realised how angry she'd probably seemed to the other girls.

Eugenie laughed. 'I like this one.'

She had a faint accent that Frankie couldn't place. There was a book poking out of her right blazer pocket. She could see it was something by Agatha Christie.

'Murder gave her a baptism,' said Trixie.

The other girls gasped.

'What, already? I got mine after my seventh week, though I'm fairly sure she only did that because of my accent. Austrian,' she explained. 'She seems to hold me personally responsible for the war.'

Trixie's lips thinned, 'She's vile.'

Marie nodded. 'I g-got mine because sh-she said it would c-cure my stutter. But it only gets worse when I'm frightened.'

Frankie felt her heart twist for the bigger girl.

Eugenie squeezed Marie's hand.

'But don't worry, we'll show you how to avoid it next time. It's annoying but once you play by her rules, she leaves you alone.'

'Thank you,' said Frankie.

Frankie felt grateful, but she couldn't help thinking that it wasn't right. Sister Mourdell shouldn't get away with what she did.

The 'rules' were simple.

'The easiest way to get Murder on your back is to make a mess or to be late for anything. So, keep your bed neat and fold away your clothes. Same goes for your appearance,' said Trixie.

'Cleanliness is next to godliness,' intoned Marie, in dull tones.

Frankie had heard the nun say that a few times now.

'And never, ever "backchat,"' said Eugenie. 'That means, don't ever offer an opinion, the only thing Murder wants to hear is "yes, sister" or "no, sister" – anything else is considered backchat.'

'Got it,' said Frankie.

There was no way she wanted to eat any more of that vile soap.

Trixie and the gang made it all bearable. She missed home with an ache that she was sure might never go away but without them she wasn't sure she would have survived.

Every particle in her being had to resist answering Sister Mourdell back when she said or did something that made her skin crawl.

Following the girls' advice, Frankie managed to get through her first few weeks without another incident.

But she soon discovered another rule, one that was to prove the most challenging.

One night, Sister Mourdell overheard her speaking about her life back home to the other girls.

They enjoyed hearing about her life on the farm. So different from theirs. Trixie had grown up in a wealthy part of London, and both Eugenie and Marie were from big towns.

'Your father actually bought you a plane?' exclaimed Trixie, her eyes shining. 'For your birthday?'

Frankie nodded. 'An old plane we had to restore, but that's what made it so fun, because when it was finally ready, it was ... oh it was bliss,' she said, her face alight with the memory of taking the plane out for the first time, seeing her father and Michael's face. She frowned, then swallowed. It still hurt to think of him.

Eugenie scoffed. 'The only thing my father ever bought me was an incomplete set of encyclopaedias. I will never know what mysteries the letters M–Q hold.'

They all laughed.

'What's it like t-t-to fly?' asked Marie.

So Frankie told them. 'It's like all your troubles fall away; they become smaller and smaller as you drift up in the clouds. You feel as if you are weightless, in the air, and part of another world, like the birds—'

Sister Mourdell's voice interrupted them. 'Francesca, follow me, now!' she spat.

Frankie looked at the others. Her knees turned to water. What had she done wrong now? She stood up reluctantly and followed the sister down the corridor to her room, which was sparse, with one bed pressed up against the corner and just behind the door there was a table and two chairs.

'Sit.'

Frankie did as instructed.

The nun sighed then steepled her red fingers together as she peered at her with her hard, seed-like eyes.

'We don't tolerate liars or braggarts in this house, do you understand?'

'Sister?'

'Many of these girls come from poorer households – your friend, Trixie notwithstanding. They are respectful girls, who know their place. They do not attempt to be what they are not, as you do.'

'Sister?' she said again, confused.

'You are a girl, Frankie, and yet you seem to have forgotten that.'

'I haven't—'

The nun's eyes flared. 'You think that you can live the life of a boy – flying planes and doing whatever it is you want? Worse, you think you can put those sorts of dangerous ideas in the other girls' heads? I will not allow it, do you hear me? You were sent to me for correction by your parents.'

She sighed, her tone softening somewhat. 'But it is not

completely your fault. They encouraged this in you – and now they want us to fix their mistakes. Well, so be it. If I ever catch you even thinking about flying again, you will be punished, do you understand?'

Frankie felt a wave of anger wash over her.

'You can't control my thoughts,' she snapped.

It happened so fast, Frankie didn't even see it coming.

Her seat was knocked out from under her by the nun's legs and she went crashing into the hard linoleum. As she lay there dazed, a bruise formed on her wrist. The nun loomed over her.

'We'll see about that, child.'

The months passed by slowly.

Sister Mourdell was true to her word. She watched over her like some bird of prey, ready to pick at Frankie's words, in case she said anything that she found fault with. Anything that would indicate that she was still thinking about flying.

At night she lay in her bed and thought of Michael, how she was here because of him.

How he'd helped to send her to the wolves.

Sometimes she woke up with her pillow soaked from crying herself to sleep.

Her one source of comfort was the girls, but even so Frankie was losing weight, and sleep. She had grown silent. It was safer to listen than to share her inner world with the others. Sister Mourdell's eyes watched her every move, and she felt like her shoulders were pinned to her ears from the constant stress of watching over her back.

She didn't answer the first few letters her family sent her. She didn't know what to say. The girls told her that Sister Mourdell read their post and the letters they wrote to their family.

'There was a girl who tried to report Mourdell to her parents. She wrote about her and what she does to us – let's just say she paid for it, for weeks,' warned Eugenie.

'The refectory only served her porridge for months and she took away her bedcovers, even though it was winter.'

Frankie gasped. 'What? That's horrific.'

Eugenie nodded. 'Just – well, bear it in mind. Like we've said, she's fine if you play by her rules. But there are ways around them. I've been thinking ... something changed after the day Mourdell asked to see you.'

Frankie bit her lip.

Eugenie continued. 'She said something to you after you were talking to us about flying, she told you to stop, right?'

Frankie nodded.

The others looked amazed.

'So that's what's been wrong,' breathed Trixie. 'That's why you've been reading *Jane Eyre*.'

It was true, she often re-read her favourite book when she was troubled. Lately, that had been often. Jane gave her strength, and the belief that one day things would change for her too like it had for her. Though she had never imagined, that one day, like Jane, she would be made to experience her own version of the harsh Lowood School...

Frankie looked at them, saw their concern, then whispered, 'She said I wasn't to give you all dangerous ideas.'

She surreptitiously rubbed her wrist – the pain from when Sister Mourdell pushed her was long gone, but the fear remained.

Trixie snorted. 'I don't need you for that, Frankie, I have dangerous ideas all on my own.'

Eugenie smirked. 'So do I. Which is that apart from French and English the nuns can't speak another language, especially my native tongue, which is why I think it makes sense for me to teach it to all of you – that way we can speak without them ever knowing what we're saying.'

It was an ingenious plan. They'd all started learning French in school. Frankie had struggled at first, because of her dyslexia, but the teacher had switched to a method of teaching spoken French, and getting her to memorise things that way when she saw her struggling and it had helped enormously.

So when Eugenie decided to teach them German, she used the same approach, but unlike French they were much more motivated to learn from Eugenie, because it offered a small taste of freedom, as well as rebellion.

Over the months, every letter Frankie received from Michael she tore up without reading.

One morning, before lessons, on a cold day in late November, when the windows were covered in frost and the trees were bare, she was shuffled into the Mother Superior's office. It was a large room, with oak panelling. There was a single picture on the wall of Jesus on the cross.

The windows overlooked the grounds, which stretched out towards a forest in the distance.

It was colder in this part of the country, wetter too. So different from the flat and dry landscape back home.

'You aren't happy here, Miss Chalmers.'

It wasn't a question.

'I like my friends.'

It was the only part she liked.

'You have lost weight since you joined, and you don't write to your family.'

Frankie looked over at the Mother Superior. Unlike Sister Mourdell, she had a kind face. She had blue eyes, and a mouth that looked like it was used to smiling.

'I'm fine,' Frankie lied. She had learned that the truth got you nowhere fast in this place.

'Your parents are worried about you.'

Frankie couldn't help herself. She snapped. 'If they were so worried they shouldn't have left me here.'

Mother Superior nodded. 'I can see why you think that.' She sighed. 'Have a seat.'

Reluctantly, she sat down opposite the older nun at the large desk. It was polished wood, with no decorations, apart from a photograph.

The nun saw her looking. 'This was the first group of girls we taught.'

Frankie didn't look.

The nun frowned. 'I know it hasn't been easy. Sister Mourdell has a heavy hand.'

Frankie stared at the nun in bemusement.

'Yes, I am aware.'

Frankie frowned. She was aware but did nothing? That didn't make her feel any better.

'Your parents sent you to us for your own good. This isn't a punishment. We have a reputation for helping girls like you. They just feel this is a better place for you right now, and while you may not like that, you have to respect their decision. I'd like you to write back to your family. Put their minds at rest.'

'If I don't?'

'Well, let's just say it would be better than letting Sister Mourdell know that you have been ignoring your parents.'

Frankie shrugged.

'Also – she has told me that Eugenie has taught you German. She wanted to put a stop to it. She had some unfortunate, prejudicial views about the Teutonic people that I will not repeat. I could see nothing wrong with you all furthering your education, but well, I may yet change my mind... as Sister

Mourdell believes you aren't simply learning for learning's sake but to speak of things that she would rather you did not...'

Frankie sighed. 'I will write to them.'

'Good, we understand one another well, then.'

Her first holiday back home was over Christmas.

Her family kept shooting her worried looks on the drive home, as she was so quiet and withdrawn.

All she'd wanted was to come home. But now everything was different.

When they got through the door, Emily rushed forward to embrace her, only to recoil slightly at the look on her face.

'Frankie?' she said.

'I'm fine. Just tired.'

Emily nodded. But she didn't look convinced.

From behind her there was a sound. Frankie looked up and saw Michael. He was smiling at her, in welcome. 'It's so good to see you,' he said, as if the fact that she hadn't been home for the past three months, as if everything she had endured in that place was nothing, as if it wasn't his fault that she had been sent away.

She turned her back on him, and was about to storm out of the room when his cracked voice stopped her in her tracks.

'Frankie – I'm sorry.'

She turned back to look at him, disdain twisting her face.

'I'd like you to get out,' she spat.

Emily sucked in a deep breath of air. 'Frankie!' she breathed at the same time as her mother, who looked shocked.

Frankie felt her face turn blotchy with suppressed anger.

'If you expect me to ever come home again in the holidays, *he* cannot be here, while I am, do you understand?'

'No, Frankie, this is his home too—' began her father.

'It's all right, Bill, I'll go.'

The others argued, urged him to stay.

'Let him go,' said Frankie coldly.

They watched him leave. It was like he'd folded in on himself. Frankie felt a stab go through her heart. She forced herself to ignore it, hardening herself against him, telling herself he deserved it.

14

LOIRE VALLEY, 1944

Market day in St Jude fell on a Wednesday. The stalls were set up in the cobbled square next to the stone church covered on one wall with jasmine, the heady scent of which perfumed the air, and made one nostalgic for summers past.

Antoine smoothed down his shirt, noting absently how the fabric had become loose around his middle. There had been a stage when it strained across it, the middle button open slightly to give a glimpse of a belly that had been lovingly rounded by his lifelong obsession with good food, wine and cheese. He'd pat it affectionately, it had grown from joy, and one couldn't really resent that.

Even as a boy he'd loved market day, anticipating the new flavours that would be on offer.

Before the Occupation, the tables were overflowing with olives of all kinds swimming in golden pools of olive oil, like countless jewels. There would be *saucisson* in all flavours, too, some studded with those delectable olives, or cheese, truffles or exotic spices.

Even the fruit could make his mouth water. The seller had a fortune teller's gift, holding up a melon the size of both of his fists and telling him, 'It will be ready for you on Sunday morning.'

Antoine had learned to trust those predictions, because by Sunday the house would be perfumed with the sweet scent of melon, and his family would descend upon the kitchen like a pack of wolves. The juice would run down their chins, and they would smile at one another, while enjoying the nectar of the gods.

When his wife, Jean, was still alive, they used to come to the market together. It was their ritual. His mouth would water as she visited the fishmonger, and then the fruit-seller, and predicted their culinary futures: *sole meunière*, the fish drowning in heavenly melted butter, and lemon, with just-picked parsley, followed by a dessert that was light as air, *clafoutis* from apricots with dustings of sugar, all to be enjoyed in the late summer evening, under the trees in the garden.

Before they left the market, there was another ritual, almost as important.

Jean would linger at the village bookshop, where the light in the old bookseller's eyes would slowly come alive, like one of those lightbulbs that need time to warm up before they begin to glow, as he got to chatting about their favourite authors.

Antoine would slip away for a cold *pastis*, and sit with the old men outside the bar, who'd been basking in the sun like ageing walruses, making grunting noises of encouragement to players enjoying a game of boules on the small pitch outside. Like them, he'd shoot out a few words of advice and encouragement, the taste of the aniseed liquor sweet on his tongue.

He sighed as he looked at the village scene that unfolded around him now.

Despite the warmth of the day, the atmosphere was cool. The stalls were only half filled, and what was on offer suffered from an absence of variety. Much of what the farmers produced went to the German army. It was their enemies who grew fat now on what they had so lovingly produced.

Antoine tried not to think of that. Tried to quell the anger in his heart. Especially when he saw one of Nazi officers who had moved into their village a few metres away up a cobbled path. He was the one with dark hair, who didn't bother trying to pretend he was their friend, like that blonde one, Dieter Frosch. Antoine had recently learned that this one's surname was Röber, and it seemed appropriate somehow, as wasn't that what they'd come here to do, rob their land from them?

Röber went inside the tobacconist and Antoine felt his lungs expand when he was out of sight.

As he turned his attention to the fishmonger, two elderly women, with baskets in the crooks of their arms, caught his eye. They were sisters who lived in a cottage on a farm not far from his.

They called him over.

'I have something for you,' said one. She was thin, with pure white hair and dark eyes that darted towards the tobacconist shop, making sure the Nazi was still inside.

The other woman, who was tall with grey-peppered hair, turned to block his view, should he happen to leave.

Antoine felt his heart beat rapidly. *Why were they acting so furtively?* The white-haired sister slipped her hand inside her bag, then she shoved something inside his big open palm. Instinctively, he made a fist over whatever it was. It was hard, and made of glass. He frowned, but held on, looking at them in confusion.

'It's for *Isabelle*,' whispered the white-haired woman, then winked. 'My late husband swore he couldn't live without it.'

Antoine was touched. He remembered that the woman's husband had been English. He used to teach at the school. He'd passed a few years ago now. A good man.

'It should still be good.' There were bright tears in her eyes.

'Hopefully, it will give her some comfort.' He looked down, confused, then a small smile flitted across his face. It was a small jam jar full of looseleaf tea.

Before he could thank her, the women were off, having delivered their clandestine package.

He shoved it into his jacket pocket, and felt his heart lift from their small act of kindness. The Nazi officers might have taken their village, but they hadn't yet taken their spirit.

By the time he had finished at the market, Antoine moved on to the tobacconist, which was mercifully clear of officers now. The shop had seen better days, the once-overflowing shelves – full of magazines and newspapers – only offered half of what used to be on offer and much of it was long out of date. It was to be expected, the only thing anyone used up column inches for now was the war.

He picked up a new-to-them but old *National Geographic* for Théo, a women's magazine for Isabelle and a large, somewhat illicit sized pouch of tobacco – like most things, tobacco was strictly rationed but the shop owner had a beloved cat that Antoine had performed surgery on for free and so there was always a little extra set aside for him.

Another small act of rebellion.

Antoine always gave his extra tobacco to an old friend, who'd been forced to quit against her will. She was a former librarian who lived at the top of the village, as a woman, she wasn't given a rationioning at all, which didn't strike him as fair so he did what he could to help out.

Antoine and the shop owner startled when they heard a commotion outside.

Someone was screaming.

It was the sort of cry that turned the stomach to water.

He dropped his basket on the ground, and a beet rolled

outside and down the street, but no one paid it any attention, including Antoine.

The two Nazis officers were dragging a family out of a stone house surrounded by overflowing baskets of bright red geraniums – the incongruity of the pretty house and the ugliness of what was happening would stay with Antoine afterwards, like some dark fairy tale.

A man and woman with two young children were forcefully pulled outside, their faces marked with terror. They were followed by an older woman with short curly hair. She was wearing a white apron with bright strawberries dotted all over it on top of a sky-blue housedress.

She was the one screaming, he realised, as the officers dragged her family into the street.

He knew her well. Madame Avril's talents with needle and thread were renowned in the village. She was the one everyone went to for outfits for special occasions. She had made the christening gown for his daughter and his wife's wedding dress when she was just out of girlhood herself.

Antoine stared at the scene in horror.

Around him there was a hubbub of confused whispers, as people came rushing from the market and out of their houses to witness the scene.

Soon there was a van approaching, and several more Nazis descended onto the street. As they climbed out of their vehicle, like a swarm of brown ants, they began to speak to each other in rapid-fire German, offering each other salutes, like it was some compulsive tic.

Antoine swallowed in fear. *Why were they here? Surely they hadn't needed reinforcements for this? They must have come from the nearby town of Cagnes Sur Mer.*

Antoine didn't know the man or the children, but he recognised Madame Avril's daughter, Therese, though it had been some years since he had seen her as she had moved away once she got married.

He felt his chest tighten as he remembered... she had married a Jew.

Oh God. Is that why they've come?

His heart began to beat rapidly.

No one even knew Therese and her husband were living there now. He certainly didn't... Madame Avril must have decided to hide them away.

Madame Avril's voice turned pleading. She clung to the blonde-haired Nazi, Frosch, who shook her off, like he was batting away a fly.

'Please, she's my child. They haven't done anything wrong. Please, please don't do this.'

'Madame, it's the law,' said the blonde officer, Frosch, his face impassive. He could have been discussing a rise in taxes, not imprisoning a family for the crime of being a different religion.

'Please,' begged Madame Avril twisting her apron in her hands. 'Please don't take them.'

Röber looked at her with disdain.

'Harbouring a Jew is a crime as you all well-know. Let this serve as a lesson.'

Then before anyone had a chance to react, he pulled out his pistol and fired it into the older woman's forehead.

Antoine cried out helplessly as he watched her fall as if in slow motion. He wasn't the only one.

Her daughter's screams were ear-splitting as she fell onto her mother's body, trying to pick her up, leaving trails of blood on the pristine white apron as she howled and railed against the Nazis.

There were muffled cries and shouts from the onlookers, followed by the sound of crying.

One of the Nazis pulled the woman off her mother, his

expression unchanging even as her legs and arms reached back for her.

Antoine felt rooted to the spot, his stomach churning. Behind him the shop owner swore, his face white.

'That dark-haired Nazi officer has been coming into my shop for a week now. He comes in, stands there by the magazines and stares at Madame Avril's house. He must have realised there was someone else living there. He was just biding his time.'

Antoine watched as the officers shoved the family into the van.

They left the body lying in the street.

A warning to them all.

As the van rolled past, Frosch caught his eye, then nodded politely.

The fact that he could act so naturally sent a further chill down his spine.

For a long while Antoine couldn't move. His hands and legs were shaking and he had to fight the urge to break down in sobs. Around him, many of the villagers, including Madame Avril's friends, were in a similar state of shock and horror.

'We should move her,' said one of her friends, a woman with rust-coloured hair, who like Antoine had dropped her bag of shopping onto the floor. Her freckled face had turned white, and her voice was strained with emotion. 'She doesn't deserve to be left like that.'

It was the rallying cry they needed, as everyone suddenly sprang into action, including Antoine. He and the shopkeeper, along with the priest, carried Madame Avril's body to the church.

They were followed by several of the woman's friends.

'Sh-she wouldn't want to b-be buried in that,' said a small

dark woman who wore gold-rimmed spectacles, looking at Madame Avril's body in her housedress and bloodied apron.

She went inside Madame Avril's and returned a few minutes later with a change of clothing. He recognised it as the outfit she often wore to church, a smart navy dress with a jacket.

Antoine nodded, feeling choked up again. 'Of course.'

Though all he could think was that she shouldn't have had to be buried at all.

Hours later when he returned home, he found Frankie asleep on the sofa. Opposite her Théo was reading a book about astronomy, Saint's big head in his lap.

Today had been a reminder of just how great a risk it was that they were taking having Frankie here.

The boy looked up, only to frown. 'Is everything all right? You've been gone all day; I was starting to get worried.'

The sound made Frankie stir, she went from asleep to instantly alert, and on edge. She took one look at his face and her eyes widened. 'What's happened?'

The events of the day were written on his face. A part of him wanted to spare them from what he'd witnessed, but it would be useless, they'd find out soon enough.

He stalled, wanting to extend the quiet domestic scene he'd found, a world not yet shattered like his own had been, just that little bit longer.

His hands fiddled with his pocket, and he frowned as his fingers traced over a bulge. The small jar of tea. He swallowed past the lump in his throat. It was hard to imagine that that had happened only this morning. It felt like a lifetime ago already. A lifetime ago when he'd imagined that the Nazis hadn't yet taken their spirit from them.

How wrong he was.

'The Germans shot Madame Avril.'

15

Théo had taken to spending hours alone in his bedroom, with only his old copies of *National Geographic* and Pip, the blackbird, for company. Frankie tried to entice him away by making his favourite food, fresh baguette with scrapings of precious butter, vine-ripened tomatoes, basil and slivers of *port salud* cheese, but he only picked at it.

Madame Avril's murder, following so soon after the fire, had brought a pall to the village.

Antoine was often to be found haunting his vines. As if there in their symmetrical rows, where the *grolleau* grapes grew fat in the sun, he could find sense where there was none.

Frankie felt helpless, like the ground had shifted beneath her once more.

Saint had taken to sitting with her as she worried about them.

At first, she thought that the boy was fearful that the Germans would discover her real identity, that he worried that they would share Madame Avril's fate if the Germans found out that they had been harbouring her.

But a few days later, she found out that Antoine and Théo

had been keeping a secret of their own. One that, if discovered, was just as dangerous as the one they were all keeping by pretending she was someone else.

It was this that had made the boy so taciturn and withdrawn following Madame Avril's death, because like her they were hiding a similar secret.

She knocked on Théo's door, and made her way painstakingly into his bedroom. Putting pressure on her ankle was agony, the seared flesh screaming out in pain. But she reminded herself that the pain was her friend. Antoine had told her that. If she didn't feel pain, it would be a sign of nerve damage and more serious third-degree burns. She had to keep reminding herself that it was a good thing.

Théo looked up when she approached. He was sitting at small desk beneath a window that overlooked the vineyards, Pip perched on his shoulder. His hair was a mess and some dormant maternal instinct inside her longed to reach for a brush and pull it through those dark curls, but she resisted. She looked around the room with fresh eyes.

The walls were painted a midnight blue and had cut out pictures of constellations from magazines on one of them.

She took a seat on the bed. 'Théo, you and your grandfather have been incredibly brave, and kind, keeping me here. But I think—'

Théo looked up at her sharply. 'Don't!'

Pip chirruped in surprise and the boy took him off his shoulder, placing him on the desk.

She frowned.

The boy's face grew animated with concern.

'Don't. I know what you're probably thinking, you think we're worried about them finding out about you. But it's not that.'

She was not convinced. 'It's only natural, Théo, after everything that's happened. It was bad enough before but now that we know what their response to this sort of thing is, it would be foolish of me to stay, to put you all in such jeopardy.'

Théo slammed his fists on the desk, startling her.

'No, don't you see? After what happened, no one will betray you now! They would be much too afraid. Besides. You can't let *them* win. Please promise me you won't leave.'

'But—' She was confused.

He ran a hand over his face, then sighed. 'There's something we haven't told you,' he said.

They heard the sound of slippered feet in the corridor.

Antoine stood in the doorway. His face looked drawn, as if someone had pulled the plug out from him, to drain away his colour. But his expression was resigned too.

He nodded, as he listened to the boy. 'It's time you knew the secret that we've been keeping from you.'

'A secret?' breathed Frankie.

Antoine sighed, then came to take a seat on the bed next to her. The small bed with its red coverlet sagged from his weight. On the floor, Saint looked up at them all, as if to encourage them to tell the story.

'My daughter, Marie,' said Antoine, picking up the framed portrait of Théo's mother that lived on the boy's bedside table. He smiled faintly as he looked at it. The way one might even when their heart is broken.

'We didn't think we would be blessed with children, Jean and I. We tried for years, but it just never happened. In the early years of our marriage that was hard. It was hardest on Jean. Every time she miscarried, I felt so helpless. I wouldn't wish what we went through on anyone. It was hard to watch her suffer, watch her long for something that as time went on, felt like it just wasn't part of our destiny.

'At some point, we just decided to pour all that love we

might have had for children into each other, and the animals we looked after in our practice. It was hard for Jean to give up the dream of becoming a mother but in time she was like a mother to all the animals she cared for, and she made peace with the thought of never having a child of her own.

'But then, life has a funny way of rolling the dice, because just as she began to go through the menopause, she fell pregnant. One of those strange, wondrous miracles of life.

'Of course, we worried about the pregnancy, due to her age, the risks involved, but it all went smoothly, and in our forties, after twenty years of marriage, we welcomed our precious child into the world. Marie.'

He smiled faintly as he touched the glass. Tracing the features of his beloved girl. His chin shook. 'I still feel like I see the little girl she was, out of the corner of my eye, sometimes. Hear her laughter, when it is just the wind. You don't just miss the person you lost but all those memories you had too.'

Something stirred within Frankie's chest as he did. As if his loss touched some shared pain within her heart.

For a moment, her lungs forgot to breathe and her world felt rocked by pain.

She had lost someone precious to her too.

Antoine took a deep, steadying breath.

'Marie was such a happy child. Creative and sensitive. She loved music, and could turn her clever hands to any instrument. But the violin was her favourite.

'When she was fourteen, she won a scholarship to a prestigious musical academy in Vienna. She was there for three years, and that's where she met Théo's father, Claude Schneider, a talented conductor who was also a German Jew. Had the Nazis not come into power, he would no doubt have become a celebrated maestro in time.

'They married when she was only seventeen, Théo arrived a few months after the wedding.' His eyes clouded. 'They were very in love, and Jean and I were happy for her.' His breath caught, and his chin wobbled.

'They died in a car crash shortly after Théo turned one. I suppose it is a small mercy that they were not around to experience what would become of this world of ours, and how the Nazis would view a love like theirs as wrong, as opposed to what it was, something beautiful.

'Jean and I raised Théo, until she died a few years later. Then it was just us two, Théo and me against the world. And it felt like that, too, especially after war broke out. As his legal guardian, I have the power to "correct" details on his birth certificate.'

His eyes begged her to understand.

'It was shortly after France was occupied. I listed his father as someone who had been killed from our village. A Christian. I hate myself for doing that to dear Claude, rewriting history, but I felt I had no choice. I *had* to protect Théo.

'I was informed that they were checking our records and making a note of the Jews. We had heard the tales of what they had done to their Jews. Stories of the night of crystal glass the year before the war broke out, of Jews losing their homes, stripped of their rights, their jobs, and being forced to live in ghettos. It chilled my blood. This was before I had even heard about the camps.'

He shuddered.

Frankie felt her blood chill and put her hand over his.

'You did what you had to.'

'I know. But what if they find out that we altered his records? What if they find Marie's marriage record and work it out?'

Silence followed.

No one knew what would happen then.

16

SUFFOLK, 1938

It felt good to be up in the air.

The wind was cool and crisp, the sky impossibly blue, the farmers had planted rapeseed and lavender, making lush carpets of gold and purple below.

For just a moment she forgot her sorrow.

The Moth had taken some coaxing this morning, but the old plane was as familiar to her as ever.

Whatever objections her mother had had to her flying, she kept to herself. As an adult, at nineteen, Frankie was free to do what she wanted. The irony was that right then she would have given anything – *anything* – to rewind the clock and be a young girl again.

A part of her wanted to stay up here for ever.

Up here, for just a little while she could pretend that nothing had happened. That she was still that young girl, with her first plane, and that when she came in to land in front of the big old barn with its peeling paint, her father would be there waiting for her, a crooked smile on his face, and mug of steaming tea in his hand. 'Frankie-beans,' he'd say, grinning, 'you're as natural as a bird up there.' He'd hand her a cup of tea, then put his arm around her, while she glowed from his praise and company. 'Get this in you, nothing like a lovely cuppa to warm up those bones.'

Then they would make their way to the barn, which always felt like a haven. The radio would be playing in the background, and she would watch his feet keep time to the music. Despite having only one hand, he was the best dancer in town; her mother and father were always the first onto the dance floor at their country parties.

There in the barn they would talk about everything and nothing, and when she came home for the holidays from school, it was the one place she felt as if time had stood still.

Her father and mother had reached a sort of truce about her flying. Her mother got her way by ensuring that Frankie was exposed to other things – to school and the outside world, but when she was home, she turned a blind eye to her flying, so long as she didn't take unnecessary risks.

Frankie had learned her lesson, and became more cautious as a result. She knew that the truce was a delicate thing and didn't want to jeopardise it. She would never admit it, but it made her a better pilot.

But now, those precious times were over.

Her lip trembled, and fresh tears pooled down her cheeks.

He wouldn't be waiting for her. He would never be waiting for her ever again.

She swallowed and her eyes glazed over with tears.

'I hate this, I hate this so much,' she whispered. 'Why did you have to take him?'

She would have gladly traded in years of her life to keep her beloved father.

Up here she could allow herself the tears she didn't shed at home. It was like a mausoleum without him, like the colour had evaporated out of their world.

Her mother looked as if she had been cut down at the knees. Ageing overnight, unable to do even the smallest tasks by herself.

It was Emily and Frankie's turn to be strong for her now. Washing her mother's hair, and putting her to bed.

Frankie missed the fire in her mother's eyes. The strength she had taken for granted from this sharp, but kind woman.

Frankie and Emily arranged the funeral when everything inside her railed against his loss.

Everyone told her to be grateful that he went peacefully. He'd been doing what he loved, restoring an old plane, when his heart simply gave out. He clasped his chest and fell, and by the time he hit the ground he was gone.

It was quick. She supposed she should have been grateful for that. But she wasn't.

It felt like all the warmth had gone from her world. Like she was left with an endless winter.

She didn't know how she was supposed to live in a world without him in it.

She took a shaky breath and wiped her eyes on her sleeve, then brought the plane in to land.

She was already late for the funeral.

It was dark in the church. The only colour came from her father's favourite flowers, bright yellow sunflowers. Frankie knew he would have hated the traditional white lilies.

'When I go, I want people to remember me in life, not frozen in death.'

Frankie sat in the front row pew of the church and listened to the vicar speak about a man he'd likely only met for a combined total of three hours. His words were kind, but they weren't really conjuring up her father – the sort of person who made everyone smile, who was spontaneous and charming, who made her believe that anything was possible.

When he mentioned her father's disability for the third time, and how he 'overcame' it she had to stop herself from shouting at him. Her father was so much more than that. Yes, it was a part of him, but so was the smile that lit up his face on Christmas mornings, how he would be the one to wake them up excitedly so that they could unwrap presents. Or the twinkle in his eye when he teased his wife when he made her think he had bid in an auction for a small lot of 'just thirty old planes'. She turned white until he came clean and told her, 'But see now it doesn't seem so bad when I tell you it's only five, right?' He giggled as she chased him around the kitchen table flicking a dishrag at him while she threatened, laughing, to 'whip his hide'.

From behind her she heard someone grunt, too, when the vicar again mentioned his arm.

Frankie felt an affinity with whoever it was.

Her mother held onto her hand so tightly her fingers felt bruised. Her sister, Emily, was quietly sobbing on her other side.

When it was finally over, and she made her way out of the church, numbly shaking the hands of friends and family, she looked up when she saw a familiar pair of warm brown eyes and she realised who had been sitting behind her.

She hadn't seen him for almost a year because he'd been away at university.

She had been the one to phone him to tell him what had happened. The way his voice had broken on the end of the line haunted her thoughts still.

She felt her eyes fill at the naked pain on Michael's face. It was too much to bear.

It wasn't just her that had lost a father.

He had too.

The only one he'd ever known.

Before she knew it, she was hugging him, and he was clinging to her like he might never let her go.

17

SUFFOLK, 1939

The Suffolk Swifts was a small flying club with just over ten members. The name was somewhat misleading, as there was nothing particularly swift about them.

Most were well into their dotage and spent more time playing chess and telling old war stories than actually flying.

Their hangar was a rickety barn in the middle of a decommissioned airport.

The facilities were such that it was best to bring your own cup, tea and probably your own kettle and gas stove, too, as the one they had was about as reliable as a sunny day in Britain. The green tweed armchairs were moth-eaten and full of dog hair from the arthritic golden retriever who'd been nicknamed 'Major Gold' because he was always there to oversee them, having years ago decided to wander over from the nearby farm where he lived to establish order.

Despite its lack of charm (Major Gold notwithstanding), Frankie loved everything about the club. There were few places where she felt able to just be herself and this was one of them. Since her father died, she had been spending much of her free time at the club. But even here, the outside world, and the growing fear of war trickled in.

One cold March day, she climbed out of the cockpit of her old Moth and made her way with frozen extremities into the hangar and the doubtful allure of the tiny three-bar heater. She proceeded to peel off her leather gloves and stretch her hands in welcome relief, as feeling returned to her fingers. Just then, she was greeted by two of the regulars who had set up camp in the old armchairs for the day. There was a packet of Marie biscuits well underway on the coffee table before them.

Major Gold heaved himself off one of the chairs with a grunt, to receive his obligatory pat, only to lean against her and almost knock her off her feet. She didn't mind. The friendly dog and his warm bulk were welcome.

'Post Office treating you all right?' asked retired General Tom Beccles, who had lost his leg but not his will in the war, and like her father, hadn't seen any reason to let it stop him from flying. He had an impressive moustache that he was fond of twirling while he considered his next chess move.

Frankie shrugged. 'Yes.'

She'd got a job at the village post office a few months earlier. It was supposed to be a temporary measure until she got a position where she could put her flying skills to use, but so far no one had seemed that interested in taking on a female pilot.

'Don't worry, someone will eventually snap you up,' he said, as if reading her mind.

'I hope so.'

'K-k-kettle's boiled – s-s-mall miracle,' said the General's companion, a thin man in a worn suit, named Abe, with deep purple bruise-like shadows beneath his eyes. He, too, had come back damaged from the last war, except all his wounds were etched into his soul and like many the only way he found solace was in a bottle.

He seemed sober now, though; she'd heard he saved most of

his drinking for the evenings when the terror of the trenches still haunted him.

'Thanks, Abe,' she said, and went to make herself a cup of tea.

When she came back, she sat down opposite them with a tin mug filled with tea, and Major Gold's head resting against her knee.

The trousers she wore were an old, comfortable pair that used to belong to her father. She'd taken to wearing them when she flew, so that he was with her, in some small way, and to the credit of the flying club, no one had even raised a brow.

General Tom jerked his head towards a newspaper next to the biscuits, where the headline declared PEACE IN OUR TIME.

'Do you think he'll stick to it?' he asked.

Frankie didn't need to ask him who he meant. It was all anyone spoke about. Hitler and his expansion plans, as well as Europe's latest attempt to appease him and thus prevent war, this time by ceding parts of the Sudetenland to Germany.

For years, news of the brown-shirted radicals who were stirring up nationalist views and causing trouble in Germany was dismissed by most as a passing concern.

The prevailing view on the street was that those right-wing nationalists who called themselves Nazis would soon be given short shrift as common sense would prevail – no one wanted another war, least of all ordinary Germans who had lost so much.

But most people, Frankie included, had underestimated the bitter pill that Germany had been made to swallow after the last war from the Treaty of Versailles, which crippled their economy as they paid reparations that left many starving and out of work. That coupled with the economic crash had led to a unique breeding ground for radical ideas like Hitler's to take root, as many longed to throw off the yoke of the failing country they'd been left with.

For millions, his approach was seen as the answer. By the time the rest of Europe woke up to the threat he presented, the idea of another war no longer seemed as inconceivable as it had only a few months ago. Many were starting to see it as inevitable.

Frankie considered Abe's question.

'Honestly, I'm not sure. But I don't think Hitler's the type who is satisfied with concessions.'

Abe nodded. 'I a-agree. I d-doubt he'd be satisfied until he's got all their former territories and rebuilt the empire.'

General Tom twirled his moustache. 'I hope you're wrong.'

Frankie took a sip of tea, and frowned. 'Me too.'

Despite prime minister Neville Chamberlain's assurance that he'd helped secure 'peace in our time', for the first time in history, army conscription began during peacetime.

Everyone was on tenterhooks for what might unfold.

But in July, for a little while at least, in their pocket of Suffolk, Frankie and her family's focus turned instead on a long-awaited event that brought a twinkle to almost everyone's eye in the village.

Frankie's older sister Emily was getting married. She'd met her sweetheart, Stuart, on the train journey up for her first week at Cambridge University, after they noticed they were reading the same book, Daphne du Maurier's *Rebecca*, and the two had been inseparable since. Everyone in the village was invited to the wedding.

The festivities had given her mother something to focus on, and in recent months, she had clawed back some of her fighting spirit, as she organised everyone and everything around them.

Frankie, with help from Trixie, her old chum from St Cuthbert's, took on the task of arranging the flowers, many of which were grown at the farm.

Trixie had often been a guest at their farm over the years, along with the other girls. Her parents had been bemused at their tendency to slip into German every so often, a habit they kept up all through their schooling years, so that now all of them were pretty fluent.

Frankie had taught Trixie how to fly, and she'd become so enamoured that she had paid to have further lessons herself, gaining her pilot's licence shortly after Frankie. The other girls' parents had strictly forbidden them from learning, much to their chagrin.

But so far, despite visiting every so often, none of them had met who they termed the 'elusive Michael' who had been instrumental in sending Frankie to boarding school and with whom there had been tensions for years now.

He'd kept to his word and stayed away whenever she was home from school, something she had regretted asking him to do since almost the first moment she'd told him to. Over the years, she had only run into him a handful of times since.

Michael was to be the one who walked Emily down the aisle, taking the place of her father.

It was an honour that had brought tears to his eyes when Emily suggested it. Frankie knew her father would have approved, and she felt a lump in her throat thinking about it. Her sister had looked her in the eye and said, 'You're all right with it, him walking me down the aisle?'

'Of course, Em.'

She felt guilty that her sister had to ask. As they set up their displays around the altar in the village church, Trixie, who was dressed in a pale-blue dress that set off her white blonde hair magnificently, whispered to her other school chums, Marie and Eugenie, who had been roped in to help with the wedding too.

'Do you think Michael has horns?'

'I think he's covered in green boils,' said Eugenie, who looked pretty in a pale pink gown, her dark eyes mischievous.

'You d-don't have to be ugly to be a villain,' said Marie.

Frankie rolled her eyes. 'He's not a villain, trust me.'

The others looked similarly nonplussed. They had heard the tale of his betrayal often enough while they were growing up. For years Michael hadn't dared to visit when she was around, so understandably this about turn was something of a surprise.

The truth was, whatever anger she'd felt towards him had faded, and she regretted how petty she'd been. She missed their friendship. The easy relationship they'd had when they were younger, and how natural it had been to see him every day.

Ever since their falling-out it was like there was a hole in her life, which had only grown larger when she lost her father.

She knew he would want her to repair the damage, to forgive him. She could almost hear her father's voice whispering in her ear. 'Oh, Frankie, there are plenty of people in this world who don't deserve the time of day, who offer false promises, and never show up when you need them. Don't go on hating one of the few whose only fault was caring so much about you that he'd rather have you hate him and know that you were safe than stand back and watch you put your life at risk...'

And it was a risk. She realised that now. The chances she took in her plane, the tricks she did. She still wouldn't change that, and she would always be the type of girl who was perhaps more spontaneous than sensible, but she could see now that he hadn't persuaded her mother to send her away out of malice.

She should have forgiven him a long time ago, but her pride hadn't let her.

Over the past few months, they'd made tentative steps towards establishing a friendship, but it was still a fragile thing, the ease they'd had in each other's company had gone, replaced now with an awkwardness that made her feel oddly shy around him.

Trixie, who was repositioning a long-stemmed pale pink rose, paused, her blonde brows shooting upwards.

'Since when?'

She looked at Trixie and said, 'For a while now. It's complicated.'

The others all shared puzzled looks, but soon the church was filling up with guests and they all went to take their seats as the organist began to play the Wedding March.

Emily appeared in the entrance, the sun casting a halo around her. She was beautiful, in a simple white dress, and a string of pearls around her neck, highlighting the darkness of her hair.

But it was the appearance of Michael at her side that caused the girls around her to gasp.

He was resplendent in a navy suit. Tall, with his dark hair and eyes, he was looking down at Emily with a smile that made more than a few church members wish they could take her place.

Trixie tutted next to her. 'I say, you sly fox, now I see why it's suddenly "complicated". Here I was expecting horns, not bloody Clark Gable.'

Later that evening, in a barn that had been converted into a dance hall, the wedding guests swayed along to the local band that played some of their father's favourite crooners.

Trixie had been dancing up a storm with several of the men from the village who were besotted with their glamorous guest and was fanning herself as she took a seat on a haybale with a glass of champagne.

'You country folk do know how to throw a party,' she teased. 'I'm not sure I'll be able to walk on these feet tomorrow.'

Still, that didn't stop her saying yes to another dance from a handsome man with a faint moustache a few minutes later.

Frankie swayed along to the music. Like Trixie she'd been almost as popular with the local boys, but she was happy to sit back and watch. Especially when her mother was led out onto the dance floor by a local farmer, and proved that she still had the moves that had at one time made her and her father famous at local dances.

She was still smiling when Michael caught her eye across the dance floor as the band began to play 'Cheek to Cheek'. A patchwork of emotions passed over his face, from sorrow to joy.

Both of them could recall the day the song had come on the radio and her father had started to sing it and then twirl each of them around the barn while they were fixing up the Moth, and the way they'd laughed until their stomachs hurt, while Bill soppily put his face next to Michael's.

Before she knew it he was at her side, holding his hand out to her.

She felt a flutter of nerves that she squashed down.

Frankie fitted just under his chin, and as they began to sway to the music, they didn't speak.

The awkwardness that had been between them for some time fell away, as he sang softly in her ear, and she found herself looking into his eyes.

At some point the song changed, without them realising it, and she looked up in a daze to find Emily looking at them oddly.

Michael's mother, Irene raised a brow at them. Irene and her mother had grown closer since her father's passing. Frankie found herself blushing at the look on the other woman's face.

Frankie was about to step back, when he tightened his grip. 'I wanted to tell you—' She glanced at him, his tone had suddenly become serious, he hadn't seen Emily staring at them. 'Um, it might come as shock, and I'm sorry if it does, but well, I've joined the RAF.'

Frankie stopped dancing, to blink up at him in shock. 'You've volunteered?'

He nodded. 'I mean, there might not even be a war, but if there is, I just thought—'

She pushed herself out of his arms. 'That what – you'd be first in line to get yourself killed?'

She saw red.

'Frankie—'

She shook her head. Her jaw tensed, and she felt her face mottle with anger. 'For years you were against me flying because I could get killed, like your father, which I understood. I hated that you thought I was reckless, but in time I came to see your point... As I was taking unnecessary risks, only for you to turn around and do *this*?'

'Frankie, please, don't be like this.'

'Like what – like you?' she snapped, storming off. He caught up with her near the exit.

She didn't care that they had drawn a few onlookers, including her friends. Later, she would be embarrassed, but right then she was full of liquid fire.

He sighed. 'Frankie, I've learned to fly, and to conquer those fears, and I have experience that they could use, I can't just stand aside and not do anything just because of what happened to my father. He gave his life fighting for what he believed was right. I can't not do the same out of fear.'

She shook her head. 'I could get that, Michael, if we were at war, if we had no other choice, but volunteering to me just feels like you're asking to be first in line to be fed to the wolves.'

A week after the wedding, he came past the farmhouse to see her. It was just the two of them there.

Her mother was at Emily's new house, helping her to set up. She and Stuart had bought a little Suffolk pink cottage at the edge of the village, in need of some restoration, that the pair had decided to take on themselves. Frankie was just changing into her overalls and preparing to go down and help when she heard a knock at the door.

'I'm glad you're home,' he said. Taking off his fedora, and stepping inside the small hallway, his tall body loomed over hers. He smelled of lemon verbena soap from the little village shop, and it made her head swim.

'I'm sorry for what happened the other night. I shouldn't have told you at the wedding.'

She shook her head. 'I'm glad you told me.'

He nodded.

'Look, I just wanted to say goodbye, before I go. I'm being sent south for training, I'll be based down there for a few months.'

There was a long silence where no one said anything.

He frowned, then turned to leave.

Frankie closed her eyes for a beat, then shot out an arm to stop him, then pulled him in for a hug.

His arms tightened around her and she breathed him in.

'Just – if we do go to war – just promise me you'll come back alive, all right?'

'I promise.'

18

Two months after Michael had left, Frankie saw an application for an experienced pilot with at least 250 hours flying to take part in a new initiative known as the Air Transport Auxiliary (ATA) that would use civilian pilots to help ferry military planes from factories to airbases across Britain.

It was pinned up on the noticeboard at her flying club, the Suffolk Swifts.

It was early morning, before her shift at the post office, and she was cradling a cup of tea when she spotted it.

As she paused by the circular, General Tom elbowed one of the other members, an older woman who had learned to fly as part of a circus act when she was younger. Her name was Carol. Despite her adventurous past, and the stories that she no doubt had, she was someone many in the club avoided, as she was the sort of person who confused telling the truth with an excuse for being rude.

'Told you Frankie would be interested,' said Tom, chortling.

Frankie grinned. She certainly was.

'Apparently, the ATA was established in order to provide a civil reserve of pilots during wartime, who would not otherwise be eligible for the RAF, due to age or their circumstances, but whose skills can be used for a range of transport tasks from delivering mail, dispatches, news, medical supplies, civil authorities, medical officers, ambulance work and co-operating with police and fire brigade,' said General Tom.

Frankie looked at him, her eyes shining at the possibilities. 'I'd love to help with any of that.'

Carrol scoffed. 'Yes, well, you might love the idea, but I reckon when they receive an application from a woman, they might not be quite so keen.'

Frankie frowned, feeling suddenly deflated, looking at the circular again. 'But it doesn't say anything about these pilots needing to be male – just experienced.'

Carol laughed. 'Just because they forgot to specify "only males need apply" doesn't mean that's not what they mean.'

'I'm going to apply anyway.'

'By all means waste your paper and stamps, sweetheart.'

To Frankie's frustration, as the weeks went by and she heard nothing back regarding her application she began to see the bitter truth in Carol's words.

As more female pilots sent in their applications the idea of using them for the war effort began to fill up angry column inches nation-wide.

The editor of *The Aeroplane* wrote a scathing reply to a letter from Lady Bailey on the subject of female fighter pilots.

> *We quite agree with her that there are millions of women in the country who could do useful jobs in war. But the trouble is that so many of them insist on wanting to do jobs which they are quite incapable of doing. The menace is the woman who thinks that she ought to be flying a high-speed bomber when she really has not the intelligence to scrub the floor of a hospital properly,*

or wants to nose around as an Air Raid Warden and yet can't cook her husband's dinner...

The irony was not lost on Frankie that the women they were dismissing were already highly skilled pilots with hundreds of air miles under their belts, whose expertise could certainly be put to use if war broke out.

Three days before the outbreak of war, an Air Navigation Restriction Order was introduced preventing civil aircraft from flying over Britain without a special permit.

Frankie and her flying club were effectively grounded.

It came as little surprise then, when on 3 September, after Germany invaded Poland, Britain declared war.

The news that they had been dreading was met with rallying cries across the country, and the mood turned to one of determination to do their part.

Frankie couldn't help worrying about Michael, but she heard that they weren't immediately being sent over to fight just yet, and she couldn't help but feel a sense of relief at that.

Christmas that year brought a pinch of light that saw them through the rest of the winter.

Michael got leave to come home for two days, and it put her mother in one of the best moods she'd been in for months. She whistled carols while she adorned the house with all the homemade Christmas decorations Frankie and Emily had made when they were children, from baubles to trees made of wood and moss and in Frankie's case, a papier-mâché Santa Claus delivering presents in a plane made out of wooden popsicles.

When Michael arrived that afternoon, Frankie opened the door and inhaled sharply. He looked so handsome in his navy

RAF uniform. His face looked more angular, he'd lost weight, and it made his dark eyes seem even bigger as skin crinkled around the corners as he smiled at her in a way that made her stomach swoop.

He took off his peaked cap, then pulled her into a hug and sighed in pleasure, 'I can't tell you how good it is to be home, Beans.'

He smelled of soap, and forgotten summers, and she closed her eyes and breathed him in.

The hug lasted perhaps a beat too long. But neither of them pulled away, not until both their mothers came rushing into the hall. Irene gasped in delight, 'Michael, you're home,' as Frankie broke away, her cheeks flushing slightly.

They looked at one another for a beat and then Frankie's mother arched a brow, and said, 'Come on in, lunch is nearly ready.'

They sat down to one of the best meals anyone had had in weeks, complete with sprouts, roast potatoes and gravy. The only thing that would have made it better was if her father was there. She looked over at her father's seat, empty since he'd been taken from them, and now it was tradition to leave it open for him.

They all laughed though when Scrappy chose that moment to claim the chair as his.

'Excuse me, you little gobshite, what do you think you're doing?' exclaimed her mother, her mouth falling open in shock at the dog's audacity, while they all howled in laughter.

Michael snorted, then leaned over and whispered in her ear. 'I think he would have loved that.'

His breath caused shivers to run down her neck.

She grinned. 'Absolutely.'

Afterwards they all opened presents by the fire in the living room. Frankie's mother came over and gave her a fierce hug when she opened up her present from her, which was an oil painting she'd commissioned from General Tom, who was a wonderful artist, of her parent's wedding photograph.

'It's beautiful, thank you,' she said, and couldn't stop staring at it.

'Well now, I feel bad for just making you these,' said Emily, indicating the overalls she'd sewn her with gardening tools embroidered on the chest.

'Don't be a gobshite yerself now, you know I love it too,' said her mother, and they all giggled.

Michael opened his present from Frankie, a collection of poems by Wilfred Owen, and he looked touched as he his hands traced the green cover. 'This is perfect, thank you.' Owen was an English poet and soldier who'd died in the last war, and her father had told her how much his poetry had meant to him.

When she opened his, she frowned as she tore the brown paper. It was a lurid green mass of wool. She picked it up and unfolded a very lumpy-looking, long scarf.

'Um, thanks?' she said. 'It's an interesting colour,' she continued, just as Emily hooted, 'Oh my god, did you knit that yourself, Michael?'

He pressed his lips together to stop himself from laughing, and nodded.

Frankie's mouth popped open. 'You made me this?'

'Yes, sorry.'

She grinned, then looked at it anew. It was objectively ... rather ugly, but it must have taken him weeks. The thought that he had spent that long making it just for her made it one of the best gifts she had ever received.

She wrapped it around her neck, raised her chin and declared, 'It is beautiful.'

'Isn't it just,' sniggered Emily and they all broke into hysterical laughter apart from Frankie, who tossed a length of scarf over her shoulder and said, her lips twitching as she tried not to laugh, 'They're just jealous,' which made Michael clutch his stomach, tears of laughter spilling down his cheeks as he declared, 'Oh god, I might wet myself.'

Later when she went up to bed, she saw Emily and Michael speaking privately near the stairs. Michael's face looked sombre, and he nodded. 'Not if it'll change things.'

'You know it will, if it ends badly…'

Frankie frowned. What were they talking about?

'Is everything all right?'

They startled when they heard her.

'Yes, fine. I was just asking Michael's advice for something regarding Stuart.'

Frankie nodded, but she had her doubts. Whatever they were speaking about, it hadn't sounded like it had to do with Emily's husband, who hadn't got leave for the holiday. Whatever it was though, they didn't want her to know about, and she wasn't going to pry. So she bid them goodnight.

Frankie wore her ugly scarf every day that winter. It was lovely and warm, and a source of comfort for her. She lived in hope that she would be able to leave her boring job at the post office in the village and finally get to do her bit for the war effort.

It was a cold day in January when she visited her grounded flying club and shared a pot of tea with General Tom and Abe. The two men were playing what seemed like a never-ending game of chess.

She took a seat on the old sofa, next to the bar heater and the old Golden retriever, Major Gold, who took the opportunity to lay his large head on her feet, providing an instant source of warmth as well as a mood lift.

As Abe's fingers hesitated over his next play, he said, 'S-so did y-you hear, C-carol has had t-to eat her words?'

Frankie, who had just popped a Marie biscuit into her mouth, looked up in surprise and mumbled, 'Mmmh?'

General Tom looked up at her askance. 'Don't tell me you haven't heard – it's in all the papers. They're finally letting girls fly!'

Frankie started to choke, and she had to beat at her chest, so that bits of biscuit went flying onto the floor, which Major Gold helpfully hoovered up.

'What?' she cried.

General Tom, bent over towards a small table next to him, and then chucked a newspaper at her.

Her eyes fell on an article where a huge photograph of a group of women posing next to a plane, all dressed in uniform, dominated the page.

Beneath the photograph it said they were the first group of civilian ferry pilots for the women's section of the ATA, which was established under the leadership of Pauline Gower, a respected and experienced pilot.

Frankie read the article hungrily. It said that the qualifications for enrolment were the same as for the men, and like them, the women considered had to pass a flight test. If they passed, they would undergo a training course that would allow them to learn how to fly a variety of aircraft, as they would be expected to transport a range of different planes from the factory to the airbase where they were needed.

'Apparently they'll be ferrying Tiger Moth planes,' said General Tom.

Frankie looked up sharply. 'I could do that. I don't think it's that different from my old moth.'

'I think you're right. Perhaps they'll recruit more women to ferry them soon.'

Frankie looked up at him, eyes shining. 'I hope so.'

Frankie couldn't help being disappointed to not be one of these trail-blazing women, but over the course of the next few months she soon saw that being first also came with a considerable backlash, as the press had a field day with the introduction of female pilots. There were scathing articles and letters and it seemed that most people thought it was a bad idea.

Still, she would have rather dealt with the bad press and be a part of the first eight female ferry pilots than not.

She couldn't help chuckling, though, when she opened a letter she received from Michael, where the only thing inside the envelope was a cut-out of one of these articles, on which he'd scribbled, 'Don't let the buggers get you down.'

She put it in her purse as a daily reminder.

Back in September, many believed that as soon as war was announced an all-out battle for the skies would follow, government included, but that hadn't happened as yet. Journalists began to describe this time period as the Phoney War, where there were no major hostilities as no land operations were undertaken by the allies or Germans after they had invaded Poland in September and quickly defeated them, resulting in a stalemate that would last for months.

At home, the country had been bracing itself for an attack by the Germans. Air Raid precautions were put into effect as well as civil defence plans, but as the threat didn't materialise there was a sense of anti-climax in the streets as people were living under a set of restrictions such as food rationing that began to feel unnecessary.

Frankie came home from her job at the post office one wet and miserable day in March, to find her mother grumbling. 'I wanted to make an Irish stew, but the gombeen butcher wouldn't sell me any beef – said I'd already had me rations for the week! Fair play if it was feeding active soldiers, but we haven't fought anyone yet... so why should we all have to suffer while we wait for them to get a move on?'

Frankie let her moan. It was how she knew her mother was back to feeling more like her old self.

'We could always use beans,' she suggested.

Her mother narrowed her eyes. There was a flicker of humour about her lips. 'I haven't fallen that low just yet, thank you very much.'

Frankie chuckled, then went to get changed out of her work clothes.

Back in the kitchen, she defrosted in front of the Aga and helped her mother with dinner.

'I got a letter from Michael.'

Frankie looked up from chopping the carrots. For a moment her heart skipped a beat, *Was he being sent somewhere?*

'He said the training has been going well. His squadron is based down south but he wouldn't say where.'

Frankie's heart rate slowed.

'It's probably a precaution. They probably don't want it known where the airbases are in case the Germans find out – it would be an easy target.'

Her mother turned pale. 'I didn't think of that.'

Frankie nodded. 'I hear it a lot at the post office – letters arrive with information blanked out. I had one angry woman come in and accuse us of tampering with her mail – my manager had to explain that it wasn't us.'

'Irene came past this morning.'

Frankie looked at her mother, her brow raised.

Michael's mother had become something of a friend, she seemed to want to help her mother after her father passed, and was always suggesting she join some new project she was involved with.

'She suggested I get involved in the Land Army project, with the farm. She said she'd help.'

Frankie bit her lip. It made sense; at some point when the war actually began there was likely to be food shortages, as they could no longer import what they didn't grow themselves. Small farms around the country were being asked to support the government-backed scheme.

But at the same time, it would be a lot of work for her mother. Their farm manager was busy enough with the demands of running the farm and ensuring the crop of potatoes and sugar beet filled the quotas needed as most of it was going to the army.

Frankie looked at her mother. 'What did you say to Irene?'

Her mother pursed her lips. 'I said I'd think about it. Apparently, if I signed on, they would send us some workers to help – girls mainly who would be part of the Land Army,' she said with a small smile. Then she squared her shoulders. 'I think Irene is right. It's a good idea, and it might be good for me. I know your father would have got a kick out of it.'

Frankie gave her mother's shoulders a squeeze. Her throat constricted with unshed tears. 'Yes, he would.'

One of the other side-effects of the phoney war was that people were once again beginning to question the need for female pilots.

It made Frankie despair that she might never be taken on for the war effort as a pilot. When she went to visit her flying club friends, one wet day in March at the airbase, where no one was allowed to fly but they all ended up visiting anyway, mostly to commiserate with each other over a cup of tea, General Tom seemed to read her mind. 'They'll change their tune soon enough about the need for more female pilots when the war starts for real, trust me. They've all just got too much time on their hands now, so that's what taking up press time – soon enough they'll have far bigger things to worry about than a tiny group of women.'

It seemed the head of the ATA women's division Pauline Gower shared his sentiments, as she replied to a letter from

Frankie enquiring if there would be opportunities in the future for further female ferry pilots.

21 March 1940

Dear Miss Chalmers,

Thank you for your letter. At present, the question of employing more female pilots has only met with resistance. But I have been assured that 'should the so-called war develop into a real war, it will not be long before there will be openings for experienced pilots.'

So right now, we are to wait and see. The Air Ministry have said not to be on standby, but I am sure you will ignore that advice as will I.

Sincerely,

P. Gower.

Frankie set the letter down and sighed. It was frustrating because she had heard via her now-grounded flying club members that the ferry pools were taking on men with far less experience than she had. But she also knew that Pauline Gower had a point: once the war began to quicken in earnest, there would likely be a change in attitude as men were shipped off to where they could fight.

In April, everything changed.

Norway was invaded, and the newspapers were full of reports of Britain's delay in sending troops to help in time, resulting in the resignation of the prime minister, and the appointment of Winston Churchill. He took office on the same day, just as the Germans invaded France, Belgium, the Netherlands and Luxembourg.

Emily and Stuart had come over to listen to their radio when she heard their new prime minister speak for the first time. Frankie couldn't help feeling something inside her stir as he promised, during this dark hour, to 'wage war against a monstrous tyranny' and offer the people his blood, toil, tears and sweat.

'He's who we need now,' her mother said.

'Yes,' said Frankie.

Soon afterwards, their new prime minister cemented this belief, not just in her mother's heart, but in the nation after he led a successful rescue and evacuation of British and French soldiers who had found themselves trapped by the invading German army on the coast of France and Belgium in Dunkirk. Everyone who could got involved, sending boats and doing what they could to help rescue the soldiers. Saving thousands.

That summer, the war became personal for Frankie.

The phone rang and before she picked up the receiver she knew it was Michael.

'We fly tomorrow,' he said, keeping his voice neutral. She sucked in a breath. Not knowing what to say, except, 'Michael...'

'I'll be careful.'

'You better.'

There was a soft chuckle from down the line.

'Tell my mother for me, Beans? I don't think I can.'

'I will.'

'Michael?'

'Yes?'

'Promise me you'll come back alive.'

There was a swallow.

'I promise.'

Afterwards it was like a part of her heart was up in those skies, exposed, and the daily sighting of planes overhead, and the distant rumble of bombs, brought the war home. Some nights she went to bed haunted by dreams of Michael dying the way his father did and she had to get up and pace the farmhouse and try her best not to think about it. Some days she just couldn't make the image fade away.

It was during those fraught days that Frankie received news that the government had finally given the go-ahead to add more trained women pilots to the ATA and she was being considered for one of the positions.

On the day the letter arrived, inviting Frankie to join, she sat at the bottom of the stairs as two 'land girls' passed her by on their way to the farm. The girls had arrived a few weeks ago, to help her mother and Irene as they turned a section of the farm over to the Land Army initiative. Frankie had been helping in her spare time away from the post office, and she enjoyed the company of the girls, and how they had brought life to the house, especially with her mother, who was in her element organising them. Irene had been right. It was good for her, and she was grateful to Michael's mother for suggesting it.

'You all right?' said her sister Emily, who had been roped in by their mother to join. Her hair was tied up in a scarf. She wore the regulation uniform of a brown coat and shapeless trousers, which she somehow managed to make look good.

She came to take a seat next to her on the steps, noting the letter she was clutching tightly.

Frankie nodded.

The letter offered Frankie a position in a new all-female ferry pool which would be based in Hatfield. She would be leaving in a week.

Frankie took a shuddery breath. Now that it was here, she felt a mixture of excitement and nerves.

'It's finally happened,' she said, showing her the letter.

Emily gasped, just as her mother came in from outside, pausing in the doorway, a streak of dirt on her face. Her eyes showed a mixture of worry and resignation, but then she smiled.

Frankie could have kissed her for that brave smile.

'It's come, then?'

'Yes.'

She got up off the stairs, and joined her mother and sister in a hug.

'You be careful now, do you hear, Frankie-beans,' whispered Emily in her ear.

Frankie's lip wobbled at the use of her father's nickname for her.

'I promise.'

19

Frankie sat in the passenger seat of the old farm van with her battered box suitcase on her lap. It contained all she possessed. It wasn't much. Her stomach churned with nerves.

In her pocket was the folded-up letter inviting her for her flight test in Hatfield. She would only be allowed to join the ferry pool if she passed.

It was a beautiful summer's day. The frothy white cow parsley was in bloom along the county lanes as they drove through the flat landscape of Suffolk towards Hertfordshire.

Emily held out a slim hand to touch the lacy blooms, an indicator of how slow the van was.

Many of the road signs were gone, one of the measures taken to prevent the enemy from being able to recognise landmarks while they were flying overhead.

They'd had to study the map beforehand in order to make sure they would be driving in the right direction, studying map routes was something that Frankie knew would likely be a big part of her life, should she get the job.

She swallowed.

'You'll get it, don't worry,' said Emily, sensing how her sister was feeling as she changed gears.

Frankie nodded.

But she didn't feel as confident as she pretended. She was an experienced pilot, yes, but that was during peacetime, when the stakes were low and the only thing she had to concern herself with was flying through a landscape she knew as well as the back of her hand.

This was an entirely different beast.

Every day new enemy bombers appeared in the sky, recognisable when there was a dull thud of a nearby explosion.

She would be expected to transport planes from a factory to airbases across the country, navigating dangerous flight paths with German planes overhead, while landmarks were obstructed. Defensive balloon barrages filled the sky, and the smog and smoke from industrial towns along that path would make visibility near impossible.

That young girl who hadn't known a moment's fear in a plane had gone.

She was all too aware of what could go wrong.

When the van came to stop at the airbase, Frankie climbed out on somewhat shaky legs, her hands turning white while she clutched her suitcase handle.

She hugged her sister goodbye, feeling her eyes smart with unshed tears, then made her way inside the base.

Twenty minutes later, she was given her flying check by one of the original eight female ferry pilots.

Frankie climbed into the cockpit of the Tiger Moth, which was what was being produced by the de Havilland factory nearby. She along with the other ferry pilots would be tasked with transporting it across the country.

As she took the plane up, the sky opened up around her, and she felt joy at being airborne after so long.

When they came into land, the older woman looked at

Frankie, then shook her head. For a moment, Frankie felt her world tilt. She hadn't made a mistake. Had she? Had her old recklessness resurfaced without her realising, in her excitement at being in the sky? She knew that the ATA weren't interested in daredevils. Daredevils got themselves killed and wasted the valuable equipment they were transporting.

She had vowed to keep that part of herself firmly under lock and key.

She bit her lip, waiting for the woman to speak.

The other woman smiled. 'I'm sorry it's taken so long to get you on board. You're a natural, and if this was a just world, you'd be snapped up by the RAF. No one else will probably say this to you, but we're lucky to have you.'

Frankie's throat constricted for a moment at the praise. 'I feel lucky to be here.'

The woman chuckled. 'Steady on. Let's see how lucky you feel in a few months.'

She led Frankie to the base where she would be staying with the other new recruits.

She walked fast, and Frankie hurried to keep pace. 'The flight check was your first test, but you're not permanent until you do the refresher course in two weeks. That's when you'll get your official uniform.'

Inside, she was introduced to the others, including Pauline Gower, and she was soon to discover how different it would be to fly during war time. 'The coastline is to be avoided at all costs, as it has been defended in every way possible. Navigation will be harder than what anyone is used to, as everything is obstructed. Sign posts, as you know, have been removed, but airfields are also obstructed at sunset with anything available, such as farm equipment, so if you aren't sure that you will be able to make it in time, you will likely have to make an emergency landing somewhere else along the route...'

Frankie listened as Pauline Gower and some of the senior women explained the strict protocols of flying in wartime.

While they were speaking, she was handed a small pistol. Despite living on a farm, she had never held a gun in her life.

'Sort of makes it seem a bit more real now, don't you think?' whispered one of the other new girls on her right, a pretty woman with black hair and almond shaped brown eyes who had introduced herself as Harriet Mathews.

Frankie nodded.

It would be small consolation against an enemy bomber.

She tuned back in to the rest of the protocols they were expected to follow.

They would need to fly at all times within sight of the ground so that they were recognised. And they had to stick to routes in areas that were defended by a barrage balloon. They were also instructed to fly in gaggles, with someone following by car.

The next morning was her first mission. She, along with several other girls, including Harriet, were to drive to Perth and take a batch of Tiger Moth planes to their various destinations across the country.

The drive took six hours, long enough for her to get to know Harriet and some of the others a bit better. She liked her new companions.

As they neared Perth, however, the sun was nearly about to set, and the airbase was being obstructed for the night. They spent the night in a hotel nearby. Frankie shared a room with Harriet, and they stayed up playing cards and sharing the stories of how they'd learned to fly.

Harriet picked up a card, then said. 'I read Geography at Cambridge, and my grandmother left me some money after she passed. She said in her will that she wanted me to do something bold with it.'

She grinned as she took a sip of red wine from a bottle she'd managed to squirrel away inside their room, unbeknownst to their commanding officer, who would certainly not have approved. Frankie had already seen that the atmosphere at Hatfield was a bit like a school dormitory with the rules to match.

'We won't have the whole bottle,' Harriet promised, 'but one glass won't hurt.'

'Neither will two,' said Frankie with a grin, and Harriet guffawed. 'I knew we were going to get on.'

Harriet continued on with her story. 'My gran was a character. So, I thought, well, something bold I'd always wanted to do was learn to fly. I figured if I had my licence along with my degree, maybe I could make it my career. Soon after I qualified, I got a job with the army doing aerial photography.'

Frankie was impressed.

Apart from Trixie, her friend from school, who'd taken a shine to flying, too, and had gone on to get her pilot's licence after Frankie taught her how to fly, she had never been around girls who loved flying like she did.

Harriet was amazed when she told her about how her father had taught her when she was a young girl, and Michael too. She found herself telling her new friend all about them both, pausing only when her throat became constricted with unshed tears.

'He sounds wonderful, your dad.'

'He was.'

Harriet grinned. 'I think he and my gran might have liked each other.'

Frankie ginned back. 'I think you're right.'

. . .

Unlike the other new girls, Frankie was the only one who wore trousers to fly. She'd been wearing them for some time now. The rest, before they would be given their uniforms, wore skirts, including Harriet.

'Oh gosh, I envy you,' she said in the morning, as they made their way over to the base. 'It might be June but this is not warm. I'm looking forward to my first ever pair of trousers.'

Frankie grinned. 'They're as good as they said.'

Harriet laughed.

The official uniform was a navy sweater, a Sidcot suit – a huge boiler suit effort with a separate lining – that almost no one wore, a tunic with a gold strap, a belt, a skirt and a pair of trousers – which they were only supposed to wear on aerodromes.

At the airbase, the girls were all given their 'ferry chits' – a document that included their name, details of their licence and what they were allowed to fly as well as the aircraft they were to transport. It would need to be signed when they delivered the plane.

Frankie's destination was a small airbase just over three hours away. She would need to refuel en route as the Tiger Moth only held fuel enough for two hours' flying. They were told to study their routes from a master map that was kept behind lock and key, and they had to memorise roads, railways and any special features along the way. As airfields were camouflaged this made it trickier.

The map they were given didn't contain any of these recognisable landmarks, and they were forbidden from marking them in any way, in case they got into the hands of the enemy, who would now have important, classified information – the safe air routes around Britain.

Each map was marked with their pilot's number, so if it went missing, and was found, the ATA would know exactly who the irresponsible pilot was.

Considering the pressure the female pilots faced, from a barrage of scrutiny, they were warned not to make any mistake that would bring all of them into question.

It was a huge responsibility, and not for the first time did Frankie envy the men who were free to make the sorts of mistakes they could not because they weren't all blamed if one of them messed up.

Her first trip went off without incident. At first, her 'gaggle' consisted of two other girls who were going west, they set off together to refuel en route at a small airbase, then went their separate ways, and she was alone for the first time, flying solo. It felt good, and she felt a sense of freedom as she cut through the skies and headed towards the flying school, which was her destination, where the new Moth would be used to train new recruits.

When she came into the circuit, and jumped out of the cockpit, one of the ground crew stepped forward in shock and Frankie learned how to take a compliment even if it was a little backhanded.

'You're a girl,' he said, eyeing her and the plane with some level of shock.

'So I've been told,' she said drily.

'Sorry,' he gawped, blushing, 'it's just that, I haven't actually seen one of you yet, and I... mean, erm, well done. I mean... not that you—ah, sorry.'

He was blushing. 'Thanks. It's my first time with a delivery, so we have that in common. Where do I get this signed off?' she asked, showing him her ferry chit.

'Through there,' he said, pointing.

Her ferry chit was processed and she made her way to the nearest train station, where she caught a sleeper back to Hatfield.

. . .

Over the next two weeks, she realised that the process was never quite as straightforward as her first trip had promised. A few days after she joined, she was tasked with taking a Tiger Moth to an airbase down south. She refuelled en route, only to have to find an empty field in which to land when she neared her destination as they had already obstructed the airbase for the evening. She rented a room in a small bed and breakfast, and in the morning, when she made her way back to the field, it began to rain, and the visibility was so poor it was impossible to take off. The downpour persisted all day long, and she was forced to spend another night at the hotel.

She had only brought an extra shirt with her, and she was longing for a proper change of clothes.

In the morning, the weather cleared, and she was finally able to drop off the plane. By the time she returned to base, it was four days after she'd set off.

One of the senior pilots who passed her on her way back to her rooms said, 'Glad to have you back. Next time, take as much extra clothing in your bag as you can – I hate to say it, but what you experienced happens more often than not. Poor visibility, the airbases being obstructed, getting lost – it can all delay you. Don't worry, though, it's completely normal. Even now I never know if I'll be gone a day or a week when I set off. Keeps it interesting.'

Frankie laughed. It certainly did.

When her first two weeks were up, she along with Harriet, did the official acceptance test with the ATA chief instructor at Whitechurch, which was a large circuit. After the sort of flying they'd all been doing, it turned out to be hard to fail. Even so, it was a milestone. Frankie now was officially a part of the ATA and could receive her uniform. She was one of them.

. . .

Over the next few months, Frankie was kept busy, ferrying planes across the country, and sometimes having to take the ferry plane to collect the others. In August, however, she got a welcome surprise as a new member joined their ranks.

After a long, hard week, she came back to base to discover a familiar face beaming at her.

'*Trixie?*' she cried.

'In the flesh! Couldn't let you have all the fun now, could I?'

In many ways, glamorous Trixie with her tiny frame, her never knowingly under-lipsticked mouth, and her shock of white blonde hair appeared to some as an unlikely candidate for a pilot. She was everything the sort of men who wrote letters of complaint about female pilots feared. Someone who collected fashion magazines, could and did tell you exactly how to pose for the best photograph, and matched her handbags and head-scarf to her uniform. But that was just the surface: she was fiercely intelligent, kind, adventurous and a really good pilot.

It was wonderful having Trixie be a part of her ferry pool. She had the sort of indomitable optimism that could make a tough day just that bit easier to bear.

Like the day they were all to take a batch of Tiger Moths to Birmingham, and they found themselves in a boarding house in the Pennines en route, with a landlady who gave each girl a blanket that looked about as thin as a musty old sheet and made them pay extra for the privilege.

While the other girls grumbled, Trixie modelled the blanket, like it was Paris couture, and tied it in various ways around herself. 'This delightful garment, made from a collection of quite interesting muddy-toned fibres, is a bargain at only tuppence... A truly versatile piece for the dashing lady – why, see here, it's a day out at Ascot, flying over it, you understand,' and then she tied it around her shoulders, 'while here it is, of course, a cape the likes of which one could join Robin Hood and his band of merry men...'

They were all soon howling with laughter.

'F-flying over it, you understand,' repeated Harriet, holding onto her stomach as she giggled, along with the rest who broke out into fresh peals of laughter, which only intensified when they heard the sound of the landlady's broom hitting the ceiling at the noise.

Soon it was hard for any of them to imagine not having Trixie around.

While she enjoyed her first few months, despite the challenges, Frankie was keenly aware that she had joined during a perilous time in the war – during a period that would become known in time as the Battle of Britain. The bombs were often dropped near the airfields, and it was impossible not to feel a sense of apprehension any time she heard the distant thud of a bomb.

She thought of Michael often, of what he was doing, how he was faring. Telling herself that no news was good news, something they all subscribed to.

In September, the Blitz began, a bombing campaign by the Nazis with mass air attacks against British cities.

For Frankie the term seemed horribly incongruous. A small, almost cheerful word for something so monstrous. Whole areas wiped out, countless lives lost, along with history and architecture, razed to the ground due to some madman's attempt to control the world.

On a rare weekend off, Trixie proposed going to London to take photographs with her of the city's landmarks, in case they never saw them again, and it was one of the most depressing day trips of her life.

They walked the streets of the East End, where it had been hardest hit, not long after what became known as 'Black Saturday' when hundreds of bombs were dropped on East London's warehouses, docks and homes. She saw a woman picking through the rubble where her home used to be, while another brought over a cup of tea. The other woman smiled as she accepted it.

Frankie was amazed that she could find it in herself to smile.

But as the day wore on, she saw a mixture of responses, from intense grief as people sobbed in the street, as well as others acting normally, going about their day.

It was the latter that stayed with her longest, adding more fodder for her nightmares.

In October, nothing could have prepared her or her friends for the devastation that was to follow when a batch of bombs were dropped on their base in Hatfield.

The air raid drill sounded at the same time the bombs fell. Frankie and her pool ran to the air raid shelter just as a bomb dropped. Thankfully, it did not explode on contact or she along with Harriet and Trixie would have been lost.

But others nearby were not so lucky. In the factory workshop, one of the bombs killed twenty-one people and injured over seventy.

The event rocked them all.

Frankie tossed and turned for the next few nights, waking up when she heard quiet sobbing. She found Harriet, who was always stoic and composed, shaking. 'It was nearly us,' she whispered.

Frankie could only nod. The same thing kept her awake too.

It would, for a long time afterwards.

20

PRESENT DAY, LOIRE VALLEY, 1944

Frankie's memories were coming back slowly. Every day she recalled something new. The face of a friend. The airbase where she was first stationed and once, the gut-wrenching grief when she remembered losing her father.

It felt like some awful trial, as each day she was confronted with a memory that she was forced to relive.

Antoine was sitting with her under the shade of an oak tree, in the sunshine. For just a moment they could fool themselves that the war was far away, but not for long.

It had been a few weeks since he and Théo had confessed to her the secret they'd been hiding about the boy's Jewish heritage.

They were all still reeling after the murder of Madame Avril, but Théo had at least left his room, and was nearby with Saint, throwing a ball for the dog to catch.

Frankie glanced over at the boy. Even from a few metres away, she could see the shadows beneath his eyes. She knew that he was worried that the Nazis might look further than his later birth certificate or notice the discrepancy. She wasn't sure if the boy knew.

It had haunted her ever since.

The thought of them coming here to take Théo away or killing Antoine was too much to bear.

She bit her lip; something had to be done.

The next morning, she asked Antoine to take her to the village. He was shocked. 'But Fr— *Isabelle*,' he corrected himself, 'what if someone sees you – no one in the village knows what you look like, they might not realise that you're the woman they are supposed to be pretending is Isabelle! If one of the Nazis saw them acting strangely around you, they might get suspicious.'

She bit her lip. There was no excuse she could give that was likely to satisfy the old man. She couldn't even feign needing feminine hygiene products because he'd already thought of that and had quite casually mentioned that the bathroom cabinet was stocked with anything she might need.

She had been touched with his professionalism and thoughtfulness, and his lack of embarrassment.

She didn't want to tell him the truth, she didn't want to get him involved if anything went wrong, but if she was going to do it she needed his help.

'I'll be careful, I promise. I only need to get something from the Mairie's office.'

He looked at her askance, his eyes widening. The Mairie was the mayor's office; it was where all the records were kept.

'What?' he asked, suspicion clouding his eyes.

'Anything that could threaten my young friend's life.'

Antoine swallowed. 'I'll help.'

She shook her head. 'If you get caught—'

'It's the same thing if you do, better we do it together. Besides, I think I might know a way I can bribe our way in.'

. . .

The Mairie was a white building that in peacetime was adorned with the French flag, with window boxes filled with pansies the colours of liberation: red, white and blue. The caretaker now, it seemed, didn't have the heart to maintain them and filled it instead with white lilies, as though the building, with its Nazi flag flapping in the wind, was in mourning.

Perhaps it was.

The old man who greeted them at the desk was thin and wiry, with a long patch of grey hair that he had combed over to one side to fill the rest of his bald pate.

He was shocked to find Frankie there.

'Antoine?' he whispered.

'Good morning, Monsieur Cheval. We're here for the deed record for the old Smithy, in case Isabelle ever needs to prove who owned the property.'

'But it's completely burned down – it's not like it would be of any use.'

He eyed Isabelle with curiosity.

'Even so,' said Antoine, glancing around towards the back office to ensure no one else was around. 'If we could just take a look, we'd be most grateful. Just to be sure that our information is the same as that on record.'

'We'd really appreciate it,' said Isabelle.

Monsieur Cheval hesitated. 'Technically, I'm not meant to let anyone near the records any more...'

Antoine slipped something towards the man. It was a small bag of sugar, which was heavily rationed in the war.

'We'll be in and out so fast, it was like we were never here.'

Monsieur Cheval's fist closed over the sugar greedily. He nodded. 'Five minutes, not a second longer,' he warned.

They made their way into the room where the records were kept.

They consulted the marriage register, where every marriage was recorded by hand in a log book.

Antoine flicked though the pages, then paused with shaking fingers when he found it.

'Here,' he said, tracing the record with his unsteady finger.

Marie Duvall and Claude Schneider at St Jude Church on 1 May 1932.

His hands shook further as he reached inside his jacket pocket for a pen and prepared to blot the log record.

'Don't!' said Frankie, coming forward, moving quickly despite the agony in her leg, and snatching it away from him. 'That will only make it obvious. Here—' she said, then began to very carefully pull out the page so that the casual observer wouldn't notice at first that the log for all marriage records for the years 1930 to 1932 were completely missing.

'They'll see the page is gone, but they won't know why.'

Antoine nodded, still looking shaken. 'Yes, that's much better.'

Then she carefully folded it up and stuck it inside her brassiere for safe-keeping.

'We'll need to get the marriage certificate too.'

On the shelves were hundreds of files that were neatly dated and clearly marked. Antoine hurried over to the one that covered the marriages for the area, and began to scan the shelf for the correct year.

'Got it,' he said, pulling out the heavy file that covered the marriages from the early thirties.

He paged through, until he found the marriage certificate. It didn't take long; there were only five others from the village who got married that year.

'It's here,' he said, pausing.

'It was such a beautiful day, her favourite roses were in bloom, the Pierre de Roussard ones that grow by the wall over the farmhouse, and her bouquet was picked fresh from them.

She wore her mother's wedding dress, Jean was so touched that she did that.'

His lip wobbled, and Frankie reached out to squeeze his hand.

They heard a cough from outside.

'I'm sorry, Antoine, but we must hurry.'

He nodded, dashing away a tear with the back of his hand. Frankie folded up the certificate and put it in the other cup of her brassiere.

The quickly tidied up, removing all trace that they had been there.

Then they made their way out of the office, Frankie following behind Antoine, only to slam into his suddenly still form.

She looked up in confusion, only for her knees to turn to jelly, as she found herself face-to-face with the blonde-haired Nazi officer from the village, Dieter Frosch. The one who'd brought them food, when he'd heard that Isabelle was injured. The same one who Antoine had seen wave politely at him, after his colleague shot Madame Avril in front of him.

'What were you doing back there?' he asked, his blue eyes clouding with suspicion.

His usual polite smile was gone.

'I – I,' Frankie hesitated.

Monsieur Cheval came in from the kitchen, a mug of tea in his old hands, and turned white.

Antoine thought fast. 'There was a delay in getting Monsieur Dubois's death certificate. Mademoiselle Dubois and I called at the front desk, but there was no answer, so we thought Monsieur Cheval might be in the records room, and we went to check, but no one was there...'

'Sorry, I was in the kitchen,' said Monsieur Cheval, 'my

hearing isn't what it used to be. Let me find out what has happened to that certificate, dear Isabelle. I apologise for making you come here.'

'It's no trouble,' said Frankie, her stomach churning, the hidden papers scratching her skin.

Dieter Frosch watched the exchange with a frown on his face.

'Villagers are no longer allowed in the records room.'

'I didn't know,' lied Frankie. Her heart thudded inside her chest. She felt nauseous with fear. If he came forward and checked that she hadn't stolen anything, she would be responsible for the very thing she was hoping to avoid. Putting the lives of the young boy and the old man who had become so dear to her in danger.

Her legs almost gave out when he nodded his head. 'I'm sorry it wasn't sent to you sooner.'

There had been delays of these sorts of items due to the war.

Frosch wore the polite veneer well, his face looked friendly now, but she couldn't help thinking of the woman that had been killed in the village, and how Antoine had described how chilling it was that his face had betrayed no reaction whatsoever, as if killing someone's grandmother in front of a crowd of friends and family was just a normal part of daily life for him now.

The thought terrified her.

Her voice was strained, as she tried her best to act normal. 'Thank you.'

A few minutes later, Monsieur Cheval came out with a manila envelope. 'I found it, the death certificate is here,' and handed it to her.

Frankie and Antoine turned to leave, in relief, only to stop when Frosch placed a hand on Frankie's shoulder. She had to school her face to hide the thrill of revulsion she felt. Her stomach dropped, uncomfortably.

'I wonder, Fräulein,' he began, as the blood rushed inside her ears, 'I didn't ask before as you were still recovering from your injuries, but now that you are, would you care to join me for dinner sometime this week?'

21

Frankie stood rooted to the spot.

'I—' she began, looking up at the Nazi officer who had asked her to dinner.

He waited patiently for her answer.

Was it wise to decline? How could she possibly accept?

Suddenly, a face flashed before her eyes. A pair of warm brown eyes that crinkled at the corners. She frowned.

'Forgive me, officer, but I am not free, you see there is someone else.'

He frowned. 'Someone from the village?'

She swallowed. 'He is... away.'

His expression cleared, and he chuckled. 'You mean he was fighting us, and now he's likely captured somewhere. He might not make it back, Fräulein.'

Frankie blinked. Anger bubbled up within her and she had to work hard to not show it. He must have caught some glimpse of it, because his lips twitched slightly, like he was amused.

It was the moment she went from simply fearing him to loathing him.

'Very well, you likely need some more time, I shall ask you

again, later. Consider my invitation, as our American friends say, my attempt to put my hat in the ring.'

Then he bid her farewell.

Frankie stood, momentarily rooted to the spot.

His words made another face swim before her eyes. She saw a tanned face, and a wide smile, and felt something inside her stir, as she heard a midwestern accent in her mind say, 'Well, doll, I've heard some whoppers in my day, but that sure beats all.'

She blinked.

She had no idea who that was.

Whoever it was, though, she was sure of two things. That the man with the American accent meant something to her.

The second was that the Americans were *not* their friends.

22

BRITAIN, 1940–42

The winter of 1940–41 was dismal.

There were no weekends or holidays for the ferry pools, and Frankie spent her first Christmas at the base with the other girls. It couldn't have been more different than the year before.

They made the most of the occasion. Wrapping up warm, in her long, lurid, lime-green scarf, Trixie took one look at it and winced. 'I swear that scarf just gets uglier the more one looks at it,' and Frankie rolled her eyes at her friend, hiding a grin.

'You know, now that I mention it, I have always wondered about it ... you always look so stylish, Frankie, with that glorious hair ... but that thing—'

Frankie put her hands on her hips. 'I don't know, I think it sort of matches the colour of my eyes,' but she had to fold her lips together to stop herself from snorting.

'If your eyes were the colour of bile, sure,' said Trixie, raising a brow.

Harriet sniggered.

It was hard to explain that she loved it because it was hideous, because it had been made for her, because it made her feel close to Michael because it had been made over countless hours by his fingers, just for her.

She didn't tell them any of that though because she knew there would be no end to the teasing.

After their roast dinner, they drank sherry and played games, eating mince pies and unwrapping the presents they had got each other. Harriet had knitted Frankie a maroon jumper that was lovely and warm, and Trixie gave her an engraved lipstick case with her name on it. She had given each of them a book.

She'd found out a few months before what their favourite novel had been growing up, and she gifted each of them a copy. Harriet's was *The Secret Garden* while Trixie's was *Anne of Green Gables*, and they each hugged them to their chests. For much of her childhood, books had been something that Frankie approached with fear, a symbol of her failure, but as she learned to manage her word blindness, she'd come to see books as the sort of friends one needed to get through the storm. In these dark days of war, they brought hope and comfort. An escape from a world turned mad.

'It's perfect,' said Trixie.

Harriet nodded, swallowing, unable to speak.

Later that evening she telephoned her sister. Her mother had gone to spend the holiday with Emily and her new husband.

'It's horrible that you're not with us,' said Emily. 'I felt perfectly miserable when I found out you weren't getting leave.'

'It's all right, Em, we've made the most of it.'

'Glad to hear it. Did you hear about Michael?'

'No?' her heart began to race. Her mind raced with the horrible possibilities. 'Is he all right?'

Emily's voice sounded bubbly with delight. 'Perfectly. He's met someone, apparently. All the girls in the village are going to be broken-hearted to find out he's finally off the market!'

Frankie felt her stomach drop.

He'd met someone? He was with someone else?

Ever since her sister's wedding it had felt like there was something between them. Something more. Had she just imagined it?

She felt her throat constrict with emotion. She struggled to breathe. The scarf he'd knitted felt like it was suffocating her, and she pulled it away.

There was too long a beat of silence.

'Frankie?' said her sister. Her voice concerned.

Frankie shut her eyes. *I will not cry*, she told herself.

It must have all been in her mind – her stupid heart seeing something that was never there. Michael had never said anything or done anything to indicate that there was something more between them, not really, nothing concrete anyway, she told herself, while her mind whispered *but what about the almost kiss after the wedding when they danced* – she must have read it wrong, she realised now, bleakly. Or maybe it just didn't mean as much to him as it had to her. Maybe he'd just had too much to drink.

'Sorry,' she said, putting on a bright, false voice, 'got distracted by someone walking past,' she fudged, then forced a laugh. 'That's true.'

'Irene said it might be serious. Isn't it the best news, just perfect for Christmas!'

'The best,' agreed Frankie hollowly.

When she climbed into bed that night, she dreamt of the night she and Michael had danced at Emily's wedding.

When she woke up, her eyes were filled with tears. She was a fool to think it was anything more than what it was.

She couldn't bring herself to stop wearing the scarf he'd made her though, even though its significance had changed in her mind. She had seen it as a sign of more of a romantic affection for her, but now she saw it as he likely meant it, a token of friendship.

January arrived with a fight, the weather turning from bad to worse. It would be one of the coldest winters on record, and Frankie told herself that it was only the miserable weather that was making her feel out of sorts.

But she kept thinking of Michael.

Even when she admonished herself not to.

In the autumn, she'd been given a conversion course to learn to fly the bigger Oxfords and Masters at Upavon. Despite Frankie's experience, the course was stressful, and whatever confidence she had in herself was tested thoroughly.

The Central Flying School course was difficult, the new planes were entirely different to what she was used to – from coping with a twin engine, to the constant speed propeller, retractable undercarriages, and coming in to land at the speed of 90mph which was as high as the cruising speeds that they were accustomed to, it was just sheer bad luck that they switched over to ferrying the more difficult planes during the worst of the weather.

Like the other pilots, Frankie had to memorise the routes before she set off, and in time, the woods, rivers and country mansions became printed on her memory, so that years later if she heard a place name she would picture in her mind a vast swathe of countryside viewed over a thousand feet from the air.

The planes were not fitted with radios; all navigation was to be done from sight alone.

It was a hazardous, stressful business.

In early January, she was sent to deliver a Master from Reading to the flying school at Ternhill, but the weather turned as they approached the Birmingham area, creating a grey so shapeless it was hard to make out anything in the haze, and as she was thinking that things couldn't get worse, it began to snow.

She swore.

It was terrifying. The snow came on so suddenly, closing the route in front and behind, leaving her unsure where to turn to get out of it.

There was no way she would be able to see where she was headed.

She turned back and ended up at Little Rissington, where she left the aircraft with the maintenance unit. Before her the Cotswolds were covered in snow. It was beautiful, but freezing, and her bed for the night was in a WAAF officers' house, where the pipes were frozen solid, and there was no heating. With only a thin blanket for warmth, she shivered miserably all night. The following day, she found the plane frozen, and the weather unchanged, the idea of another night in the cold room was unappealing, but she had no option. She wasn't prepared to walk through several feet of snow to look for a hotel, so she spent another miserable night in the freezing cold room, and couldn't help thinking of the instructor who'd said, "Let's see how lucky you feel after a few months as a ferry pilot."

Right then she felt anything but lucky. She would have sold her soul for a warm bed and a bowl of her mother's rich Irish stew.

As soon as the weather broke, she got the Master started and was able to deliver it to the flying school. Afterwards, she met up with Harriet who unlike her had spent the past few nights in a comfortable hotel and delivered the unwelcome news that they would have to take a pair of Harvards to Oldham. They were old and in need of repair. Frankie's airspeed indicator was broken but once she was up, there seemed no point in delaying taking it. So she went on to Oldham, where to her abject relief, Trixie was waiting with the ferry plane to take her and her cold hands and feet back to base.

The luxury of a warm bed, a heated room, flowing water, and a proper shower and change of clothes was heavenly. She was reluctantly dragged away by Trixie to go out to the pictures, but was soon laughing and eating popcorn, though she did fall asleep on her friend's shoulder.

That night she slept like the dead. Shortly after she woke the weather once again worsened. They heard the awful news that one of their ferry pool pilots had died; she'd crashed due to poor visibility. A woman named Amy Mollinson or Amy Johnson as the papers called her. It hit them all hard. Soon after that they were all suspended from flying in the inclement weather.

The best part of being grounded was the knowledge that so were the Germans.

When spring arrived, it felt like she had been given a new pair of lungs from which to breathe. The relief of being able to see and avoid the barrage balloons was enormous.

By the summer, women were cleared to fly operational aircraft, Hurricanes and eventually Spitfires too. The Hurricane, she discovered, was not much different to the Harvards and Kestrels she'd learned to fly the previous year but, of course, politically there was a sense that only ace pilots could fly fighter planes, and it was seen as a turning point for them. Within two years, women would even be flying bombers, but that July the thought of that to Frankie and her friends would not have been conceivable.

The Spitfire was the aircraft she dreamed of flying. On the ground, it was a trickster during take-off, but up in the air it was a forgiving machine, and most people enjoyed it, Frankie included. The cockpit was barely wider than her shoulders, and she thrummed with excitement at the thought of the power she had at her fingertips.

The first chit she was given to ferry a Spitfire was during the autumn. The weather had turned hazy as she set out from her base, making her think she might need to stop somewhere before moving on the next day, but as she flew to Dumfries and caught sight of the canals and the railway, she followed the lower ground to the hills and Barnard Castle, finding that she was able to maintain her position despite the haze, setting a course and managing to refuel before delivering it to the squadron at an airbase on the south coast.

She made her way to the ops room to get her ferry chit signed off, thinking that she would catch a sleeper train home. Only to be greeted by a low whistle.

It was a tall man with dark blonde hair, and a dazzling smile.

'I'll be damned,' he said. 'You realise you're the only one who made it here today?'

She frowned. 'Really?'

The man nodded enthusiastically, while the CO frowned at him, holding out her chit for him to sign. Clearly, he wasn't a fan of the American man's brand of enthusiasm.

Frankie found it refreshing.

'Yeah – a gaggle of Americans who were ferrying some here had to turn back. I cannot wait to tell them about you,' he said with a wink. 'I'm Steve, by the way, Steve Morris.'

'Fr—' she began but someone from behind them got there first.

'Frankie,' said a familiar voice, and her heart leaped.

She turned slowly in shock to see Michael.

He shook his head, a small smile playing at the corners of his mouth. 'Why am I not surprised that you were the only one stubborn enough to show your face today?'

She grinned, feeling a bubble of joy at seeing him again flood her senses, and she winked. 'It's nice to see you, too, Michael.'

There were a few guffaws from some of the men who had come in behind him.

Michael grinned back.

'To be fair it's a nice face, cap,' said Steve.

'Careful now, lieutenant,' said Michael.

'Always, cap,' said Frankie. There were more sniggers.

'What he means to say is – why don't you come in and have a cup of tea?' said Steve.

'Oh God, she's flown for over two hours in this horrible weather, she doesn't need to be punished by your excuse for tea, Morris,' said Michael.

Steve shrugged, then grinned. 'Well, shucks,' he said, his American twang thickening. 'I just don't know how you can make the swill taste any worse than it already does.'

Frankie grinned. 'That's fighting talk, that is.'

Steve grinned back. 'For you, maybe I'll even use a fresh teabag.'

They all groaned at that. The American invention of teabags had not caught on here at all.

She laughed. 'Come on, cap,' she said and Michael led the way.

The men weren't lying. Steve made a truly awful cup of tea.

But she didn't mind.

She was enjoying the friendly welcome, and it certainly beat what she was usually offered after a plane delivery. Which was precisely nothing.

Steve took a seat opposite her, and grinned sheepishly as she took a sip, and winced slightly at the tea.

Michael guffawed. 'Told you.'

'It's lovely,' she lied, pulling a face.

The men around them laughed.

'You can be honest,' said one.

'I've had worse,' she said, then grinned, 'but not by much.'

They all howled.

'Cut to the quick,' said Steve, feigning a stab wound, but grinning widely. Frankie couldn't help smiling back.

'So how do you know cap?' he asked. 'Who, as you know, is technically not a cap, but our CO... but we call him cap because he is so fond of rule breaking.'

Frankie, who was taking another sip of tea, snorted some of it at that, as she tried wildly to suppress a giggle.

Michael looked at her with mock offence. 'Why is that funny?'

She waved a hand. 'No reason.'

He chuckled.

It was good to see him. Especially here in his environment. It was clear that he was well liked and respected by his men.

She couldn't help thinking of the girl he'd met, the fact that it was 'getting serious'. A part of her wanted to ask, but a bigger part of her didn't want to hear it.

She had been staring, and so she looked away, noticing that when one of the others laughed when he held his cup, his fingers shook slightly.

She had seen that on some of the pilots, the strain of what they were doing evident. Many managed with alcohol.

All of them were the lucky ones, the ones who made it back.

'We grew up together,' said Frankie, answering Steve's question about how she knew 'cap'.

'So you're like siblings?'

'God, no,' said Michael.

Frankie looked at him, a small frown between her eyes.

Steve raised a brow and looked around at the men meaningfully. 'Oh, it's like that, huh?'

Michael didn't say anything, but she saw him shoot Steve a look. Steve then held up his hands as if in surrender.

Frankie felt herself blushing, 'Michael has a sweetheart, so I've heard,' she said, catching Michael's eye.

He took a sip of his tea and frowned. 'Yes.'

'Emily said it might be getting serious.'

The others quietened. Michael bit his lip. 'Maybe.'

Frankie found she didn't really want to know more, not yet. So, she changed the subject. 'Tell me about you,' she asked Steve, 'what are you doing on this side of the pond?'

So far the Americans had remained neutral. There were some who had come over to volunteer, but they had done so independently. Some had been recruited by government for pilot ferry duties but a large number were here because they wanted to make a difference. Like many, Frankie was grateful to those who chose to volunteer to help when they didn't have to. Like the brave South Africans, Indians, Australians and others who had signed on to fight.

Steve nodded. 'Well, I felt like they were just taking their sweet time joining, back home. A lot of folks feel that way.'

Frankie shrugged. 'You can't blame them for wanting to stay out of it, not after the first war.'

Steve nodded. 'I know, but it's hard to stay neutral when half the world is fighting... and you've got the resources to do something to help... to put an end to this madman. The stories of what is happening in Europe under Hitler's regime chilled me. I got tired of just talking about it, you know, so I decided to volunteer. I grew up on a ranch in Montana and learned how to fly by dusting crops.'

Frankie grinned. 'I had a similar childhood.'

'I knew there was a reason I liked you, apart from the obvious,' he said, waggling his eyebrows, so she blushed faintly again.

'Steady on,' spluttered Michael.

Steve grinned.

Frankie finished her tea; she needed to get going if she was to get the sleeper train home.

'We're having a dance on Friday night here. You should come, if you're free,' said Steve as she was about to leave. 'Please come.'

She bit back a smile, then glanced back at Michael who nodded at her, the expression in his eyes unreadable.

'I'll try.'

Frankie smoothed down her borrowed dress. It was one of Trixie's, green with a shimmer to the fabric, that fell below her knees and had a sweetheart bodice. It was a bit tighter on her than she would have liked, as she was at least a foot taller than the smaller girl. 'Va-va voom,' was her friend's pronouncement. 'That was how that dress was meant to be filled out,' she said, approvingly, and wouldn't hear of Frankie changing into something more 'sensible'.

'Time enough to be sensible when you're dead.'

They laughed at that.

Harriet drove them in her car. They'd been given leave for the night, a rare treat.

The party was in full swing by the time they arrived. There was a whoop from some of the officers as they spilled out of the car and made their way inside the mess hall.

Seeing Trixie's pale blonde hair, and grinning smile, one called, 'Here comes trouble.'

She grinned. 'Funny how they all seem to know my middle name.'

Harriet groaned, then adjusted her skirt and sweater set. She had resisted Trixie's cajoling to get her into a cocktail dress.

'You look like a librarian destined to spend all night on the sidelines.'

'That's perfectly fine by me,' she said as they made their

way into the hall. It had been cleared of the tables and a stage had been set up near the back where a band was currently performing covers of the hits of the day.

It was packed, and warm, as many couples were dancing. The air was full of heat, the scent of smoke, beer, and the heady mix of perfumes and wild abandonment, as if tonight may well be the last night they had, so they might as well enjoy it.

Frankie smoothed down her dress again and took a glass of sparkling wine from a tray that was being circulated.

Before they had even found a table, Trixie was being whisked onto the dance floor by an eager young pilot who looked a few years younger than her.

Frankie had looked around for Michael but hadn't seen him yet. She took a sip of champagne and turned when her shoulder was tapped.

'Well, this evening sure brightened up,' said Steve.

He was just as handsome as she remembered. His smile infectious. The light overhead bounced off his hair, burnishing it gold.

At his side, was a skinny man who looked like he had an apple lodged in his throat as he swallowed nervously while he worked up the courage to ask Harriet to dance. It was clear from the besotted look on his face as he eyed woman before him, that if he had his way there was no chance of her spending the night sitting on the sidelines.

'Care to dance?' asked Steve.

She grinned and let him lead her onto the dance floor.

As she followed after him, the smile froze on her face, as she saw Michael, dancing with a beautiful black-haired woman in a pink dress.

He hadn't seen her, but the look of happiness on his face, as he smiled down at the woman in his arms, stopped her in her tracks.

'Yeah,' said Steve, seeing her looking. 'He popped the question earlier tonight.'

Frankie's heart thudded painfully. 'Tonight? He's *engaged* now?' she whispered.

As Steve looked at her, she forced a smile.

'That's wonderful.'

She swallowed. She shouldn't have been surprised. She knew he had met someone, and he'd said that it was getting serious, but just a few days ago he hadn't, as yet, been engaged...

Steve pulled her into a lively jazz dance and whispered in her ears, 'There's nothing between you two, is there?'

Frankie shook her head. 'No, I was just surprised, as last we spoke he didn't say anything.'

Steve shrugged. 'Ah well. That's how it is nowadays, isn't it? People getting caught up – you'd be surprised at all the proposals flying around here, getting special licences to marry over a weekend... people want to live while they can.'

She nodded, then tried to force herself to enjoy dancing with the handsome man who was currently in her arms. To not watch Michael dancing with his beautiful fiancée.

She accepted another glass of champagne.

Then another, as she danced with several more men, but Steve made sure that he filled out most of her imaginary dance card. He was an excellent dancer, and she found herself keeping up with him, twisting and being lifted up, and carried away by the music, the alcohol, and the handsome man who was giving her his full attention. She ignored the desperate desire to think about the fact that Michael was engaged.

Unfortunately, this wasn't to be, as Michael spotted her and brought over his fiancée to introduce her.

'Frankie, this is Alice,' he said.

Frankie stared at the girl, who was beaming at her. 'I've heard so much about you,' she gushed. 'I've never had a sister, and now I'm going to have two!'

Her heart dropped as she realised Alice was referring to her and Emily. She looked up at Michael who was frowning slightly as she looked at him. She looked away, unable to meet his eyes in case they betrayed how hurt she felt.

'Look!' Alice squealed and held out her hand towards Frankie, who could see the ring glittering on her finger.

Frankie sucked in her breath, and forced a smile. 'I just heard – congratulations,' she said.

She was saved from Michael's reply by Steve who dragged her back to the dance floor, and she left gladly.

It was hot and the wine was flowing and she was getting steadily more inebriated as the night wore on. Determined to have fun even if it killed her. She would not let it show that her heart felt like it was breaking in two.

At one point Steve whispered in her ear, 'By God, you're the most beautiful woman I think I've ever known. if I wasn't this drunk, I'd ask you to marry me on the spot too.'

She giggled. 'If I wasn't this drunk, I might even accept.'

They laughed, and he pulled her in for a kiss.

Her head swam, as the taste of him flooded her senses, a mix of cologne and alcohol.

He rested his forehead on hers and her world began to spin suddenly, as he was ripped out from her arms. When she looked around, she found Michael standing in front of them, his face twisted with rage.

Before she knew it, he punched Steve, who fell to the floor with a thud. Behind Michael, his beautiful fiancée screamed his name, just as Frankie did.

'Michael, what the hell—!' she cried.

He looked up at Frankie, his fists balled at his sides.

'He was taking advantage.'

'It was just *a kiss*.'

'He was mauling you in front of everyone!'

They were drawing a crowd.

Steve grunted as he sat up on the floor. He looked up at Michael with a sardonic smile as he wiped the blood from his mouth. 'Nah, I think you just suddenly realised you wished it was you in my place.'

Michael was about to launch himself at Steve once again, but he was pulled back by several of the men standing around.

'Is that true?' said a small voice.

Michael immediately stopped fighting against the men as he turned towards Alice who was now looking from him to Frankie, suspicion clouding her eyes.

'Alice—' he said.

But her eyes filled with tears, and she turned and ran from the hall.

Michael looked up at Frankie helplessly then rushed after his fiancée.

Frankie held a cloth wrapped with ice over Steve's lip.

'Do you think she's forgiven him?' he asked.

She knew exactly who he was talking about.

'I'm sure. He's like a brother figure to me. Alice will understand that he was just being protective.'

She knew that was most likely what had prompted his outburst.

'Na-huh,' said Steve, waggling a finger at her. 'He made that very clear on the first day we met.' Then he grinned, only to wince. 'I wonder why.'

'It's not like that. Trust me. He's just always been protective, that's all.'

Steve sighed. 'Up until he landed me one, it was just about the best night I'd had since I got here.'

She blushed, looking away. It had been such a confusing night for her, filled with mixed emotions.

She couldn't let herself think of why Michael had punched

Steve. He'd made it clear by running after Alice that that was where his affection lay. For a moment she had allowed herself to hope, but she'd been a fool. She was the one who'd had a crush on him for most of her life, not the other way around. He cared about her, and considered her family, that was all.

'Can I see you again?' he asked.

'That depends.'

'On what?'

'If it's not going to cause bad blood with you and Michael.'

No matter what happened, she couldn't be at odds with him now, not with the state of the world. She cared about him too much.

'I'll make it right, scout's honour.'

She grinned. 'You were a scout?'

He narrowed his eyes, mock affronted. 'Like you even have to ask.'

She gave a small giggle.

A few weeks later, Frankie discovered that she, along with the others, would be moving out of Hatfield to a mixed pool in Hamble, and for the first time, they would be flying with men.

The new base was a big change from their old one, and had the feeling of a flying club, rather than a strict school with rules.

The men, to their surprise, were gracious about flying with them, and didn't object when they were assigned to fly under the command of more experienced female commanding officers.

It was here, one evening, after she'd finished work for the day, that she was told that she had a visitor.

'There's an RAF pilot here to see you,' said a girl, coming to find her. 'He's been waiting a while, so I gather.'

Frankie gawped at the woman in surprise. She found herself smiling, and was slightly nervous as she smoothed her uniform and hurried out into the reception area.

She hadn't seen Steve since the dance. He must have tracked her down. Being a pilot, she wouldn't get into the amount of trouble she might have if he had been a civilian, as they were not supposed to be aware of any of the locations of the airbases.

She made her way out into the lobby, only to halt in surprise.

It wasn't Steve.

It was Michael.

His dark eyes looked troubled. 'I had to see you.'

23

He stepped forward, and Frankie saw that he was nervous.

'I should have come earlier – but I haven't had a chance to get away. I've got a few days leave, so before I head home, I came straight here. I just – I wanted to say sorry.'

Frankie swallowed. 'It's all right.'

He ran a hand through his hair, and she saw the purple shadows beneath his eyes. 'No, it's not. Alice almost called off the engagement.'

Frankie's heart stalled at the word 'almost', a chill sliding down her spine.

'So it's back on, then?'

She felt her stomach drop. For just a moment she had dared to hope ... but now her heart sank to her toes.

Why did she always do this to herself when it came to him? Why did she persist in the childish fantasy she'd had since she was a girl that one day he would look at her and fall in love the way she had?

She only hurt herself by hanging on to the wish that one day he would feel about her the way she always had about him.

You're a fool, Frankie, she admonished herself. A blind fool.

Tears pricked at her eyes. She'd worked so hard over the past few months to get over him, and now, this. It was like she was back at square one, listening to her sister breaking the news that he had met someone. That what she'd convinced herself was the start of something between them was all in her head.

'Yes. But I had to come make it right with you – I know how it must have looked, like I was some jealous—'

'You don't have to explain!' she snapped, not wanting to hear that he didn't think of her that way. She couldn't bear it.

'Frankie,' he said, running a hand through his hair, looking askance. 'I embarrassed you, Steve, and Alice – I feel dreadful. I just saw red when he kissed you.'

She looked up at him, then blinked. For a moment, he *did* sound jealous. She cursed her heart for lifting optimistically, only for it to come crashing down around her as he continued in a rush.

'I mean – it's just you are like family, and of course, I want to look out for you, but I took it too far. I'd been drinking, and it probably looked like I'd come over in some... jealous rage. I know that's how Alice saw it. When that's not it.'

She nodded. That she knew. Just like she had always known that the lingering feelings she'd had for him since she was a young girl were only ever one-sided. Still, to have it put so baldly, made her feel worse. She forced herself to look at him. 'You didn't need to come here to tell me this.'

'No, I did, I had to make it right. Steve told me you'd only go out with him if I put things right with you first, he didn't want to cause friction between us, but I assured him we're just friends.' Then he gave her a lopsided smile. 'I don't want to be responsible for getting in the way of your love life.'

She gave a faint smile at that. If he only knew.

'I appreciate that.'

'Yeah, well. I suppose at some point I need to remember that you're grown up, and capable of looking after yourself.'

'To be fair, you've always had trouble with that,' she said softly. Which was partly why she had trouble of letting go of the hope that one day he would feel more for her than he did.

He grinned cautiously. 'Touché.'

'I'm not that young girl you have to worry about any more.'

'I know, but that doesn't mean I'll stop worrying about you.'

He pulled her into a hug, and she held on tight.

She broke free. She had to let him go. He belonged to someone else.

'I'll see you around, Beans,' he said, using her father's nickname.

She nodded, and turned to leave, unable to speak. Afraid she'd blurt out everything that was in her heart.

'Say, what do you call an Englishman with hot sauce in his mouth?' said Steve, calling her at the base, as he'd begun to do every second night.

'What?'

'A Spitfire.'

She groaned. 'Your jokes are terrible.'

'Nah, you love 'em.'

She sort of did.

On their first official date, they compared stories of growing up on a farm.

He guffawed loudly when she told him about collecting chicken eggs in winter, and how her Irish mother didn't believe in heaters, just more layers. 'I used to look like the Michelin Man, I could barely move my arms and legs...'

'You think that's cold? Your winter is like autumn in Montana.'

'Impossible!'

'Oh yes, it snows until April, and even then, the temperatures are well into minus by the time spring strolls around, taking its sweet time, in May.'

'May? You're kidding. It sounds horrible.'

He shook his head, eyes dancing. 'Nah – best place on Earth. Wild, untamed, so beautiful it stops your heart. Like your face.'

She blushed. She wasn't used to compliments like that.

'I'm not beautiful. My friend Trixie—'

'The little blonde?'

She nodded.

'She's a doll, sure, but you're the beauty. It's sorta sad that you don't know that,' he said, reaching for her hand.

She looked away. 'My sister Emily is the beauty in the family. The brains too,' she added.

He whistled. 'This coming from a lady pilot? It's not easy what you guys have to do, navigating by sight alone, no radio, hell... if you only knew how many men fail at that...'

'Thanks. Still, I wasn't clever like Emily growing up. I struggled with school.'

'Oh God, who didn't? I hated it! Wanted to be out on the ranch, or up in the air, anywhere but stuck in a classroom.'

She grinned. It was refreshing to hear someone who felt the same way she did.

'Actually, speaking of intelligence...' he began to whisper. 'Well, have you heard about the Moon Squadrons?'

She lowered her voice to match. 'Moon Squadrons? No?'

'Well, they've heard of you.'

She stared at him.

He grinned. 'Mainly because I told a friend of mine who's in one about the clever girl who flew a Spitfire in an autumn haze when every other pilot had to turn back.'

She felt her heart begin to thud. Was he talking about what she thought he was?

'Who are they?'

'Let's just say they are a secret government organisation, who might have a special mission for you.'

She blinked up at him.

Then she whispered, 'Are you talking about the SOE?'

It was not something the public were aware of. It wasn't part of the regular Secret Intelligence Service. The Special Operations Executive was a force that waged a secret war overseas. They sent agents there to sabotage and subvert operations from behind enemy lines.

'Could be.'

He handed her a card – there was no name on it, just an address.

'If you're interested, you're to report here – show them the card, tell them Morris sent you.'

It was a secret airbase in Tempsford, north of London. Frankie felt conspicuous in her ATA uniform, and wondered if she should have worn civilian clothes instead.

She handed the card to the reception, and waited.

Soon a tall thin man with dark hair in a boiler suit came to meet her. He looked both stressed and tired. Like he was carrying the weight of the world on his shoulders.

'You're the ATA pilot Morris mentioned?'

She nodded.

'Heard a lot about you.'

She quirked her lips. 'Can't say the same.'

She wasn't meant to know, considering that he was part of a secret organisation.

He laughed. Then held out his hand.

'I'm John McCall. There are two squadrons based here. We fly Halifax bombers, and Lysanders – can you fly a Lysander?'

'I can fly almost anything. It's part of the requirement for being a ferry pilot.'

'Very good.'

'On nights when the moon is full, we fly behind enemy lines, and land on makeshift airfields. We drop off agents and pick them up, mainly in France. You will never know the real identity of the agents we transport, and they will never know yours. We fly by the moon as we need it for visibility over the landing zones and drop zones.'

She was used to flying in similar conditions.

'I won't lie, it's dangerous – if you're found you could be shot and killed, but as an ATA pilot, those are risks you're used to. Still, you'll be taking them to enemy territory, and that in and of itself is a far more dangerous prospect. I'll understand if you decline.'

Frankie bit her lip.

Ferrying planes was useful, she knew, but this was something else, a chance to actively play a part in stopping the war and distract herself from thinking about Michael.

'I'd like to join.'

McCall smiled.

Which is how, a few weeks later, her heart in her throat, she joined the Moon Squadrons at Tempsford, and found herself standing in front of a Lysander that had been painted black in a mixture of black, grey and green, so it was easily camouflaged in the sky.

Part of her couldn't believe she was really doing this.

As far as her family and friends at the ATA were concerned, she had been reassigned to a different base.

No one would know what she was really doing.

She couldn't help feeling a small jolt of guilt. She had promised Michael and her family that she would be careful.

But it was different, she had an opportunity to really do something to help stop the war.

She squared her shoulders, and smiled as the tall figure of McCall walked across the runway with a group of three people at his side. 'Here are your guests.' She was advised to call them all 'Joe', male and female alike, and told she would be collecting two more when she landed in France. They had been housed in a special country house in the vicinity.

She set off to the forward base at Tangmere which was around a hundred miles south of Tempsford. The base allowed the squadron to fly deeper into France. Her eventual destination was just outside the Loire Valley near the town of Blois.

McCall had told her that she could expect to spend a week at base before and after her mission. But tonight, she would be making a clear run, due to the moon – it was too good to waste. He flew with her and their guests to base.

When she returned that evening she would be billeted at a cottage opposite the gates of the RAF station. McCall got out and they refuelled for the next part of the journey. He wouldn't be coming with them.

The thought of flying on without him, with a group of agents who didn't know her name, and she didn't know theirs, filled her with trepidation. She wished McCall would join her, just for the first one, but she knew if she asked, he might change his mind about taking her on.

Her hands shook. Frankie couldn't help looking at the agents. One of them was a very beautiful woman with dark hair and a lipsticked mouth. The other two were older men. She couldn't help wondering what they would be doing.

All too soon, it was time to go. Frankie's stomach churned at the prospect.

McCall smacked the side of the plane in farewell, and she set a course for France with the light of the moon her only guide across the ocean.

It wasn't unlike her flights for the ATA, except now she was flying directly into enemy airspace.

The Joes were speaking softly to one another, making small talk, but Frankie was concentrating on her route, air speed, and checking all her gauges, while keeping one eye out in case they encountered company.

She was told that the BBC broadcasted coded messages to let the Resistance know when they were sending agents over. Frankie had been surprised. 'It's all a code?'

'Some of it is,' said McCall, 'They pepper code words and names, or short phrases or sentences into news bulletins. Sometimes there's tailored programs to transmit information to a specific group. Music means something too – Beethoven's Fifth for example, is a code for victory. Sometimes the choice of music sends a code – if you play a certain song the Resistance is waiting for, it might mean they are being given the go-ahead to blow up a certain bridge.'

Frankie had stared at him in shock. It was a whole world of subterfuge she hadn't realised before.

'What if the radio presenters played the wrong song?'

He'd run a hand through his hair, 'Yes, well, that's happened, and let's just say it can mean the wrong message gets sent, the wrong bridge gets blown up.'

'Blimey.'

'Blimey, indeed.'

Frankie had to plot her course ahead of time on her map and look out for any recognisable features, just as she did when she was ferrying planes.

The moon was bright. It was a beautiful night, studded with stars, but Frankie's heart was in her mouth.

'Your first mission, pilot?' asked one of the Joes.

Frankie nodded.

'The Allies keep Jerry pretty busy with night attacks, we shouldn't have any company.'

'So I've heard.'

Still, just because the Germans were preoccupied didn't

mean that if they weren't spotted, they wouldn't come under fire.

As she approached the site, a makeshift airstrip in the Loire Valley, the waiting agents staked out a flare path with some torches and flashed the letter M to her in Morse code. When she acknowledged the signal, they switched on the other lights.

She had been told that when she landed she had to be ready to turn the plane around in under three minutes.

'Goodbye, pilot,' said the female Joe.

'Bye, Joes, good luck,' she called.

A fixed ladder let passengers deplane and board quickly. The top rungs were painted yellow to make them easier to see.

The new agents quickly replaced the others, and she set off back to base.

When she came into land, she felt able to finally draw a proper breath.

One of the new Joes heard her sigh of relief. An older man with a faint French accent.

'I do the same, every time, pilot.'

Frankie could well imagine.

Over the next few months, she thought of that Joe's words every time she came safely back. She had a sense that she was like a cat with nine lives – unsure, though, of how many she had left.

Unlike within the ATA, Frankie had more free time between missions, as each depended on a full moon.

She spent a lot of time in the cottage or at the mess hall, chatting with the other pilots, Moon Squadron and RAF alike.

One rainy day, at the cottage, she was trying and failing to read a magazine, when one of the female Joes came to sit next to her in the communal living room.

She was an older woman, in her late forties, and she

reminded Frankie of Mrs Bell, the teacher who had helped her with her dyslexia when she was younger. She had dark hair that was cut short and kind-looking grey eyes.

'You're new,' said the Joe.

Frankie nodded. 'A few months now. How could you tell?'

The woman took out a packet of cigarettes and lit a smoke.

'You're restless. The other pilots – the ones who have been doing this for ages – seem to almost forget that they have a mission when they're off-duty.'

Frankie gave the woman a tight smile. She wasn't so sure about that. There were always signs of the stress they faced on the pilots' faces. Some numbed it with alcohol, others with other things, but if you looked closely you could see that there was no such thing as being off-duty. Not really.

'The trick is to get into a routine,' the older woman continued. 'Send a signal to yourself that you're entering normal life when you return. The first thing I do is have a bath when I get back – like I'm washing it all away. Then I climb into bed with my book.'

Then the older woman looked around, her eyes falling on one of the Moon Squadron pilots who seemed to have a habit of shaking his fingers every so often as if he was trying to rid himself of pins and needles. A nervous tic. Frankie realised that perhaps the older woman saw more that she let on.

That night she ran herself a bath, feeling somewhat silly when she helped herself to a bottle of bubble bath that had been left behind.

She sank under the warm water, forcing herself to stay longer than the quick washes she usually did, as if she was on the clock, because for years, she had been.

It felt like hours had passed when she got out, her body bright pink from the water, but it had only been ten minutes.

She did feel a little more relaxed though. But not much.

How did you create a routine that made life normal when nothing was?

She supposed the only thing to do was to try.

One morning, as she was coming in from breakfast at the RAF mess, she saw Michael.

She stopped in her tracks, and gasped.

He was standing alongside two other men, who were laughing.

'Well, hello, cap,' she called.

He turned, then his face split into a wide smile that cut straight to her heart.

She hadn't seen him since he'd come to visit her at Hamble, several months before, when he'd come to apologise. Seeing him made their last visit flash inside in her mind, bringing back the painful memory of him telling her that he didn't have feelings for her, that he'd only ever thought of her as family. She'd worked hard over the last few months to let it go, to let him go, for her own good. It just hurt too much. She would love him the way he loved her now, as a friend.

He left his companions, and steered her away by her elbow, his brown eyes full of questions. 'Does this mean what I think it does?'

Frankie felt a stab of guilt. She had promised him she wouldn't do anything risky or reckless, she could well imagine what he would think...

He could likely guess as to what it was she was doing here. The male Moon Squadron pilots could easily pass as ordinary RAF men, but the women, less so. Although there were lots of jobs for women at the base, it was obvious to Michael that she was now SOE, because he knew that she was a pilot.

'You know I can't answer that.'

He shook his head. 'God, Frankie.'

'Time for breakfast?' she asked. Thinking it would be good

to spend some time with him, help allay some of his fears. The truth was, though, she just missed him.

'Sure.'

Frankie was on to her third cup of coffee, as she'd come in late the night before, but couldn't sleep in. She was glad that she had decided to join the world of the living, or she might not have run into Michael.

He looked thinner than when she'd last seen him. The toll of what he had to face battling the skies, and living to tell the tale, was evident on his face. There were lines about his eyes that hadn't been there before.

'We lost Gibbs two days ago,' he said, when she came back with another cup of coffee for them both.

She sat down, a frown between her eyes.

She remembered him from the first day she'd met Steve – he was the young man whose fingers shook.

'He was shot down over Blois. The plane caught fire and crashed into a valley. I saw it happen. It's the third one we've lost from our squadron in a month.'

'I'm so sorry.'

He shrugged as if it was normal when really it wasn't. Death wasn't something you just got used to. There would be so many scars from what they'd had to normalise just to get through this war. It would take a lifetime to process.

She hated that they sent them out so often that the odds were so stacked against them, like fodder for the cannons. But right then they were also the main reason that Britain hadn't been invaded. It was a lot of weight to bear on such young shoulders.

'We've all got our little rituals,' he said, 'did you know that?'

She shook her head.

'They're like little superstitions that we follow, that make us feel like we're in control. Gibbs would always kick the wheel three times with his right foot before he climbed into the cockpit, but two days before he died he stood on a piece of glass, so on the day he died, he kicked it with his left.'

Michael ran a hand over his face. 'It's so stupid, but I can't stop thinking about that. Like if that changed his fate or not.'

Frankie put her arm around his shoulder, and he leaned into her for a moment.

After a while he pulled away, and dashed the tears from his eyes.

'Sorry.'

'That's the only stupid thing you've said. You don't need to apologise, he was a good man.'

He swallowed. 'Yes.'

Then he drew in a shaky breath. 'So, I er, gather things are going well with Steve?'

She shrugged. 'Yes.'

'I'm glad.'

There was an awkward pause for a moment.

'And things with you and Alice?'

He gave her a faint smile, then nodded slightly.

It suddenly became awkward between them.

'I suppose I'd better be off,' he said, then he winked at her. 'Can't tell you how good it was to see you, Beans. Just – look, please be careful.'

'You too,' she said, feeling a lump form in her throat. She didn't want him to leave. Not when he looked that sad.

24

LONDON, 1944

The jazz club was held in an underground basement near Regent's Park. The band were playing Glenn Miller's 'In the Mood' and the dancing couples were whirling across the floor in dizzying spins.

Frankie watched them, her eyes alight, her gold heels tapping along to the music as she took a sip of a honey-sweet cocktail.

It was easy, for just a moment, to forget that they were at war.

The women, dressed in their pre-war finery, dazzled in sequins, chiffon and silk, like jewels. The men wore dark suits and enough pomade in their hair to plaster walls. The smoke-filled haze was perfumed with aftershave, Chanel No 5 and champagne.

It was a dream she didn't wish to wake from.

Frankie shifted closer in the padded pink velvet loveseat next to Steve, who winked at her before hailing a passing waitress to order another cocktail.

'I'm determined to try every one,' he'd told Frankie.

'What? Tonight?' she asked, eyes widening.

His smile was infectious. 'Maybe.'

She laughed.

'Well, maybe then I'll join you.'

Frankie sat back with a smile. She was off duty for a while. One of the supposed advantages of flying with the Moon Squadron was that she was only on duty when there was good visibility. The recent cloud cover meant that she had a few days to herself.

She had no idea what to do with them.

Steve was on leave for a week too.

They'd never spent a week together before. For some reason she was a bit nervous at the prospect.

A part of her didn't quite know how to be off duty anymore. How to live without her heart rate on constant high alert. When she'd had a recent medical check-up to ensure she was fit for flying, the RAF doctor at Tempsford airbase had looked at her in some surprise. 'You're a fighter-pilot?'

It was no longer such a strange question, so much had changed in time, and now there were a handful of women who were.

'No, I just... transport people.'

'Ah,' he said, there was a knowing sort of nod as he looked at her chart, then back at her. 'That explains it.'

'Explains what?'

'Your blood pressure – your reflexes – you might be here with me now, but your body is acting as if it's still on active duty. You need to find ways to decompress when you're not working.'

Climbing up onto her hotel roof to watch the bombs being dropped in the distance probably didn't count, she thought.

She must have looked at him enquiringly because he started suggesting some ideas. 'Hot baths, walks, spending time with loved ones—'

'Whisky?'

He gave a humourless chuckle. 'Yes, there's alcohol, but you want to keep an eye on that. A lot of our boys – and girls,' he added, 'are developing problems there.'

She nodded, she had seen that herself. A part of her was getting worried about Steve – he was fun to be around, but he was drinking like it was a part-time job.

He frowned. 'I'll write you a prescription – some pills to help calm down your heart rate. Help you sleep.'

She nodded. Sleep would be good.

The first time she tried them, it was like all the worry began to leak from her eyes, and she had to excuse herself quickly after breakfast, before anyone noticed, as she found herself unaccountably crying, and unable to control it.

She rushed back to the cottage that was used exclusively for Moon Squadron, and into her room, where she stared at herself in the mirror in horror. 'What the hell is going on?'

Her squadron leader, McCall, noticed her rushing into her room, and knocked on the door. 'Chalmers, you all right? Did something happen?'

'Um?' she half sobbed. 'I seem to be having an odd reaction to something.'

'I'm coming in.'

'No!'

But it was too late.

He looked floored seeing her in tears. 'Did you get some bad news?'

She shook her head, then pressed her fingers into her eyes in mortification. 'I had my medical and the doctor gave me something to calm me down, only it's, well... it seems to have let something loose instead.'

His winced. 'Ah. God, those pills are not for the faint of heart. Cup of tea?'

'That would be nice.' Only for new fresh tears to fall at this kindness. 'Oh hell,' she moaned.

He stared at her helplessly.

'Maybe say something horrible to me, because if you're any nicer it might finish me off,' she suggested.

'Erm...' He thought hard, then looked around the room for inspiration. He spied a book on her nightstand. It was a beaten-up copy of *Jane Eyre* that was nearly falling apart it had been read so often. It was her favourite book. She carried it with her, always. Reading had never come easily to her, but the more she read and re-read that book, the more it was a part of her. Some of its words felt tattooed inside her skull.

A shrewd look crossed over McCall's face. 'I don't think *Jane Eyre* is a patch on *Wuthering Heights*, personally. Emily Brontë was by far the more talented writer.'

Frankie's tears stopped, mercifully.

'You don't mean that.'

He shrugged. 'I do.'

It did the trick, as for the next twenty minutes Frankie waged war on Heathcliff and Cathy while they drank their tea.

Once the pills wore off, a day later, McCall admitted he'd actually never read either and she laughed every time she thought about it.

It was after that that they became friends.

She thought that he might judge her for the incident, for being soft or emotional, but he never did. Though he did tease her, a little. After that day, whenever he made her a cup of tea, he'd offer his hankie at the same time. 'It's just English breakfast, no need to fall apart...'

And she'd mime kicking him in the shins, and threatening to torture him by giving him more lectures on Heathcliff.

But Frankie had learned her lesson. The pills were not worth it. She'd rather deal with shaking hands than uncontrollable crying.

She thought now of that doctor's words about finding ways to calm herself down and sighed. Walking wasn't restful when you were living in a bombed-out city and while having a bath helped, nothing did the trick quite like alcohol.

This was the best she'd felt all day and that worried her.

She looked at Steve. They'd only been here for an hour and he was well on his way to getting drunk.

She flagged down a waitress and asked for some water. But she was the only one who drank it. 'Water is for quitters,' he said with a wink, and she couldn't help laughing.

She worried that the side of her he'd see in the morning light wasn't the fun-loving girl he enjoyed spending time with in the evenings.

She worried that he might be vastly different too.

'Frankie?'

She blinked. Steve was staring at her, a puzzled look on his face.

He smiled, then, and extended a hand towards her.

'Your face was looking a bit too serious there. Come on, let's dance. That dress deserves to be shown off.'

She chuckled. She'd found it in a Red Cross shop that morning. It was a mid-length, gold cocktail dress with tassels that spun when she moved. It had been a spontaneous purchase, in an effort to make herself feel a bit better after she'd spent a sleepless night in a small hotel room near the airbase. Not even *Jane Eyre* had helped to bring her comfort, like it usually did. She'd been shocked at how loose the dress was on her, how much weight she'd lost without realising it.

Trixie was in town for the day and she'd offered to spot them for lunch at the Savoy, which Frankie gathered was a natural stomping ground for her glamorous friend, whose blonde hair was done up in the latest style, and her red-lipsticked mouth was turning the heads of everyone seated nearby, including some officers at a nearby table. Trixie didn't notice, while Frankie was admiring the beautiful decor – there were potted palms, starched white linen napkins, real silver, and beautiful paintings covering the walls.

Then her friend turned to her with concerned eyes.

'I know you can't tell me about what you're really doing—'

Frankie had been quick to deny it. 'I don't know what you mean, I've just joined the ferry pool at Southampton—'

Trixie scoffed. 'Frankie, come on, I know that's not true. I have friends at that base, and they've never seen you there – I know that you're part of something else—' she gave her a meaningful look, 'something here in the city... something *secret*.'

Frankie's eyes widened. It was easy sometimes to forget how shrewd Trixie was.

'I can't talk about it, Trix, even with you – I wish I could.'

Her friend held up a manicured hand. Her red nails gleamed. 'I know. But I'm worried about you – you look like you haven't had a good night's sleep in ages, if those bags under your eyes are anything to go by, and your hand keeps shaking, did you know?'

Frankie looked down at the offending appendage, then tucked it underneath her thigh. She was only too aware.

'I'm fine,' she lied. 'It's just been... a lot. I have some time off this week, though.'

Trixie blew out her cheeks in relief. 'Good.'

'I'm going to spend it with Steve.'

A strange look passed over Trixie's face that was quickly replaced by one of forced joviality.

'What? I thought you liked Steve.'

Trixie waved a hand as if to clear the air. 'Of course I do, everyone likes Steve. He's fun. I just... well, sorry to sound like an old woman, but I can't see you getting much rest when he's around.'

Frankie snorted, then looked around her in case anyone had overheard. 'Steady on,' she whispered.

Trixie laughed. 'Sorry, I just mean, well, he's a good distraction from everything, sure, but well, he does drink a lot...'

'Who doesn't?'

'It's just – be careful with that.'

'I will.'

Frankie looked at Steve now as he led her onto the dance floor. Trixie was right, he was a distraction; the good kind, though.

Soon all thoughts of how tired she was, or the worried look in her friend's eyes, melted away as they danced.

They didn't really know the moves the others did. But what they lacked in skill, Steve made up for with enthusiasm and a willingness to twirl and lift her every so often. Some of the more experienced dancers gave them odd looks, at their freestyle moves, which only made Frankie and Steve laugh all the more. By the time they made their way back to their velvet booth, Frankie was clutching her stomach from giggling so much. 'Oh gosh, I can't breathe, did you see that woman in pink's face when everyone started to do the woodchopper... and you started to pretend you were actually chopping wood?'

He snorted. 'She looked like she was ready to have me committed.'

Frankie laughed. 'I know, but actually, I prefer your moves.'

'You're the only one. Thank heavens.'

She twitched her brows, then picked up her waiting cocktail, which had beads of condensation forming on the glass.

Steve had ordered a Moscow Mule and she'd chosen something called the Bees' Knees, which turned out to be delicious. They drank them down like water.

'I seem to see a pattern when we get together and go dancing – where you very quickly get me drunk,' she observed.

He winked. 'It's a tried and tested method.'

Her eyes widened in mock affront. 'Mr Morris! That hardly seems the sort of thing a Boy Scout would do!'

'You'd be surprised, our motto is "be prepared".'

She laughed.

He came in to kiss her, and her head swam from the alcohol and his nearness.

After a while she broke away to catch her breath.

She made a mental vow, no more cocktails that evening.

'Can you believe it's been eighteen months since I first kissed you? It still feels like the first time for me. Although I am glad cap's not around to come in for another punch,' he joked.

Perhaps it was the rush of alcohol to her brain, or the fact that they had lost so many young men to this blasted war, but her face paled slightly at that. Her body started to shiver. She didn't like the idea of not having Michael around, it felt fatalistic.

Steve looked at her askance. 'Sorry, I just meant – not around at the dance, not...'

'No, I know.'

Get yourself together, you fool, she admonished herself.

She forced a laugh. 'I think I just need some more water – too much alcohol.'

Usually she wouldn't have given his words a second thought, but they had lost so many people. Especially in Steve and Michael's squadron. Losing them was such a source of fear for her.

She toyed with her cocktail.

'The last time I saw Michael was at Tempsford airbase, several months ago. It was just after you all lost Gibbs.'

A shadow passed over Steve's face. He nodded. 'Yeah, that was horrible.'

It had, unfortunately, only got worse. Right now, Steve and Michael were the only ones remaining from their original squadron, something that weighed heavily on them both.

Steve had taken to drinking more. Hence, his quest to try every cocktail, as if he could blot it all from his mind.

She wasn't sure what Michael was doing, but she worried about him often.

As if he could read her mind, Steve took a sip of his cocktail and then sighed.

'I think maybe that's why Alice called it off.'

Frankie stared at him in confusion.

'Called what off?'

A line appeared between his brows, and he studied her reaction. 'Their engagement. I thought you knew.'

Frankie blinked at him in shock. 'No. I didn't. What happened?'

Steve shrugged. 'I'm not sure.'

Frankie stared at him. 'What do you mean you're not sure? Didn't he tell you why? I mean, they've been engaged now for eighteen months... his mother was starting to plan the wedding...'

The last time she'd seen him, Michael had looked so sad. The thought that Alice had caused him further pain twisted at her heart. Her cheeks flushed in sudden anger. 'I can't believe she'd just break it off, especially now, knowing what he's facing out there. Did she even think of that?' she spat.

Steve shifted uncomfortably. His eyes darted to the dance floor, as if he was hoping he could rewind time to when they were out there enjoying themselves. The mood had shifted so fast.

He ran a hand through his hair. 'I don't think that's fair, I gather it wasn't entirely her fault.'

'What do you mean?'

He took a sip of his drink and Frankie's leg jiggled.

Steve noticed, and she willed her limbs to still. It was clear he regretted bringing the subject up, but there was no way Frankie was going to drop it now.

Steve sighed. 'Well, she was getting frustrated with him. He wouldn't agree on a date for the wedding, and in the end, she said that if he didn't set one she would call off their engagement. I think she was trying to call his bluff, and it backfired.'

Frankie stared at Steve, a puzzled look on her face. 'Why wouldn't he set a date – was he worried that something might happen to him? He didn't want to leave her a widow?'

It was the sort of thing he might do... but surely, he could have explained that to Alice. Surely, she would have understood?

Steve shook his head. 'Yeah, I don't know. I think his heart just wasn't in it, and she could tell that that was why he kept delaying. I mean, most couples are rushing into getting married nowadays, it's more common than not to get a special licence to do it fast. I think her friends were starting to ask questions...'

'Oh,' she breathed, then took a sip of her cocktail. She felt lighter suddenly, as if something heavy had slipped off her shoulders.

Michael didn't want to marry Alice.

Steve was looking at her oddly. She couldn't meet his eyes.

Frankie smoothed her skirt, feeling her cheeks redden. 'I'll just be a minute,' she said, 'need to go to the ladies'.'

She quickly made her way to the bathroom. It was tiled in pink and green with gold accents. There was a large velvet sofa on which to relax, or fix one's shoes. She made her way to the sink and turned a gold tap on, splashing cold water on her face, in relief. She didn't care about her make-up.

Her cheeks were flushed, and her heart was beating rapidly.
Michael was single.

She thought back to the last time she'd seen him, how he'd leaned against her, how natural it had felt to have him in her arms. How easy it was to speak to him. How right it felt when he'd looked at her that way he did that made her feel like she was the only person in the world that mattered to him – an unfortunate trait that made every girl fall for him, she knew. She shut her eyes, squeezing them tight. Just because he wasn't marrying Alice didn't mean anything. He had made it clear that what he felt for her wasn't romantic, it was protective.

Besides, she was with Steve.

She adored Steve.

'You all right?' asked a pretty blonde girl in a green cocktail dress who came in to re-apply her mascara, staring at her from the mirror from behind wide-lashed black eyes.

'I'm fine.'

'If he's pressuring you, you don't have to give in – we're at the table next to you if you need a lift home.'

Frankie smiled at her. 'It's not that. He's a lovely man.'

'Well, then, feel better,' she said, turning to leave.

'Thanks.'

Alone once more, Frankie took a deep breath, then dabbed at her face with one of the clean facecloths that were stacked nearby. It had been sprayed with lavender oil, and she breathed the scent in, a welcome respite from the chaos in her mind.

When she made her way back to their table, she found Steve slumped over in his seat, his tie undone, and a hard set to his face.

She felt her stomach twist in dread. 'Steve?'

He didn't look at her when she sat down, and her heart started to thud in worry.

He'd got himself another drink. A whisky. She noted the change with a frown.

'I – er – thought you were going to try all the cocktails,' she said, making her voice light, joking.

He exhaled a short sharp breath. 'Yeah, well.'

She swallowed.

'Is something wrong?'

He looked up to the heavens and scoffed. 'I don't know, Frankie, is something wrong?'

'Wh-what do you mean?' She reached out to touch his shoulder in concern, and he jerked away.

'Steve? What's going on?'

He looked back at her in disbelief, an expression of contempt on his face that shocked her. He'd never looked at her that way before. 'So that's how you're going to play it – like nothing just happened?'

Her stomach flipped uncomfortably. 'What do you mean – what happened? I just had to go to the bathroom.'

He stared at her incredulously. 'Sure, sure.' His eyes were like gimlets, skewering her in place. 'That's all that happened,' he said sarcastically, as he toyed with his glass, looking down for a moment then back at her, eyebrow raised. 'It wasn't the fact that when I told you that another man broke off his engagement – a man that once punched me for kissing you – your face lit up like a damn Christmas tree.'

Frankie sucked in a breath. 'It – it didn't!'

'Yeah, I just imagined it, right? Or the fact that that you looked so happy you had to go calm yourself down?' he said, taking a long sip of whisky then slamming the glass down with a heavy thud.

She flinched.

'It wasn't like that,' she said in a small voice.

People were starting to stare. The girl in the green dress was looking at her in concern. She blushed, mortified to be the cause of a scene.

'Maybe we should go outside, get some fresh air—'

Steve's face was twisted in pain. He ignored her suggestion. 'I saw what I saw – I must have been blind before! You keep denying that there is something between the two of you, but—' he exhaled heavily. 'That's just a *lie*, isn't it?' he hissed.

Frankie winced. 'Please, Steve, calm down.'

'Do not tell me what to do,' he said, coldly.

He ran a hand through his hair, making it stick up wildly. He was extremely drunk, she realised.

She reached out to touch his arm again, and he pulled away once more.

'Just be honest with me!' he snapped.

She blew out her cheeks. 'Steve, Michael is one of my oldest friends, of course I care for him. But there's nothing more between us than that. He's always been protective of me, he doesn't have other family besides his mother and she wasn't around much when he was growing up. He's not interested in me, in that way, I promise you.'

He stared at her for a long moment. Then he gave a low whistle as if he'd just realised something.

'What?'

'You do hear yourself, don't you?'

She frowned. 'I don't know what you mean—'

'*He's* not interested... but you are, right?'

Her eyes widened. She swallowed. There was an uncomfortable pause. She took just a beat too long to protest. Perhaps he could see the truth in her eyes, the pain.

'It's – well, it's—'

'It's what, Frankie – a crush?'

She bit her lip, then ran her hands over her face. She didn't want to do this. Not here. Not now. She wanted to go back to half an hour before when they were happily dancing and drinking cocktails.

'Just tell me.'

She reached out a hand to console him, but he was like stone. He stared at her hand and she reluctantly removed it from his arm.

She blinked back tears. How had things turned so horrible? 'It's – well, it's complicated. I did, when I was younger... but that's gone now.'

He sighed. Then took a sip of his drink. Then stared at her hard for a long while. 'Jesus,' he ran a hand through his hair, then let out a short, humourless laugh, 'the sad part is that there's this bit of me that's screaming at me to just shut up, to let it go, so I'll still have you—'

'But you do still have me,' she said softly.

'Darling, I don't know who you're lying to more now, me or you?'

She dashed away a tear.

'Steve, don't do this, there's nothing between Michael and me. I care about you, Steve, I love being with you.'

He closed his eyes tight in pain. Then opened them wide. 'You care about me?'

She nodded.

'But you love him, right?'

She paled.

He pinched the skin between his eyes. 'I suppose I always knew, deep down. I saw the way you look at him. The way he looks at you too.'

She shook her head in denial.

'You only *care* for me, while I've been in love with you since the day we met...'

He sounded so broken. 'Steve—' She reached for his hand, and this time he didn't pull away.

She couldn't see, the tears were falling so fast. It was like with one move he'd exposed the secret she'd hidden for most of her life – how she felt about Michael, and all she wanted to do was stuff it back in that top corner of her heart where she'd never allowed herself to look.

She cared so much for Steve. She hated hurting him like this.

'Steve, please, you mean the world to me,' she said, her voice breaking.

He closed his eyes for a moment, and when he opened them they were hazy with unshed tears.

'I will l-love you, I know I will, please,' she begged, 'just give me time.'

He rubbed his fingers across his eyes, pulling the skin tight.

'Frankie,' he said, softening. 'I just – I just don't want to be with someone who has to force themselves to feel that way. Some people might be able to settle for that, but I couldn't, it wouldn't be fair to either of us. I'd just end up resenting you, wanting you to change something you can't... 'cause if you haven't managed to stop caring about him by now, I don't think you ever will, and I can't just wait around and hope, it'll just hurt too much.'

Her chin wobbled. He was right, she knew that. It wasn't fair, but was it fair that she had to give him up, for something she couldn't help? For something she'd felt her whole life that would never be anything more than what it was... was she destined to be alone as a result?

He took a deep, steadying breath, then stood up, and closed his eyes as if schooling himself, then he kissed her forehead, and left.

She sat at the table and sobbed.

Around her, couples were dancing and laughing, and she felt as if her world had split in two.

25

It was a misty spring morning as the train hurtled through the green and gold Suffolk countryside. Frankie leaned her head against the window. Her green box suitcase was in the luggage compartment above her head.

Her eyes were swollen from crying.

She toyed with her battered copy of *Jane Eyre*. Then flicked over to the inscription on the inside.

> *There was a reason you were drawn to her.*
> *She got through her troubles just as you did.*
> M

She closed her eyes as the memory washed over her, a few months after she had turned twelve, of when Michael had given her the book. How it had meant the world to her. How he'd gone to another town, almost an hour away, just to get it for her. It had got her through so much, this story.

As the train pulled into the station now she closed the book. She had spent a sleepless evening at her hotel room, unable to get the look on Steve's face out of her mind. She couldn't believe it was over. That it had ended so horribly. She'd stumbled into bed sometime after three in the morning and had lain awake reliving the whole sorry affair.

She was meant to be spending her leave with her boyfriend, getting to know a different side of him; instead all she could look forward to was a week in a single bed in a cheap hotel, and feeling more alone than she'd ever felt in her life. As dawn broke, she had made her way into the lobby and inserted coins in the telephone box. As soon as she heard her mother's voice, she started to cry.

Her mother listened to her for a few minutes then said, 'Come home.'

Her sister was waiting for her outside the station, leaning against the door of the blue farm van. Her dark hair was tied up in a black and white polka dot silk scarf and she was wearing the uniform of a land girl, but it couldn't disguise a tell-tale bump beneath her shirt.

'Em—?' cried Frankie, dropping her suitcase in surprise, her sadness giving way to unexpected joy in a heartbeat.

Emily smiled widely. 'Surprise! You're going to be an auntie.'

Frankie rushed over to embrace her, breathing in the familiar scent of home, clean linen, the lavender soap from the village store and the scent of earth from where she'd been working in the kitchen garden.

'How long? Tell me everything!'

'Six months. It happened when Stuart got leave in the autumn,' she blushed.

'I'm so happy for you.'

Her sister looked at her, then hugged her tight. 'You look terrible.'

'Well, thanks.'

'It's going be all right.'

Frankie broke away. She knew she was talking about Steve and her break-up. She hadn't told them the details over the phone, just that it had ended, rather suddenly.

'Is it?'

Emily nodded. 'It will. Is there a chance you could work it out?'

Frankie pictured Steve's stricken face and sighed. 'No.'

'Was there someone else?'

Frankie looked at her. '*No*. It wasn't like that.'

Emily raised a brow. 'Maybe not for him.'

Frankie stared at her sister, then frowned. 'What do you mean?'

'Well, it's just, I always thought that if there was anyone you'd given your heart to it was Michael...'

Frankie squeezed her eyes shut in mortification. *Did everyone know how she felt about him?*

She sighed. 'That was the gist of why Steve ended it.'

'Oh, Frankie, I'm sorry.'

She glanced out the window, as her sister began to drive. 'Look, I didn't think it would be a good idea, what with everything that happened between you two when you were kids, and how it affected the whole family, but with Michael, I think he's always—'

'Don't, please,' she begged, not wanting to hear how he didn't feel the same way. She was all too aware. 'I don't want to talk about it. I'm just glad to be home.'

Her sister nodded.

Soon they were riding along bumpy farm tracks, surrounded by hedgerows that were full of the signs of spring, with new green leaves, and cow parsley just coming in to bloom.

She had missed this.

'Check the glove box, Frankie.'

Frankie frowned, then did as instructed. There was a small bar of chocolate inside.

Emily smiled. 'It doesn't solve anything but it helps everything.'

Frankie snorted. 'I'm all right, thanks.'

She gave her a pointed look. Clearly, she did not believe her.

Frankie broke off a piece of dark chocolate with nuts and popped it into her mouth. The burst of sweetness was enjoyable but she would need to drown herself in chocolate to make her feel better about what had happened.

When they got through the front door, her mother rushed towards her. Her hair had turned more grey, but her skin was tanned and healthy from being outside so often. She looked fit and strong and she hugged her tight. Emily joined in.

This was far better than any chocolate.

Her mother made to let her go and Frankie held on tighter. 'Not just yet.'

Her mother smiled into her hair. 'Oh darling, you're going to be all right. I know it hurts like hell, but you'll get through this, Beans,' she said, using her father's old nickname for her and it was like he was there, holding her too.

That night was the best night's sleep she'd had in weeks. In the morning, she made her way downstairs, in her nightgown, bleary-eyed, to find the kitchen a hive of activity as her sister made breakfast for what looked like a small army.

She waved a wooden spoon that had a face drawn on it at her in greeting. 'Scrambled eggs?'

'Just coffee.'

'There's a fresh pot over there,' said her mother, coming in from the garden. She was dressed in overalls, and she was followed by Michael's mother, Irene, who greeted her warmly, a shrewd look in her brown eyes.

'Your mother says you'll be home for a few days, so you'll be around to help us plant our spring crop?'

'Irene—' admonished her mother. 'Frankie isn't home to work, she's here to—'

'No, it's fine, Mum, I'd go mad without something to do.'

'Work is sometimes the best thing for it,' said Irene, kindly, squeezing her shoulder.

Over the next few days, along with two land girls who were living at the house, she helped prepare the field to plant their spring crops. She wore a pair of her father's old overalls, tied up her hair in a scarf, like her sister, and worked muscles she hadn't used in years, removing rocks that would catch in the plough, along with the others.

It felt good to be in the fresh air, and in the company once again of women. It reminded her of her time in the ATA, which she missed.

Her sister and the others were full of stories and gossip. Like the one about her mother's new 'gentleman friend'.

The first time she'd heard of it, her heart had squeezed tight, and she couldn't help thinking of her father. The thought of him being replaced made her throat constrict.

'What do you mean? What gentleman friend? Have you met someone?' Frankie exclaimed, looking at her mother, who was preparing a patch to sow carrots.

The older woman sighed, then rolled her eyes.

'She's talking about your old friend from the Suffolk Swifts. With an emphasis on old. I'm sure he was a general in the Boer war,' piped her mother.

Frankie laughed, in relief. Only to feel a stab of guilt for feeling so. Her mother wasn't old, she could still find someone else, but the thought of it, even now, five years after her father's death, felt too raw, too soon.

She realised her mother was talking of General Tom Beccles. 'No, he just looks like he could have been with those sideburns.'

'And the fact that he's about a hundred and two,' said her mother.

Frankie smiled. 'He's been calling?'

The thought cheered her somewhat.

'Yeah, pops in every now and again in his old plane to come visit, brings the dog. I think, if anything, he just comes to hear about how you're doing.'

She felt a lump form in her throat. The old man had been a kind friend after her father had passed. She was glad he visited her mother.

Frankie grinned. 'The Major comes?'

Emily laughed. 'I think Major Gold has it as bad for Mum as the old General.'

Frankie grinned, then winked at her mother. 'Just proves they've got good taste.'

Her mother threw one of her gloves at her.

That night, while everyone was asleep, Frankie opened up the boot cupboard, which was full of jackets and pairs of old wellingtons.

Her father's old waxed coat was still hanging on its peg, the one sleeve rolled up to fit over his missing arm. It was like it was waiting for him to come back.

She picked it up, and buried her face in the worn fabric. Tears sprang in her eyes, it still smelled of him. Like engine oil, and sunshine.

She put it on, and didn't unroll the sleeve, only to smile at herself as she could imagine him laughing at her, and she smiled, through her tears.

She put it back. She liked the idea that it was there, if she ever needed it.

Frankie heard the telephone ring shortly after dawn. It was like being woken by the sound of a bullet and her heart roared into life.

It was a strident, urgent thing, and she was out of her bed and flying down the steps before anyone else had stirred.

Her hands had started to shake before she picked up the receiver.

'Hello?'

'Frankie?'

Frankie recognised the voice immediately. She heard the anxiety too.

'Trixie. What's wrong?

There was a small intake of breath. 'I've been calling all over to try and find you.'

Frankie's heart began to thud.

'What is it?'

'Steve has been trying to get hold of you. He didn't know where your farm was.'

She felt her throat constrict in sudden fear.

'Why has he been trying to get hold of me?'

She gripped the telephone so hard her knuckles turned white. She had a sick feeling in the pit of her stomach.

Oh God, please don't let it be that.

Please let him be all right.

'It's Michael.'

Frankie's knees gave out. The blood began to roar in her ears.

'What happened?'

'Oh Frankie, I'm so sorry, Michael's plane was shot down.'

Frankie felt her world tilt on its axis. Tears were beginning to fall without her even realising.

'He— he's dead?'

'No, I don't think so. Steve said he saw his parachute go down as they were flying over France. Michael managed to get out of the plane before it crashed.'

Frankie drew in a shuddery breath. Her limbs were shaking. He was alive.

'Did Steve go back for him?'

'He couldn't, the others had gone ahead to their target in Germany, a factory there, Steve said he was taking on too much fire. It would have been impossible to land and search for Michael. He barely got away as it was.'

'When did this happen?'

'A few hours ago.'

Frankie sucked in a deep breath. 'So there's still time.'

'What—?' came Trixie's surprised voice. 'What do you mean?'

'Did Steve say where he was?'

'At Tempsford airbase.'

'I'll call you later,' said Frankie.

She had a train to catch.

Two hours later, she was running onto the secret airbase, frantically searching the building for Steve. It had started raining and her hair was plastered to her face. She didn't care, she had to get there, had to find Steve, and find out where Michael was.

Her heart was roaring in her ears when she found him in the mess hall. He was sitting by himself, nursing a cup of coffee. The sight made her heart flip slightly. He looked so lost.

'Steve,' she cried.

'Frankie!' he cried in response, standing up, awkwardly. His arm was covered in a bandage. 'You heard?'

His face crumpled, when she ran to hug him.

'I couldn't go back for him – I took on so much fire.'

Her eyes filled with sympathy. 'I know. You're hurt?'

'I'm fine,' he said gruffly.

'I'm glad, truly.'

He looked at her and there was so much pain in his eyes, it was still so raw the way they'd ended it. She hated that she had been the cause of it, and couldn't help feeling a flicker of guilt at what she had to ask him to do now.

'Steve. Can you tell me where he was shot down?'

He frowned. 'It was near the midi.'

She nodded, then took her rolled-up map from where she'd shoved it at the back of her trousers and spread it before him, a pencil in her hand. 'Do you have an idea of where, exactly?' she asked, searching his face.

His eyes widened.

'You can't be serious.'

She drew in a shaky breath.

'I have to go and find him, Steve.' Her voice broke. 'I have to at least try.'

He closed his eyes for a beat. Pinched the skin of his eyes, then sighed. When he opened them he looked anxious.

'We were flying over this area, near the Dordogne – it's full of forest, and heavily patrolled,' he said, drawing around an area near the Périgord region.

'His parachute went down somewhere near here,' he said, indicating a massive stretch of forest.

'So he could have gone into hiding,' she said, relieved.

'Maybe. But he'd be surrounded and if you go after him it'll be like trying to find a needle in a haystack while a dozen armed officers bay for his blood.'

26

Steve's words were whirling in her mind but they didn't deter her. First, though, she needed to steal a plane.

In broad daylight.

Taking one of the Lysanders, meant for night flying during the full moon, and flying into enemy territory without permission wasn't just a fireable offence, it could get her into serious trouble. She could even be sent down, have her licence revoked or face prison time.

But she had no choice. She couldn't leave Michael alone out there. The thought of him dying at the hands of the enemy was a far worse fate than whatever trouble she might face right then.

Steve wasn't able to go with her, his injuries were too bad, but he was able to get her flight cleared with the control tower.

She felt a stab of guilt; if anyone found out that he'd covered for her, he'd be in trouble too.

She'd just climbed into the plane, a plane that she had so far flown several missions in, when she saw something that caused her stomach to drop down to her toes.

It was her commanding officer and he looked furious.

McCall came sprinting towards her on the runway.

'What the hell, Chalmers,' he cried. 'I got a notification that someone is taking out one of our Lysanders from my squadron and I had no idea... Jesus, what's going on?'

Frankie climbed down, her heart churning.

'McCall, it's Michael – my friend, he was shot down near the Dordogne, his squad couldn't turn back for him—'

He stared at her incredulously. 'So you decided you'd steal a plane and go and look for him yourself?'

His face showed a panoply of emotions from anger to fear.

'You realise you could get sent down for this – stripped of your licence!'

She winced. 'McCall – I know. I promise you, I'm not doing this lightly. He's – like family, I can't leave him there, not if there is some way I can help.'

McCall's anger seemed to wink out. 'But it's dangerous, Frankie – the area is probably crawling with Nazis, all looking for him.'

'I know, but see, that's why I need to try to find him, I know how he thinks where he might choose to hide – there's a forest near where his parachute landed. He could be somewhere in the woods.'

When they were younger, they used to play hide and seek in the bluebell woods near the farm.

She knew the way he thought, the types of places he chose to hide.

It used to drive him mad that she always found him so much easier than he did, she was stealthier, from years of living on a farm, and from hiding her flying from her mother.

'And what if you get captured? Frankie—' His eyes were huge, scared, he never used her first name. 'The risks for you as a woman are not the same, they could torture you.'

She reached out to squeeze his hand. 'I know.' Her hands shook. She couldn't think of that. 'I have to take the risk, I'm sorry. I have to find him, he'd do the same for me. Please,

McCall,' she begged, her voice breaking. 'Please let me at least try to find him.'

He breathed out through his nose, closed his eyes for a beat, then nodded at last.

'Just – come back in one piece, that's an order, Chalmers.'

Her chin wobbled, 'Thanks, McCall. I'll try.'

When she climbed back in the cockpit, she drew in a deep, steadying breath and then squared her shoulders.

He banged twice on the side of the plane, which was his signal to take off.

Frankie's heart churned. She turned on the ignition, and the Lysander roared to life, she taxied down, and began her long journey to the last place Michael had been seen alive.

Please, she begged the heavens, *let me find him alive.*

She'd studied the route beforehand. It was in the heart of the Périgord Noir region of Dordogne, a rural landscape of deep forest and meadow near to the Vézère Valley.

She would be attempting to land in a small clearing about three miles from his last known location.

'You'll have to cover the difference on foot, if you try to land anywhere near there and they are patrolling where he parachuted down, you'll be shot down before you get a chance to land,' Steve had said, as they mapped out her route.

'There's nothing around there, just a clearing near the start of the woods.'

Hopefully she could find him, and get him out.

She had plotted out a path that would see her land in a strip of grassland far away from any houses. That was the hope, but she was aware that the reality could be vastly different.

The terror of flying into enemy territory had never left her, even after all her months flying for Moon Squadron. But today, she felt as if the fear was coming off her so thickly, she could smell it.

She flew low to the ground. It was a misty afternoon, the sky grey, with visibility impacted.

'The only advantage you have is that you're one of the few people I know who can actually fly in weather like this,' Steve had said, before she left.

The wind was picking up from the east, and she had to correct her course constantly so as to avoid flying over any of the towns that were heavily fortified.

Her eyes strained from squinting in the grey light, picking out landmarks, towns, rivers, lakes, valleys and chateaux from the map route she'd memorised.

As if her fear conjured it like some dark force, she heard high above her the sound of an enemy fighter plane, and the shadow it cast, twice the size of hers. She'd come to recognise them on sight and sound, but thankfully, it appeared not to have spotted her below – or it would have begun to fire.

She was in the perfect position for a bomb.

She scanned the skies in case there were others, but it seemed to be flying solo, and she slowed the engine to almost gliding speed, and listened to the fighter hurtle away, then she pulled above the clouds, for better cover.

She took shallow breaths of air, unable to calm down, her hands shaking so much the steering wobbled. She felt sick.

She had to double back, as she lost her way, but twenty minutes later, she had arrived, at last.

She could just make out a long grassy strip near a forest of trees.

She brought the plane down, and it bounced on the grass, for a teeth-rattling stop. She sent a grateful prayer heavenwards, and after a minute, she taxied the plane towards a bank of trees, and cut the engine.

She climbed down the ladder, then landed on the soft earth, with jelly legs.

There was the smell of wet earth, and pine trees.

It had been over five hours since Michael had parachuted down.

He could be anywhere.

Doubts flooded her. The forest stretched on for miles, she might never find him, and she could get caught. McCall's words about what could happen to her, as a woman, flickered in her thoughts. She squashed it down.

The forest stretched out like sharp, pointed teeth across the horizon. The nearest town was several miles away.

The shadows were closing in, and every sound seemed amplified.

The hoot of an owl, and some faint rustling, caused the hair on the back of her neck to stand on end.

Where are you?

Had he found somewhere to hide in this endless forest? Did he turn from here and find a barn somewhere – or had he been found by the enemy immediately after he landed?

The misty sky had offered no clues as she flew.

She felt her heart twist in despair.

The chances of her finding him, here, in this vast landscape, she knew were slim, but the canopy of trees overhead and the deep rural atmosphere gave her hope. If he was hiding, she felt sure he would stick to the forest.

He always had when they were younger, choosing one of the biggest trees to climb.

There was no sign of houses nearby, she had chosen the meadow because it seemed to be far away from any habitation. The plane, with its black and grey paint, and its proximity to the vegetation, blended into the shadows. She took out her torch.

She'd taken her pistol, which she placed in the back of her trousers now, and in a small leather satchel she carried a bottle of water, some dry biscuits, a waterproof sheet, and in the lining of her Sidcot suit there were also some bandages and rubbing alcohol, just in case he was injured.

The thought made her stomach clench in fear. How hurt was he? She couldn't imagine that he had survived a plane being shot down without incident. It didn't matter, so long as he was alive.

Please be alive.

Then she set off through the trees, her boots crunching underfoot, the smell of pine needles, fallen conkers, and wet earth heavy in the air.

The wind rustled the trees, there was the eerie sound of a creaking door, and she realised it was the heavy sound of branches rubbing against one another. A distant pigeon cooed, followed by the sound of an owl.

Every dark fairy tale she'd ever read popped into her mind, as her heart lurched with every step.

The trees dripped water onto her head, sliding down her collar, and making her shiver. Dusk had fallen, and she had been walking for over two hours, and was close now to where Steve had seen Michael's parachute drop, when she heard voices in the distance.

Her heart began to pound.

She could hear two people talking. But not what language they were speaking. Their voices were too low.

She crouched behind a massive oak tree, and looked around. She spotted people in the distance, roughly half a mile away. She turned back around as silently as she could. She began to climb, scaling up the branches of the massive tree, as quickly as she could. The oak was wide, and impossibly tall, but some of its limbs were old, and as she placed her foot on one to climb further, the branch snapped, and gave way. She swallowed a cry as she fell, grappling frantically for purchase and landing hard against the trunk. The was a resulting dull thud. She scrambled around it, and then lay low on a sturdy branch.

From below she heard the crunch of booted feet pause.

She couldn't make out what they were saying, until they neared.

She realised, in some relief, that they were speaking French.

But she had to remind herself that that didn't mean they were friendly.

They could just as easily be working with the Germans, and they could find her plane, not too far from here.

'Fresh tracks, someone has been here recently.'

It was an older-sounding voice. Male. He spoke with something of a wheeze.

Frankie cursed her stupidity; she should have disguised her steps.

'German?' said another voice, older, female.

There was a scoffing sound.

'How am I supposed to tell that?' said the wheezy voice. 'They don't all have the same feet.'

There was an impatient sound from somewhere at the back of the woman's throat. 'They do all wear the same boots, idiot.'

Wheezy voice grunted in acknowledgement.

Suddenly, torchlight beamed towards her tree, Frankie held her breath, then slowly began to reach for her pistol.

'I wouldn't do that if I were you,' said the woman.

The blood drained from her extremities. She swallowed.

It was an old woman, with long white hair that shone in the dappled moonlight. She had a strong, determined-looking face.

She had circled, silently, around the tree, followed by an older man with a whiskery face, and large belly, whose rifle was pointed at her head.

Frankie raised her hands in the air.

'Come down,' commanded the woman.

Frankie did.

The torchlight shone straight into her eyes.

'A woman,' breathed the wheezy voice.

'Resistance?' enquired the older woman.

Frankie bit her lip. Technically, she sort of was.

'Yes.'

The rifle lowered.

Frankie felt her knees buckle in relief.

'Do you have a death wish?' snapped the man in French. 'The Germans have been scouring this forest all day. What are you doing here?'

She blinked. He was right, she was an idiot.

'I – I'm looking for a pilot, an English pilot he parachuted down somewhere here.'

The rifle pointed back at her.

'The Germans are looking for the same thing,' said the man, eyeing her suspiciously.

The woman shoved the rifle away from his hands. 'Last I checked, the Germans don't have female officers, idiot.'

He frowned, then nodded.

'You flew that black plane?' she asked.

Frankie's face must have shown her shock. They had seen her. Had the Germans seen her too?

The woman shook her head as if she could hear her racing thoughts and fears. 'You flew over our house. We tracked your steps, here. You're lucky. The Germans stopped patrolling near us several hours ago, but if you'd continued on from exactly where we found you, for about an hour, you would have stumbled upon where they have set up camp.'

Frankie inhaled sharply.

The man nodded.

'There's about a dozen Nazi scum who have settled in to patrol the area, looking for that pilot.'

She would have walked straight into a viper's nest.

Her next thought was Michael.

Have they found him? Or were they about to?

The thought made her stomach churn.

'Come on,' said the woman. 'We'll speak more easily once we're sheltered, voices carry in these woods.'

Frankie hesitated. She wasn't sure if she could trust them. They could have been setting her up. But she also had no other choice.

They led her back the way she'd come, only to divert through a forest path that led to a small house, tucked away by trees and shrubs.

'Did you find him – the other English pilot? The man I'm looking for?'

'No,' said the woman.

Frankie felt her heart sink.

'But we have an idea of who might have.'

A dog barked as they approached the small grey stone house tucked away out of sight near a line of tall pine trees. It looked like a child's drawing of a house with a small pitched roof, two windows and a door. And would have been just as charming, if not for the way it seemed to skulk behind the trees, and the strip of barbed wire at the back. It was surrounded by a small cottage garden, where a dog who looked like a roll of angry brown carpet growled as Frankie approached.

'Quiet, you old mongrel,' snapped the old man, patting the creature, who quietened down to a dull roar.

'He'll calm down once he gets to know you,' said the woman.

Frankie didn't know if she was speaking about the man or the dog. She was doubtful of either.

She followed them inside the small house, which smelled faintly of wood polish, leather, and lavender.

The woman lit an oil lamp and the room came into view: it

was a small kitchen, with a scarred wooden table in the centre. On the beams hung bouquets of dried herbs and flowers. There were also various small animal pelts in the process of drying out, and from some of the hooks on the walls, she could see that these were fashioned into bags, gloves and other useful items. Whoever the couple were, they clearly lived very simply, and close to the land.

The old dog huffed as it sniffed her, and she saw two eyes buried within that wild expanse of wiry fur. It got itself comfortable inside a half-chewed basket in front of the wood stove and kept one of those eyes fixed on her.

The older woman sat down at the table, and Frankie did the same.

The old man placed the rifle on top.

'You're English?' he said.

She nodded, deciding to trust them with part of her story.

They didn't seem all that surprised that she was a female pilot, which made her think that they might have some familiarity with the Resistance, especially from the way the woman seemed to be looking at her; a shrewd look on her old, lined face.

'You said you know where he is?'

'The English pilot? We have an idea,' said the man.

'Can you take me to see him?'

They hesitated.

'Please.'

The pair looked at each other, then seemed to communicate something between themselves. 'We'll go later tonight. It's eight o'clock now, they'll still be patrolling for a few hours yet. If we set off at about one or two in the morning, there's a better chance the Nazis will be asleep.'

Frankie nodded. That made sense. But she was anxious, and wished they would go now, she didn't like the idea of waiting around when she could be doing something.

'Did you see the pilot?'

'Just his tracks,' said the woman. 'We spotted them through the forest not long after he'd come down. They started a few miles south – from what we could tell, he's injured—'

Frankie's eyes widened, and a hand flew to her mouth.

'There were traces of blood on the ground, signs that one foot was being dragged,' said the woman. 'Possibly broken.'

Frankie's heart twisted for him, he must have been in considerable pain. Then she exhaled. 'But he's alive.'

'Yes, for now.'

Frankie's heart twisted at that.

'We erased the tracks we found so it won't be easy for the soldiers to find him. I don't think they have our sorts of tracking experience, judging from the heavy-footed way they were passing through here a few hours ago.'

As if the woman had summoned them, they heard low voices carrying in the wind. They were out there now. The thought sent a shiver down her spine.

'You think they won't find him?' she whispered softly, her heart pounding.

The woman shrugged, keeping her voice low too. 'I don't know – there are a lot of them, and they are leaving no stone unturned.'

Frankie felt her throat constrict in fear.

'Where do you think the pilot is?'

'I think he's been found by someone.'

Frankie's heart stuttered, 'You mean—'

She shook her head. 'Not German, no. A local farmer. I saw his tracks near the pilot's.'

Frankie's heart pounded. *He was alive.*

She had to stop herself from demanding that they take her to him at once.

'Have you eaten anything?'

Frankie shook her head. She was feeling the effects of the

past, stressful hours, and hadn't had much besides a few sips of water all day.

After she'd got the phone call from Trixie, she'd rushed out of the farmhouse, leaving a note behind that she was needed urgently at work, and would be leaving the van by the station. She didn't have the heart to tell them about Michael, or what she had planned to do to get him back, if she could.

The woman nodded. 'You will join us for dinner.'

It wasn't an invitation, so much as a command; either way, she was grateful.

The older woman shrugged off her long coat, and placed it on a peg by the door. The man did the same.

They worked silently, alongside one another, as if they communicated more through thought than words.

As they began to bustle around the kitchen, moving from the table to a small larder to the side of the room, where they fetched and carried items, including a loaf of bread wrapped in a dishtowel, cheese, pâté and cured meats, Frankie asked, 'Can I help?'

The woman shook her head. 'No, but you can tell us a little about yourself. If we're to risk our necks for you, it would be nice to know it was worth it.'

Frankie swallowed.

From working with the Joes she knew it was best to be vague. 'I am British.'

'You are part of the Resistance. You fly for them?'

Frankie nodded.

With that information alone they could have had her imprisoned. But it was information they already knew.

'Are you involved with the Resistance?' Frankie asked.

The woman nodded. 'We help with transport.'

'Transport?'

'Yes, the safe transport of people in and out of this forest.'

She didn't offer any more details. Frankie knew it was

dangerous for them to – she could use that information against them as well.

'Have you lived here long?'

'All my life,' said the woman. 'This was my grandmother's cottage. After my parents died, I came to live with her. It was very different from my early childhood in a big town.' Bergerac, she explained. 'My grandmother lived simply, worked hard, and taught me how to make things we could sell. My husband had a similar upbringing, he didn't live far when we met. This place felt like the end of the world, far away from the madness of war, or so we thought – but these woods have seen a lot of soldiers in the first war. We lost our son in the trenches. We thought that a loss so awful had one silver lining to it – that no one would be mad enough to go to war again. And yet, just a few years later, here we are. After the Occupation, we couldn't just do nothing, we couldn't stand aside and watch them cut down our forests to build their roads, invade our villages, and steal from our land.'

Frankie nodded. 'I feel the same.'

Frankie looked around. Wondering how they survived. As if the old man could read her mind he said, 'We live cheaply and that's how we get by. Before the war we sold truffles we found to local restaurants, and made the money stretch by living simply. Now we trade with some of our neighbours – meat, produce, labour.'

'Thank you for sharing your food with me,' she said, knowing how hard they must have bartered and worked for it.

The man just tutted as if she were being silly.

At one thirty in the morning, the old man set down his coffee cup, and the old woman turned to her and said, 'It's time.'

They fetched their coats, and began to put on their boots. Frankie gathered her things and followed after them. Her hands shook. This was it, she was going to find him. Or be found herself.

They made their way back into the dark woods. Every sound was like a gunshot, twigs snapping underfoot, the hoot of an owl, the creaking door sound of branches swaying in the wind, making her startle.

It had begun to rain slightly, and the gentle patter soon began to soak through her clothes.

With every step, her heart raced uncomfortably.

She had no idea if Michael was alive. No idea of what they would find.

The old woman handed her a bunch of twigs that she had formed into a makeshift broom. 'Brush it like this,' she demonstrated, 'after you walk, to disguise your tracks.'

They had walked for a few metres when the old man snapped at Frankie. 'You sound like a bull elephant, crashing through the forest, walk like so,' he demonstrated, walking in front of her, and lifting his feet more than she had, 'you want to take lighter steps.'

It was harder than it looked.

'Thank goodness for the rain,' sniffed the old man. 'Or they'd hear you in Toulouse.'

She flexed her jaw in irritation; she was trying.

After about an hour, they headed up a concealed forest path towards a long dirt drive.

Like the couple's cottage, it was the sort of place you might never find unless you knew it existed.

To Frankie's horror, as soon as they began to walk towards a shadowy farmhouse in the distance, a large spotlight appeared.

Frankie's knees turned to water, she forgot to breathe. She couldn't see in the harsh light.

Beside her the old couple paused.

There was the sound of heavy footsteps and beyond the bright light a dark figure appeared.

Frankie couldn't see anything.

But she heard the sound of a gun being cocked and her heart began to hammer inside her chest.

The figure neared and she could make out the shape of a man, holding a rifle that was pointed straight at them.

Next to her, the old woman let out a breath in relief.

'It's just us, Tomas, stand down,' said the old woman.

There was a grunting sound. The man wasn't convinced.

'I might be old but I know how to count – who's with you?' said a crotchety old voice.

The man stepped forward, out of the glare of the spotlight, and she could make out a man with wiry grey hair and a dark beard. He eyed Frankie warily.

'A friend,' said the old woman.

'Resistance?'

'Yes. She's here to take back the parcel you found.'

There was a sniff. 'I don't know what you're talking about.'

'Come now,' she said. 'We saw two tracks that led here, looked like one was helping the other, someone who was wearing your shoes,' the woman added, pointing to his boots. 'You still haven't repaired that half-chewed heel, leaves a distinctive mark.'

The man swore softly, then muttered, 'It was from your bloody mongrel dog.' He sighed, then muttered, 'I couldn't fart in this damn forest without you two knowing about it.'

The older woman sniggered.

The man hesitated. 'Are you sure you can trust her?' he said, pointing his rifle at Frankie.

Frankie swallowed.

'You can, I promise.'

He grunted. 'So we should just take your word for it.'

She threw caution to the wind.

'I'm British, my name is Frankie. I work for the Resistance.'

He was still hesitating, then after a long pause, he narrowed his eyes.

'What's the parcel's name?'

'Michael.'

He grunted.

'Its surname?' enquired the farmer.

'Why – so you can tell it to the Germans?'

The farmer spat on the floor, 'I wouldn't give them the steam off my piss.'

'Charming,' said the old woman.

He nodded, at last, then lowered his weapon.

'How are you going to take him home?'

'We were hoping you'd give us a lift back to ours, on the farm track,' said the old woman.

'It will only take us so far, the rest you'll have to do on foot,' said Tomas.

'That's fine,' said the old woman.

The farmer scoffed. 'And then what – you're going to keep him at your cottage? You'll all be dead by morning if I let you take him.'

'No, I'll fly us home in my plane,' said Frankie. 'I'm a pilot.'

He raised a brow. 'You'll fly him home?' he repeated. Then muttered softly, 'No wonder they call the English mad. Next I'll be hearing they let their dogs fly too.'

'Maybe that's why they're not occupied,' snapped the older woman.

He grunted in assent.

'Come with me.'

The farmer took them deeper into his property. He kept glancing backwards to look at her, swinging his rifle.

Frankie followed behind the old man and woman, her heart

beating rapidly in her chest. She was following them blindly and a part of her was terrified that they'd turn on her.

Could she trust them? What if this was all a trap? What if these people were paid somehow by the Germans to bring in spies? These were desperate times, who knew what some did to survive?

She surreptitiously felt for the pistol against her waistband. She had never had to fire it, but she was glad she had it, even though it was no match for the farmer's rifle.

They walked for twenty minutes, their feet sinking into fields turning boggy from the recent rain. Frankie shivered from cold and fear.

After what felt like an eternity, the farmer stopped, then said, 'The bunker was built in the last war, by the army. The Germans don't know about it – I've made sure of that. When they came to inspect my farm, I covered the area in stinging nettles and they didn't venture further to investigate.'

Frankie couldn't see anything.

'He's there – Michael?'

The farmer nodded.

Frankie swallowed. 'He's – he's all right?

'Bit banged up, but otherwise fine.'

She felt her lungs expand at last.

'I found him early this morning, a few hours after he'd parachuted down. I saw the plane go down in the forest and went searching, hoping to catch him before the Germans arrived. There's about five billeted in the area, in the town of Sarlat, but more have been swarming in from the Dordogne since he landed. So far, they haven't come here. But I didn't want to take any chances, that's why I took him to the bunker.'

He pointed his torch towards a grassy area in the distance. At first, she couldn't make anything out, but then she noticed that a patch of grass was raised, and rectangular in shape. They approached it and the farmer flashed his torchlight on and off three times.

For a split second she feared that he might be betraying them to the Nazis. Her heart pounded inside her chest. Silence fell.

She began to breathe rapidly in terror.

'What was that?' breathed the old woman.

'My signal to let him know he's safe. Come, he's here.'

Frankie followed him on rubbery legs.

The farmer led them to a concealed entrance underground, hidden by ivy, which he pushed back to reveal a door.

Frankie's breath caught in her chest as he made to open it. It was dark inside, and she couldn't see or hear anything.

The farmer swung the torch around towards a figure crouched in the corner, a pistol in his hands.

Frankie gasped.

His leg was bent at an odd angle, and there were scratches and bruises all across his face. There was a cut above one of his eyes, which was swollen shut.

The figure's hands shook as it held the pistol.

'Michael?'

The torchlight shone in her face, and there was a sharp intake of breath.

Then a faint voice breathed out. 'Frankie?'

Frankie rushed over to him, hugging him tight.

He grunted from pain but held on just as hard.

'What – how – how are you here?' he said, his voice hoarse and strained. His hand shook as he reached out to touch her as if afraid he'd hallucinated her.

'I stole a plane, after I heard you went down, and came to look for you. I knew you'd likely stick to the woods. I know the way you think. It was worth a try.'

He gasped softly, then wiped a hand over his face. She saw tears smarting in his eyes. 'You're actually crazy.'

'Yes.' She didn't deny that this had been a form of madness.

His face crumpled. 'Thank God,' he whispered, and he was hugging her and before she knew it, kissing her, which turned quickly from something soft, his lips pliant beneath hers, to passionate, and hard as she sank against him.

Frankie's head spun. Michael was kissing *her*. He broke away, then swore, 'Oh god, I wasn't thinking, sorry, Steve—'

'It's all right, we're no longer together—'

There was a small grunt from behind and they broke away.

She swallowed, blushing.

'These people helped me find you.'

Michael turned to them. The old woman hid a smile. The old man looked equally amused.

'Thank you.'

'You're welcome. But we must go now, if you are to get home this morning,' said the old woman. 'Can you walk?'

'Yes,' said Michael with a grunt, struggling to stand.

'Good, let's go.'

They made their way, slowly, outside, the farmer putting his weight beneath Michael's other shoulder. Frankie's heart was still racing from the kiss. She couldn't believe it had happened. She was grateful to the dark night, as she was sure that everything in her heart was displayed on her face.

But just then, a sound of a twig snapping in the distance made all of that fade away, replacing everything with fear.

They weren't alone.

A deep German voice suddenly cut through the night.

'Halt.'

27

Frankie's stomach dropped.

They had been found.

The Nazi officer was waiting for them just outside the bunker in the shadows. The old woman swung her torch around and they saw that he was tall, with broad shoulders and dark, closely cropped nut brown hair. His uniform was freshly pressed, and well-fitted to his muscular body. Unlike them, he looked well-rested, and strong. His eyes were heavy lidded and cold. She swallowed, then scanned around him, to see if there were others, but he seemed to be alone, for now.

She heard the click of a pistol being cocked. The German's expression was impassive. He would kill them without a second thought, she could tell.

Her knees turned weak, and she swallowed.

Michael was leaning heavily onto her as the farmer let him go fast, and slung the rifle into his arms.

The old woman did the same.

Michael struggled to raise his pistol, grunting in pain.

'Drop your weapons,' said the German. 'You are under

arrest. The other soldiers will be here shortly. They are in the forest, half a mile away.'

Frankie's heart roared in her ears. Next to her Michael inhaled sharply.

Silence fell.

Frankie looked over at the old couple, who were scanning the shadows. The farmer was peering at the German officer, a shrewd look on his face. He scratched his cheek in contemplation.

'I think you're lying. You drop your weapon instead,' said the farmer.

The German's eyes flashed in anger.

The old woman cocked an ear towards the forest, and nodded. 'Yes, you're a frightened, lying coward. If you had company, they'd be here,' added the old woman. 'We outnumber you, you swine, you don't tell us what to do, not anymore.'

The German officer growled, then fired.

It happened so quickly. Her husband jumped in front of her to protect her, taking the bullet in her stead. Blood bloomed onto his shirt. Frankie let out a low cry, just as the old woman and the farmer fired their rifles at the German, hitting him squarely in the chest.

The German landed on the ground. His pristine uniform pooling with blood. There was a gurgling sound and then he was still.

The old woman rushed back to her husband, stifling back a sob, her hand covering her mouth as she scanned his arm. 'Are you hurt?' she asked the old man, twisting him around so she could see where the bullet had entered him. 'Why did you jump in front of me like that, you old fool?' she whispered, kissing him.

'Just my shoulder,' he said, holding it. 'I don't think I'd make it if something happened to you.'

'It's the same for me, you idiot,' she said, kissing him.

Frankie felt rocked to her core. Her hands shook uncontrollably. The old man could have died, and it was all her fault. They'd helped her and now he might die if that wound wasn't treated.

'I'm so sorry,' she croaked, her throat thick with emotion.

The old woman shook her head. 'Don't be. We chose to help – and we'd do it again.'

'But—'

The old man grunted, waving away her concern. 'I'll be fine. But none of us will be if we don't get a move on.' But his words belied the pain he was in, as his face had turned white.

Frankie bit her lip.

'Do you think the others would have heard the shots?' Frankie asked, worriedly, looking around in fear.

'Yes,' wheezed Michael. 'If there are others they'll be coming. We need to get out of here.'

The farmer shook his head. His face looked tense. 'Let's move the body first.'

The old woman winced. 'You're right, we can't leave it here.'

Frankie helped the farmer and the old woman to drag the dead German into the bunker. Even between the three of them, the dead officer was unbearably heavy. Frankie took one of his legs while the older woman took the other, the farmer bearing most of the weight in the front. They staggered towards the bunker, sweat dripping down their backs. As Frankie carried his leg, she tried her best not to look at the dead man. His eyes were open, she knew he was gone, but the way the farmer was holding him up, it was as if he was staring straight into Frankie's soul.

The image stayed with her long after they had left him inside the bunker. She knew it would haunt her for ever.

He was the first man she'd seen killed before her.

She clenched her jaw – he might not be the last, if they were to make it out of here alive this morning.

They set off as quickly as they could. Frankie took her pistol from the waistband of her trousers, and scanned the shadows, as she and the farmer supported Michael.

Their pace was slow. Michael winced with every step. The old man was slowing down too. His face was white and pinched. Like Michael, he made low grunting noises as he went.

When they saw the van, Frankie wasn't the only one to sigh in relief. It had an open back, covered with tarpaulin, and a front cab that could seat three people at a squash.

'We'll place you under the tarpaulin, in case we have any company,' the farmer said, helping Michael and Frankie to climb into the back. Then they covered them with a tarpaulin with the help of the old woman.

Soon the van stuttered into life and they set off on a winding forest trail that would take them towards the clearing and her plane.

The farmer drove without lights, and at a pace that was little better than a crawl.

With every jolt from the hard suspension, Michael winced. Frankie did her best to cushion him against her body, lifting his arm and sliding herself alongside him so that she took the worst of the impact.

She couldn't help thinking of the old man too, with the bullet wound in his shoulder. He needed a doctor. She hoped he would be all right.

Every time she closed her eyes she saw the dead German.

Michael whispered, 'Are you all right? You're shaking.'

'I'll be fine.'

His arms tightened around her. She felt his breath on her neck.

'Does that help?'

She turned to look at him.

She felt his fingers twine into her hair.

Her stomach swooped.

'I promised myself, that if I got through this alive, I'd do that.'

'What?' she asked.

He pulled her down, then kissed her again.

Her head swam, until after a while she pulled away. 'You wanted to kiss me? Since when?'

He let out a low chuckle.

'Since that day you did that trick and your plane went into a nosedive, when you were about fourteen.'

She gasped. 'What – but you told me after that incident with Steve that you saw me as a sister.'

He sighed heavily. 'I was trying to convince myself of that. I didn't want to admit the truth. Steve was right. When I saw someone else kissing you, I saw red, and acted like a jealous idiot. I was so embarrassed afterwards.'

Frankie sniffled. 'I wish you'd told me.'

'I was warned not to.'

She turned to look at him in shock. 'Warned? By who?'

He let out a low breath. 'Emily.'

Frankie gasped. 'What? When?'

'That Christmas I gave you the scarf. She saw that my feelings for you were getting more serious, and she told me that it would change everything, if I acted on it. That if things went wrong between us, it could mean that they would lose me too, and they had already been through that once before when you went to boarding school...'

Her eyes widened. She felt a flash of emotions, from amazement to disbelief, and anger at her sister. Tears pricked at her eyes. This whole time they might have been together.

'I could wring her neck.'

'Don't be mad at her.'

'Too late.'

He gave a low chuckle.

'The other reason I didn't say anything was, well, I wasn't sure how you'd react,' he said, looking at her, waiting. He looked slightly worried.

She stared at him. Did he honestly not know how she felt? 'Michael, I would have been bloody thrilled. I've wanted to kiss you since I was about nine.'

He smiled, making the lines around his eyes crinkle.

She frowned as she looked at him, then she shut her eyes in mortification. 'You knew that, didn't you?'

He laughed softly, then squeezed her tight. 'I knew you had a crush when we were young but I thought after what happened, when you went away, at just the moment I realised I had feelings for you, that yours were likely gone.'

She shook her head. 'They were bruised, but I've never quite been able to stop.'

'Me neither,' he said.

The farmer cut the engine, a mile away from their destination. They would need to do the rest on foot.

Michael clung to Frankie and the farmer as he got out, the strain on his broken leg agony, his face twisted in pain. But he never asked them to slow down.

The old man stepped gingerly out of the van. His coat was hanging off him, and Frankie could see that they had fashioned some kind of a bandage to staunch the wound while they were driving.

'We'll walk behind you, and erase any tracks,' said the old woman, picking up a stick from the ground. She handed one to her husband. There was worry etched on her face.

It had been a long night, and Frankie was feeling the strain. She was tired, and thirsty. Her feet felt as if she was stepping on glass, a blister had formed on her toe and it rubbed against her boots painfully with every step. But she pushed herself to keep going, her eyes scanning the clearing, in case they were discovered.

Every step felt like a marathon.

But at last, they neared where she had hidden the plane. It was partially concealed by the twigs and vegetation she had piled around it the day before.

'Help her clear it,' said the old man, and the old woman came forward and began to drag it away, along with the farmer.

'Come on,' said the farmer, putting his arm beneath Michael's shoulder, as they faced the ladder.

Michael breathed in sharply. Getting up there wouldn't be easy.

It was nearing dawn, and sounds from the forest were getting louder.

In the distance they heard something that made them turn to each other in panic.

Voices, low German voices, being carried by the wind.

The old woman turned her face to the side, listening. 'They're about twenty minutes away – you have to move, fast,' she said urgently.

They nodded. It felt like an age that they half dragged Michael up the ladder. At every rung his face scrunched in pain, and he let out a low grunt as he pulled himself up. Frankie felt her body tense with every spasm of pain that wracked through him.

Finally, sweat dripping down his brow, his face white, he was in the passenger seat, breathing heavily.

Frankie turned back to the others, and felt her throat constrict. Then she impulsively gave the old woman, as well as the farmer, a hug. She turned to the old man, a look of worry on her face as she looked at the dried blood on his shirt from the bullet wound in his shoulder. She lightly touched his arm, her expression one of regret for everything she had put them through.

'Thank you, for everything.'

The old woman patted her back awkwardly.

'Go, thank us by making it out alive.'

'What will you do if Germans come? If they see that you helped us?'

'It'll be the last thing they see, trust me,' said the farmer, holding up his rifle. Frankie couldn't help thinking of how brave that statement was. God knew how many others there were coming.

She nodded, then quickly raced up the ladder into the cockpit. 'Let's go,' she whispered.

Next to her, Michael nodded, his face ashen. He was close to passing out.

She closed her eyes for a moment, then took a steadying breath, her hands shaking as she switched on the ignition.

Dawn was just cresting the horizon when she brought the Lysander up and away from the clearing.

She felt her heart clamber inside her chest. She hoped that the others had got away safely. The thought of leaving them behind to face the Germans made her feel sick. But the best thing she could do for them was to leave. The Germans couldn't prove they'd helped her and Michael if they were gone. She just hoped they wouldn't find that bunker with the dead soldier. The thought of him, and his cold, dead eyes boring into hers, made her shudder.

She took a deep breath and brought the plane through a bank of clouds.

Next to her Michael was breathing softly. He was asleep.

She was desperate for some water but she'd drunk her last sip several hours before.

She was tired but alert. The sky was clearing up ahead. It would be a blue-sky morning. The perfect time for flying, which meant it was also the perfect time for company.

She soon spotted an enemy plane, up ahead, swooping in the opposite direction.

She must have gasped, because Michael jerked awake. He saw the plane. It was followed by a pool of Hurricanes on its tail.

'Just keep doing what you're doing,' he whispered, then scanned the horizon. 'We're clear for now.'

They flew past lakes, and over fields, and Frankie could pick out the landmarks on the way back to the Tangmere base where she would need to refuel.

She was about ten minutes away when she saw an enemy fighter plane heading her way.

'Watch out, he's on your tail.'

They could take on fire at any moment.

She thought fast, and she managed to pull sharply to the left, performing a trick that made the plane flip, and that ensured she was out of range, a manoeuvre she hadn't executed for years.

'Jesus,' whispered Michael.

She righted the plane, and took it up higher, so that she was now just above the fighter plane, and he fell away, not taking the chance that she might open up on him. Some of the Lysanders were fitted with bombs.

Her hands shook violently.

'I think I might be sick,' she whispered.

'You did perfectly.'

When at last she brought the plane in to land, they were both still shaking.

. . .

Frankie climbed out of the cockpit, on unsteady legs. Now that she was here, safe, her head swam and she was close to passing out. She cried out, and soon there were people running over to help.

When she next opened her eyes, she and Michael were being rushed inside the building on stretchers. 'I'm fine,' she said, trying to sit up.

'Just lie back,' said a familiar voice.

'McCall,' she whispered.

'Glad to have you back.'

Soon Michael was being rushed down the corridor to be treated by an onsite doctor.

'He'll be all right, thanks to you,' said McCall as she watched Michael being taken into a hospital room.

The relief of having him back in one piece was staggering. She was exhausted and in desperate need of a shower and some sleep but she'd give herself that luxury after she knew Michael was settled.

Despite the stress and trauma of the last few hours, she couldn't help the bubble of joy at the thought of their kiss – that he felt for her the way she felt about him. But it was intermixed with thoughts of the dead German, whose eyes haunted her, and worry for the people who had helped them escape – she hoped they would be all right.

She was taken into a hospital room of her own, where a doctor checked her over. It was the same one who'd given her a medical some months before.

'You don't seem to be injured, but you are dehydrated and exhausted. I will give you a saline drip, and then I think you should spend a few hours here recovering.'

She did as instructed.

It was evening when she awoke. She climbed out of bed feeling disoriented, and went in search of Michael.

She found him in a room down the corridor. His leg was bound in a cast and propped up, and he was sleeping.

She took a seat in a chair opposite his, just as a nurse, a stout-looking woman with kind eyes, came in. 'You're awake,' she whispered. 'Would you like something to eat?'

Frankie could have kissed her. 'Yes, please.'

The nurse paused. 'I heard that you took a plane and went to find him,' she said, looking amazed.

Frankie coloured slightly. 'Yes.'

'Well done. That was so brave.'

'Thanks, I think most people would call it something else. Stupid, probably.'

'Yes, well, there's usually a fine line between the two, right?'

Michael woke up after she'd finished eating a sandwich.

'So it wasn't a dream.'

His smile made her heart flip.

She rushed over to his side. 'You're awake? How do you feel?'

'Like I just crawled out of hell.'

She gave him a wry smile.

'Well, it wasn't far off.'

'Thank you for coming for me.'

'Of course.'

He snorted. 'There was no "of course" about it.'

'There was for me.'

They stared at each other for a long time.

He smiled, then reached out a hand for her. She climbed onto the bed and snuggled against him.

She woke up when she heard the sound of hastening footsteps. It was well after midnight.

It was McCall, his eyes panicked.

'Chalmers! There you are. I know it's a big ask, but one of the squad took on enemy fire, and had to turn back with three Joes on board. They desperately need to get in tonight. A team of important Nazi officers will be passing through Blois. They need to get there in time to stop them. I'd go myself but I'm grounded, thanks to this,' he said, showing her his bandaged hand. 'They only have tonight to stop them. The whole mission depends on it. I wouldn't ask – not after everything... but...'

Frankie sighed, then nodded.

Michael was sitting up now, alert, imploring her with his eyes to say no.

Frankie swallowed. Lord knew, the last thing she wanted was to get back in a plane so soon after everything that they'd just been through. But McCall had gone out on a limb for her; it was thanks to him, letting her take a plane, that Michael was here now.

She owed him.

'It's fine. I'll go.'

At Michael's disappointed look, she bent over him, kissing him on the lips. 'Don't worry, I'll be there and back before you even know it.'

He pulled her to him, and kissed her hard. 'Promise?'

'Promise.'

28

The stars were bright as she flew over the rolling landscape of the Loire Valley, and headed towards a small grassy field on the side of river. As she neared, the ground flickered into life by the lights of half a dozen bicycle lamps switching on from the waiting Joes, who would be taking the others on to Blois.

She waited for the signal.

A torch flickered a letter in Morse Code.

Frankie frowned.

Behind her there was a sniff from one of the Joes. A short man wearing a faded grey suit.

'It's the wrong letter. It was meant to be M,' she said, hesitating.

'N is close enough, easy mistake,' he said. 'Bring it in.'

There was a murmur of assent from the others.

Frankie frowned. She didn't have a good feeling about this. It was quiet. She scanned the field below and couldn't see anything amiss, but it was hard to see beyond the bicycle lamps.

One of the Joes tapped his foot impatiently, and Frankie pushed past her misgivings. She knew the Joes didn't have long to stop the van full of Nazi officers. She brought the plane into land and the Joes began to deplane quickly.

'Good luck,' she called.

'Thank—' began the Joe in the suit, only to stop midway, as the people with the bicycles began to open fire.

Frankie screamed.

She watched in horror as the Joe that had told her not to worry was killed before her eyes, his body fell over backwards, and blood began to stain his white shirt. She saw the other Joes begin to jerk like a macabre display of puppets on a string as the bullets hit their bodies before they too fell to the floor.

Her gorge rose, but the adrenaline coursing through her made her react fast, pushing the horror scene into a corner of her mind where she would deal with it later.

Frankie started the engine, her heart roaring in her ears, her back slick with sweat, as they opened fire on the plane. She turned the plane around as bullets began to fall like hail stones all around her.

Somehow, she managed to take off. But to her dismay she could hear something was wrong with the plane. 'No,' she begged. 'Please.'

The bullets followed as she tore through the night sky, finding their target. Her throat constricted with fear as she saw that her air gauge had stopped working.

The plane was failing.

She began to panic, struggling to catch her breath. Tears began to course down her cheeks.

The noise the plane was making flayed her nerves. She twisted in horror to see one of the engines fail, and flames began to spread.

Oh god, oh god, she whispered. *'Please, no.'*

She struggled to see past the tears. Her hands were shaking so badly, it was hard to control the plane. She tried her best to straighten it, but it was in free fall.

Frantically she looked to the undercarriage, searching for her parachute only to see in horror that it was jammed. She wouldn't be able to parachute out.

The heat was beginning to spread, the air burning up, making it hard to breathe. She began to sob. This was it, this was how it ended for her.

Her face crumpled as she thought of her family. Of never seeing them again.

Of Michael. For just a moment she had everything she had ever wanted.

I'm so sorry, she cried.

By the time she went crashing into the field, she had passed out.

29

PRESENT DAY, LOIRE VALLEY, 1944

Frankie woke up screaming, Michael's name dying on her lips.

In her dream, she'd had to get to him, to save him. Her heart pounded as she lay in the dark. It took ages for it to slow. Saint had come barrelling into the room, and dove onto the bed. For once she didn't push him off. She just buried her face into his fur, and began to cry.

There was the sound of slippered feet, as Antoine made his way into the room.

'Are you all right?'

'I remember now,' she said, softly. Her chin wobbled. 'I remember *everything*.'

'I'll go and put the kettle on.'

They spoke until dawn, watching the light as it began to illuminate the valley before them.

'But you did save him,' he said, when the sun had moved high up in the sky.

'I did.'

Then her face twisted as she recalled the night of her crash.

The night she watched the agents she had brought over shot in front of her eyes. 'I should never have landed that plane. I knew it was the wrong code letter. If I trusted my instincts they might have survived.'

She began to cry again as she thought of the Joes. They had died because she had ignored her instincts.

He reached out and tapped her knee. 'Maybe. Maybe not. Maybe they would have died when you crashed the plane. Don't punish yourself.'

She nodded, but she knew she likely always would.

A few days later, she was making dinner when Antoine came inside and whispered, 'I think I've found someone who can help get you home.'

Her hands paused while she was chopping a carrot.

'Who?'

'I think the librarian may be part of the Resistance. I'm going to see if she can help, maybe they can use a radio to let them know you're here.'

Frankie's throat constricted. 'Just be careful.'

He nodded.

'I will.'

It was a small stone building with pink roses trailing over one of its walls. It was only ever open a few days a week.

Antoine made his way inside and approached the young woman at the front desk. She was an attractive woman with black hair, wearing a pair of gold-rimmed glasses that emphasised her dark eyes.

He looked over his shoulder, making sure he was alone.

'Good day, monsieur,' she greeted him. 'Is there anything I can help you with?'

'Yes,' he said, handing her a book. It was the collected sonnets of William Shakespeare. Inside it, he'd placed a scrap of paper, with details of a British pilot who needed help. The shopkeeper had told him what to do, and say.

'I would like to return this,' he said.

Her eyes widened. Then they flickered somewhere behind him. He could see the fear in her eyes.

Antoine saw through the reflection in the woman's glasses that someone was behind him. It was the Nazi officer. Röber.

He had entered as silently as a cat. Was this a set-up? His heart thundered in his chest.

As surreptitiously as he could, he shifted his weight and hunched over the book.

'Have you read them, mademoiselle? They are truly beautiful,' he said, opening the cover, then slipping the paper into his hand, where he balled it in a fist.

'Er, no,' she said, nervously.

'Oh, you should. This one was my favourite' – and he read out a line, while he slipped the scrap up his sleeve.

There was an impatient grunt and Röber moved over and snatched the book from Antoine, shaking the pages.

Antoine turned to him with a raised brow. 'I know he's not everyone's cup of tea, but there's no need to break the book.'

Röber turned to him, his eyes narrowed.

'Is that so?' Then he looked at the librarian. 'What did he say to you?'

Antoine held his breath.

'He was just returning a book, that's all.'

Silence fell.

Antoine waited, his knees like jelly.

Röber pointed a finger at him. 'I know you're up to something, old man. I'll be watching.'

. . .

Antoine was still feeling anxious, several hours later.

'Do you think the shopkeeper betrayed you?' asked Théo.

Antoine ran his hands over his face. The cup of tea Frankie had brought him lay untouched. He didn't know how she could drink the stuff.

'I don't know. Maybe. Probably.' Then he swore. 'How could he – after watching them shoot Madame Avril in front of us? How could he be working with them, how could he turn on us?'

Frankie frowned. 'I'm not sure he has. Not completely. Because if he had, surely they'd be here, looking for me.'

They nodded.

'I don't think he would tell them that because then he would have to tell them that the whole village was keeping it a secret too,' said Théo.

'That's true.'

It was the only thing keeping them safe. For now.

But they knew they were on borrowed time.

30

'He's here – that horrible German officer,' cried Théo, 'he's just standing out there, what is he doing?' The little black bird on the boy's shoulder chirped.

They all rushed to the window to check. Röber was patrolling outside.

Frankie swallowed. 'I don't know.'

'Whatever it is, can't be good,' said Antoine, his hands in his white hair.

'Perhaps he'll leave soon,' she said.

But he didn't. Every day that week they dangled on a knife's edge. For a week straight Röber patrolled the farm. They couldn't look out the windows without seeing him. Frankie stopped sleeping through the night. She'd wake soaked in sweat, her heart racing after dreaming of the Germans bursting in through the door and killing them.

Her hands had started to shake, and there was a twitch in her left eye that didn't go away.

Even Saint had taken to cowering whenever he saw the figure lurking in the garden.

Then, as suddenly as he appeared, he was gone. They woke up one morning to find that he was no longer keeping watch.

'He's GONE!' yelled Théo.

'What?' cried Frankie, shuffling as quickly as she could towards the window, Antoine hot on her heels. The boy was right. He had left.

'Do you think he'll be back?' she asked.

'I don't know,' replied Antoine.

For the first time in days, they all breathed a little easier. But none of them dared to hope he was gone for good.

All day they looked at each other anxiously, waiting for his return, but then as nightfall came, they heard the sound of a bicycle bell, coming up the farm track.

It was the doctor, Monsieur Leclair, and his face was alight. 'It's the Allies,' he cried. 'They've come!'

Then he turned around to go and deliver the message to the others.

They rushed into the sitting room and crowded around the radio. Antoine's hand was clutched tightly in Frankie's.

'June 6 will be remembered in history as the day the war turned towards victory for the Allies...'

Théo yelped in excitement, followed by Saint who let out a triumphant bark.

'It's true,' cried Frankie, feeling overcome.

Antoine seemed unable to speak as they turned to listen once more.

'... with the largest invasion ever attempted over land, sea and air. Under the cover of darkness in the early hours of this morning, American and British paratroopers were launched into Normandy, along with the largest naval bombardment ever seen... In the coming days as more towns, villages and cities are liberated, France will soon be liberated… and in the weeks and months ahead we may soon see an end to this infernal war.'

They stared at each other, not daring to believe it was possible. Then Théo let out another cheer, and this time they all joined in, as they began laughing and crying and hugging each other.

Antoine let out a whoop, then ran into the kitchen, and back, carrying an old bottle in his worn hands.

'I was saving this,' he said, his eyes filling with tears. 'For this day. I must admit I wondered if I would ever live to open it.'

'Me too,' said Frankie.

He popped the cork, and they clung to each other. Thinking of the price everyone had paid, all the people who had made sacrifices in the war. Antoine spoke of poor Madame Avril, while Frankie couldn't help thinking of all those Joes she had watched being murdered, the couple in the woods who had helped her and Michael – it was their victory too.

31

The Germans billeted in the house they'd stolen in town woke up to the sound of booted feet, as a troop of American soldiers stormed inside.

'W-what's going on?' exclaimed Dieter Frosch, looking up bleary-eyed as a soldier pointed a gun at him.

'You are under arrest.'

He swallowed, then reached for the pistol he kept beneath his pillow, and as he did, he was shot and instantly killed.

There was movement on the stairs. The dark-haired German, Röber, tried to flee into the street outside.

'He's the one – the one who shot Madame Avril,' cried one of the woman's friends, who had followed after the soldiers to witness them storming the house.

Several soldiers captured him and tied his hands behind his back. Röber was marched through the streets while the villagers pelted him with rotten fruit and vegetables.

'Murderer!'

'Vermin.'

Antoine, Frankie and Théo watched as he was dragged

past. Antoine pointed at his eyes then at Röber, as if to say, *Now it's us, watching you.*

The Nazi stopped and sneered. He got a kick behind his legs for the trouble and fell to his knees.

'He will pay for what he has done,' said the soldier who had kicked him.

Frankie looked at Antoine. She didn't know if it would be enough, sending him to prison, not after all he'd done, all the suffering he'd caused this small village.

But then this place, like the whole of Europe, had been through so much misery. It was hard to believe it was coming to an end. That there was anything that anyone could do to make it right.

For now, however, for the first time in years, Frankie felt like she could take a full breath.

But even after the war was finally declared over it would be months, if not years, before she and the others finally felt like it was done.

She was waiting in the field in which her plane had crashed.

It was a warm day, and she was dressed in Antoine's wife's old red-and-white cotton dress. It suited her.

Shortly after they were liberated, she was able to telephone her base at Tempsford and let them know that she was alive.

She was going home. Saying goodbye to Antoine and Théo was heart-breaking, though.

'Do you have to go?' asked Théo in a small voice. 'Couldn't you just stay here?'

Her throat constricted with tears, and she pulled the boy in for a hug.

'Why don't you both just come back with me?'

Behind the boy, Antoine chuckled, then surreptitiously wiped his eyes.

'Don't think we're not tempted. But it would be a shame to leave this beautiful part of the world, now that it's finally free.'

She looked around, and breathed in the scent of summer. The lavender was beginning to bloom, and she could see the purple carpet beginning to form on the horizon, followed by the wink of a bright blue lake, and rolling fields of vineyards.

It was paradise here and part of her didn't want to leave.

Frankie smiled at him. Then her lip wobbled.

'It's not goodbye, though. You know that.'

He nodded, and his eyes misted over again.

'I'll be back soon to visit.'

'And you'll teach me how to fly,' said Théo.

'It's a promise.'

'We'll hold you to that.'

'You'd better.'

They were like Michael, she thought; some family you were born with, others you found.

They were no less precious, and she had no intention of letting them go.

After a while they began to notice movement in the sky.

Over the past few weeks, planes had passed by in triumphant formations, spreading coloured smoke behind them in the victory shades of red, white and blue.

Suddenly, they saw a small plane begin to approach. A Lysander that was no longer in camouflage and had been boldly painted red and blue.

Around them some of the villagers began to jump up. Frankie squinted as it approached.

Her heart was beating so loudly she was sure everyone around her could hear it.

It came to land, and a tall man climbed down from the ladder, smart in his navy RAF uniform, with a cast on his leg. The sunshine turned his nut brown hair auburn.

Michael turned, and smiled.

Tears began to mist her eyes.

His face was angular, with high cheekbones that made his

dark eyes look huge before they crinkled in happiness as he stared at her. Even from here, even injured, he was still the most beautiful man she'd ever seen.

They held each other's gaze and it was as if time stood still.

It was then that she knew that home wasn't just a place.

It could be a person too.

A LETTER FROM LILY

Dear Reader,

Thank you so much for reading *Her Forgotten Hours*. I really hope you enjoyed it. If you did, and want to keep up to date with all my latest releases, just sign up at the following link. Your email address will never be shared and you can unsubscribe at any time.

www.bookouture.com/lily-graham

If you did enjoy *Her Forgotten Hours*, I would be very grateful if you could write a review. It really makes such a difference helping new readers to discover my books. Also, if you'd like to get in touch or find out more about my other books, please visit my website.

Lily Graham

www.lilygraham.net

instagram.com/lilygrahamauthor
facebook.com/LilyRoseGrahamAuthor

ACKNOWLEDGEMENTS

This book was a long time coming, I first got excited at the idea of writing a story about a female pilot, and then... became a bit daunted! I am so grateful to all the wonderful people who helped me along the way, starting with Robert Alexander and Barbara Little who put me in touch with the Martlesham Control Tower and to everyone there who answered all my questions about female pilots and provided so many interesting stories, many of which found its way into this story! Huge thank you to Vicky Gunnell, who loaned me her extensive library of books that were invaluable in the research of this one, including, *The Forgotten Pilots* by *Lettice Curtis*, for which I express immense gratitude for giving me a sense of what it was like to be an ATA ferry pilot – many of the routes Frankie took in the story, were based on the ones Lettice herself did. For my research into SOE and Moon Squadrons, I am enormously grateful to *Flight Most Secret,* by Gibb McCall.

All mistakes are, of course, my own. For the purposes of the story, I did simplify some things and use a bit of poetic licence – please forgive me, especially for the scene where Frankie saves Michael, as their return would not have been possible without a refuelling session!

Of course, when it came time to actually write the book, it just wouldn't have happened without the help and guidance of my lovely editor, Lydia Vassar-Smith, who read the whole thing in a series of chunks as I worked through the story. I really do wonder if I did something good in a former life to deserve you at times. Thank you so much for your patience, kindness and support and for always knowing how to make the story better!

My deepest thanks to the Bookouture team for their hard work and support, for the gorgeous covers, and everything you do.

Huge thanks to my family, near and far, for all your support and encouragement. My husband Rui, who always believes that the words will come, and to my little furry companion, Frankie, for being with me through all the late nights and early mornings, you always know just how to lend a paw – and a name to a story.

Last and definitely not least, thank you to you – the reader; thank you so much for picking up this book, and to all the readers and bloggers who have reached out to me and been so kind and supportive; it means the world.

PUBLISHING TEAM

Turning a manuscript into a book requires the efforts of many people. The publishing team at Bookouture would like to acknowledge everyone who contributed to this publication.

Audio
Alba Proko
Sinead O'Connor
Melissa Tran

Commercial
Lauren Morrissette
Hannah Richmond
Imogen Allport

Cover design
Emma Graves

Data and analysis
Mark Alder
Mohamed Bussuri

Editorial
Lydia Vassar-Smith
Imogen Allport

Copyeditor
Jon Appleton

Proofreader
Tom Feltham

Marketing
Alex Crow
Melanie Price
Occy Carr
Cíara Rosney
Martyna Młynarska

Operations and distribution
Marina Valles
Stephanie Straub
Joe Morris

Production
Hannah Snetsinger
Mandy Kullar
Nadia Michael
Ria Clare

Publicity
Kim Nash
Noelle Holten
Jess Readett
Sarah Hardy

Rights and contracts
Peta Nightingale
Richard King
Saidah Graham

RAISING READERS
Books Build Bright Futures

Dear Reader,

We'd love your attention for one more page to tell you about the crisis in children's reading, and what we can all do.

Studies have shown that reading for fun is the **single biggest predictor of a child's future life chances** – more than family circumstance, parents' educational background or income. It improves academic results, mental health, wealth, communication skills, ambition and happiness.

The number of children reading for fun is in rapid decline. Young people have a lot of competition for their time, and a worryingly high number do not have a single book at home.

Hachette works extensively with schools, libraries and literacy charities, but here are some ways we can all raise more readers:

- Reading to children for just 10 minutes a day makes a difference
- Don't give up if children aren't regular readers – there will be books for them!

- Visit bookshops and libraries to get recommendations
- Encourage them to listen to audiobooks
- Support school libraries
- Give books as gifts

There's a lot more information about how to encourage children to read on our websites: **www.RaisingReaders.co.uk** and **www.JoinRaisingReaders.com**.

Thank you for reading.

www.ingramcontent.com/pod-product-compliance
Ingram Content Group UK Ltd.
Pitfield, Milton Keynes, MK11 3LW, UK
UKHW041420021125